D1827651

Forbidden Fruit

A Novel

Hildred Billings
BARACHOU PRESS

Forbidden Fruit

Copyright: Hilded Billings
Published: 4st September 2018
Publisher: Barachou Press

This is a work of fiction. Any and all similarities to any characters, settings, or situations are purely coincidental.

Chapter 1

Tonight's date was Jackie, a young 20-something with big breasts, blond hair, and a smile the size of Jupiter.

"This place is, like, amazing." Her big smile eclipsed the lights in the room. A bit of red lipstick was stuck to her whitened teeth. "When I tell the girls at Beta Nu about this swank-ass place, they are gonna *flip* like Tom Cruise on Oprah!"

A cackle filled the air, restaurant patrons giving Raquel and her date the side-eye. It couldn't be helped. Raquel's insatiable taste for women younger than herself often came with... unusual speech and behavior. It was worth it, even as diners looked at them as if Raquel were this girl's mother. She was certainly old enough to be, though she swore she didn't look it. But that *body*. Sure, Jackie sounded about as intelligent as a deflated balloon, but she was a champion in the bedroom. *On our first date, I took her home and found out for myself.* Soft, firm skin... tight muscles that took little maintenance to maintain... was there anything on this earth more wonderful than a young woman in the spring of her life? Jackie could talk about boy bands and frat parties for the next hour, and Raquel would listen contentedly, assured in the knowledge that by the end of the night she would have the gal's tits bouncing in bed.

"Hel-*lo*." Jackie waved her hand in front of Raquel. "Care to give me your opinion?"

Raquel took a sip of her champagne. "Yes?"

"I was asking you how cute my phone is."

A glance told Raquel it looked like any other phone available on the market. "Adorable."

"I know, right?" Jackie put it back in her handbag and readjusted her posture. This made her cleavage bulge from her strapless dress. "All the girls at Beta Nu wish they had my phone. Tres *chic*."

Dinner was fine, as always, but that was not the memorable event of the evening. It rarely was. Raquel preferred to dwell on the beauty of her date as opposed to the taste of her food. After all, food was for survival. Sex? That was for living.

"Would you like something for dessert?" Raquel picked up the tiny dessert menu. "Maybe something with cherries?" She would love to see Jackie put a cherry between those lips.

"No, thanks. I'm on a diet. I'm so damn fat."

"Uh huh. Sure." More like the most perfectly proportioned woman in the room. *Yet if there's anything I've learned as I get older and my dates stay the same age, it's that these concerns never change.* Every one of her girlfriends were self-conscious to some extent, from the softball stars to the budding magazine models. Even the science nerds! *Does it say more about me, or them?* Maybe Raquel really did prefer women who sustained themselves on compliments and being made to feel like Cinderella for a few nights. Didn't matter if they were comfortably lesbian or a little bi-curious.

"Besides, I kinda need to get going," Jackie said with a click of her tongue.

Raquel dropped the menu. "Excuse me? Do you have a test to study for?" That was the most common excuse women gave her for running out on a date. It was usually organic chemistry. Or French. For once, Raquel would love to be told someone couldn't go out with her because they had a paper due for 17th Century Chinese Lit.

"What? Hell no. I'm simply not sure this whole thing is working out for me."

"What whole *thing?*"

Jackie's face was etched in utter disgust. Her twisted nose and lip made her look like a damned fool. "You know what I'm talking about. This whole fooling around with you. I mean, like, it was fun and all, but I've gotta be serious. Why am I hanging out with you? You're like... old enough to be my grandma."

Raquel glared at her. "I am not." Neither was Jackie an example of great math skills.

"I'm just saying. Do I wanna hang out with an old lady all day? I mean, you're okay... and it was fun in bed... I guess... but if I wanna be married by twenty-five, I've gotta find someone more my age, yeah?"

The room began to spin as Raquel contained her disdain. "Are you dumping me?"

"As if! That would mean we were like... seriously dating or something!" Jackie gathered her things and stood up, her hot ass disappearing beneath her skirt as she pulled the hem down. "I mean, this is what happens when you use a dating site and don't put an age cap on it. Old ladies hit on you. If the girls at Beta Nu knew about this..." Jackie stopped herself. Good, maybe she was about to finally start talking sense again. "They don't care about the woman thing, but they would be *so* grossed out by a lady as old as you."

Raquel sat back in her seat, gobsmacked.

"Don't take it personally, but maybe you should try dating girls more your age." Jackie picked up her glass of champagne and emptied it before setting it back down again. "Bye. Thanks for dinner." The young co-ed walked off in her stiletto heels and designer dress, hair tossing behind her shoulder.

Raquel stared at the table, unable to believe that something as absurd as that happened. It was like living in some twilight zone. As she recalled, dear Jackie was more than eager to go out on a date with her after flirting on the dating site. Raquel could remember it as clear as glass. Lots of flirting. Some sexual come-ons – from *both* ends – and who could forget the nude pic of Jackie's breasts sent straight to Raquel's phone before they went out?

And the sex! *What the fuck!*

Raquel slammed her napkin down onto the table. As she sat and stewed in her rejected misery, she thought of all the girls she ever dated. Inevitably, those relationships always came to an end.

Why?

She took that question with her out of the restaurant and down the street, where she popped into a swanky hotel. She liked hotel bars. They were nicer and quieter than regular bars, and the people there wanted nothing to do with her. She could sit at the end of the bar and simmer in her disgust.

Of course, she knew the ultimate flaw in her desires. Either the girls grew tired of her, or she grew tired of the girls. As much as she wished they could both stay the same age forever, at some point, the girls matured into older women and wanted different things from life other than being some rich "old" woman's piece on the side. Besides, Raquel wasn't a total victim. More than once she let go of her flings as she realized she was no longer attracted to them.

The only thing that could console her now was another trip down Sadness Lane with a detour around Disappointment Avenue.

She pulled out her cell phone, drink chilling in front of her on the bar. Within a few touches, she accessed the dating app and looked at her profile. Over the past 24 hours, about eight young women had visited her page and sent her flirts. One even sent her a message. "*I like your profile,*" it said. "*I really appreciate a woman who likes to have fun at any age.*"

Normally, Raquel would reply with a flirt of her own. Maybe check out the girl's profile and tell her how beautiful she was. Certainly, she would be. Every girl was beautiful as far as Raquel was concerned. Especially the young ones. They were full of the energy and life Raquel craved after a long day putting around her office or traipsing about town, showing houses to people who never deserved them. She spent her days surrounded by fuddy-duddies who had nothing going on except their money. When she got off work, she wanted to kiss a girl with endless potential between her ears – and between her legs.

Maybe that was her problem. Impossible to be happy with a girl like that forever. Not that Raquel often thought in the long term. It depressed her too much. She had no issue with women who were more her age.

She dated those, too, but there was always something missing from those relationships. Some spark. Some *je ne se quoi* the women who studied French would declare. Either they acted like life was about to end the next day, or they were more concerned about finding the best tax breaks than jetting off for a romantic weekend. The thing about younger women? Everything was exciting to them. Brand-new. Even better if Raquel was their first lesbian relationship or, better yet, the first time they had been spoiled silly. Raquel wasn't a millionaire, but she made enough money as a real estate agent to live a comfortable lifestyle. That included taking women out on nice dates or on the occasional weekend getaway to Miami or Cancun. What else was she supposed to use her stash of airline miles on? Traveling the world by *herself?* Sad.

Women her age – or even a mere ten years younger than her – lost their sense of adventure by the time they met her. *"Oh, I've left those days behind me,"* the last one had said with a snort of laughter. *"I'm ready to settle down and take things slowly. Jet-setting and partying? No, thank you."*

It wasn't that Raquel wanted to live the jet-setting and partying lifestyle. Honestly, she didn't think she did. She simply wanted there to be enough room to have some *fun*. Settling down? Not her style. Never had been. Part of the appeal of dating women – of any age – was not having to worry about kids. Then again, wasn't that part of the problem with dating women her own age? Either they sobbed into their estrogen shots that time was running out now that they were in their forties, or they already had kids. School-aged or grown, Raquel wasn't a maternal soul. She didn't even have pets.

Spoiling her girlfriends was as close as it got. She didn't think of herself as their mother. Rather, she was a woman who knew what she was about and what she wanted in life. She was more than happy to spread that joy to the other women around her. So happened it was the twenty-somethings who took her up on her offers. After a while, a pattern erupted. One that hadn't looked weird to other people until the lines started showing up on Raquel's face and she saw the occasional gray hair growing out of her scalp.

I still feel like I'm twenty... Her metabolism had left the building ten years ago. She remembered the day she accepted the fact she would never be lighter than 135 pounds again. (At least she was still hot as hell!) Some fashion styles were faux-pas now that she was approaching her mid-forties. House hunting clients appreciated her experience and expertise that only being forty could bring, but it served to create a bigger divide between her and the women she ended up dating.

Deep down, I'm still a girl. She looked in the mirror and saw a young co-ed ready to go out and enjoy the day with her girlfriend. She would glance away, grabbing her hairbrush or hairdryer, and look back to see an older woman still mourning the love of her life.

Raquel needed another drink.

Against her better judgment, she looked through more profiles. Yet she remained disappointed to find it was all girls she had dated before, girls who had significant others, and girls who broadcasted no desire to date older women. Or men, for that matter.

"Having a rough day?"

Raquel looked up from her phone and saw someone leaning against the wall. In the modest light of the hotel bar, she could barely make out a blue dress and long brown hair. *I haven't seen hair like that since...* Damn, when Raquel was falling into the pits of Memory Despair, everyone looked like the old love she could never have again.

She put her phone down on the bar. "I'm allowed to have the off day now and then."

The young woman smiled at her. "You look like you could use a friend. Get dumped?"

"How did you know?"

Without an invitation, the woman sat on the empty stool next to Raquel. In the soft light, one could see the glitter in her hair and the lilac eyeshadow around her eye. Maybe Raquel's night wasn't lost yet.

"You've got that look to you." The woman flagged down the bartender from the other end of the bar and ordered a drink. "The one that says you nearly had your heart broken."

"I don't know if I would go that far." Raquel waited for the bartender to deposit the drink. "It was only our second date, but I thought that maybe..."

Laughter. "You would get lucky?"

Raquel refrained from taking another sip of her drink. "That's private."

"Only if you don't know the person you're talking to. My name is Lisa." The rim of the martini glass lightly touched lips as pink as the shade Raquel liked most. *All lips are the same color when you get down to it.* Raquel soon realized she didn't mean lips. She meant what was between them. "Now it's not so private anymore."

Raquel didn't know if she agreed with that, but she appreciated the company. After all, she thought her night would be full of flirting and desire. Maybe Lisa couldn't deliver that for her. Having some companionship after getting dumped for being "too old," however, was better than nothing. "What can I do for you, Miss Lisa? There must be some reason you came to bother my lonesome self."

"Well, when you put it that way, I sound rude." Lisa curled her lips into an exaggerated pout. On such a young woman it was like Kryptonite to Raquel's shattered soul. "I saw a lovely older lady and decided she must need some company. If I'm truly bothering you, I can leave."

Only one thing in that explanation stood out to Raquel. "Lovely older lady, huh?"

Those pouting lips pursed around the rim of Lisa's glass. Her throat pulsed with every swallow. Raquel crossed her legs beneath the bar top. "Do you not believe me when I say that? A shame. I don't find as many women as attractive," Lisa said the moment she sat up again. She batted her eyelashes at Raquel.

"Excuse me." Raquel took her phone off the counter and put it in her purse. "You're making an awful lot of assumptions." And making her heart race. When was the last time a young lady flirted with her *first?*

"What assumptions? I think we have a lot in common."

"We only met two seconds ago. I'm curious as to what makes you think I'm into women. Unless I'm completely missing the point of your overt flirtations."

"Oh, is it that obvious? I'll have to tone it down, then." Lisa leaned in closer, her long hair skirting against Raquel's bare shoulder. A pair of fingers then wrapped around her thigh, and the blood froze in a woman's veins. "I've seen you before, Miss Raquel. Five minutes ago, you popped up on my dating profile as a visitor. How sad that you didn't say hello. Nice profile, by the way. I like a woman who openly admits she likes fucking."

Raquel nearly choked on her drink. "I don't recall seeing you on there."

"Profile pic of a flower. It happens."

"I see." Raquel always skipped those girls. A woman afraid to show her face in a *dating* profile was afraid of other things. Like being seen with another woman – something Raquel had no time for. "I never said on my profile that I liked *fucking*."

"Not literally, no. But I'm good at reading between the lines... and your lines say that you love spoiling women half your age. That's pretty hot."

"I didn't say that, either." If Raquel recalled correctly, her profile said that she preferred dating younger women of all kinds, but not because it was a fetish. She was honest. She liked treating young women to things they couldn't afford or had yet to imagine. That included the shopping trips at the downtown boutiques and vacations to whatever tropical paradise they had in mind. Everything else, from the adoration to the hot sex, was a cherry on her sundae. "You're coming on strong now." Lisa's fingers continued to dig into Raquel's thigh. Soon, this beauty would be fingering a woman at a bar. Raquel wasn't sure she was into that idea, although she could get pretty kinky.

"Sorry." Lisa backed off. "I love a cougar."

This time, Raquel did drop her drink. "I'm no cougar."

"You like young women, right? Pretty sure an older woman who goes after younger people for sex is called a cougar. I mean, let's be transparent here."

Transparent? What did Raquel have to be transparent about? Furthermore, why was it any of Lisa's business? "You're starting to get annoying. First, you ask me personal questions, then you call me a cougar. Don't you know those are fighting words?"

"Rawr." Lisa laughed again, showing the white of her throat in front of Raquel's fangs. What she would give to sink her teeth there. *That* would be a cougar! "Okay, I get the point. You don't like being called out for what you are, but you make it sound like it's something to be ashamed of. I don't think that. Quite the opposite. A woman who knows what she wants and goes for it... that's fucking hot."

"I'm not sure I get what you're going for." Raquel was two seconds away from leaving. She didn't have time for games. At least girls like Jackie were blunt.

Lisa leaned in again, this time with her lips going straight for Raquel's ear beneath a coif of dark, curly hair. "I've got a room in this hotel. Let me take you up for some fun."

Something crashed into the pit of Raquel's stomach. Or maybe it was crashing into her groin. She had spent most of the evening fantasizing about another woman, after all. Now, here was some other woman at a bar trying to get under her skirt! "Are you propositioning me for sex?" She didn't mean to sound so gruff, but she couldn't contain herself. For all she knew, this was a prank.

"Gee, can't get anything past you." Lisa rubbed her hand against Raquel's bare arm. Her skin was warm, tingly. Strange. She never felt this way the other way around. A woman hitting on her? How long had it been, anyway? Raquel was so used to wining and dining young women... was this what it felt like to be wanted so badly? "I'm not looking for anything serious, if that's what you're worried about. I only want to have a good time with you."

Raquel continued to eye the counter. "*Why?*"

"Why not? I like older women... you like younger women..."

"How old are you, anyway?"

"Twenty-three."

Twenty-three! What was she doing hitting on women nearly twice her age? *No, I don't see any hypocrisy there.* "Is this a pattern of behavior for you?" Her friends that knew about her dating younger women would be in stitches to hear these words come out of Raquel's mouth. *I can't help it. This is so suspicious.* Raquel was simply a woman sitting at a bar. Sure, sometimes women flirted with her, but this overtly? When they didn't know each other? A woman as hot as Lisa, who practically oozed sensuality with the way she drank her martini and crossed her legs in that tight, blue dress? They were either picking up men or women their own age. There was a reason Raquel usually searched out her own dates.

"Maybe I like older women," Lisa said with a wistful sigh. "Maybe I like hot cougars who can eat me alive in the sack."

Lisa lowered her nose to Raquel's shoulder. More shivers ran down Raquel's back, but she wasn't sure what to do about them. "Why not date girls your own age?"

"Because they don't have the experience an older woman has." Lisa wrapped her arm around Raquel, bringing them closer together. "They don't know what they like and want in bed. An older woman has confidence. Stability. *Sex appeal.* I don't think you understand how much."

"We also have older bodies that tend to sag and wrinkle."

"Whatever. I'm sure your body is gorgeous. You should show it to me. I'll show you mine. Come on. I'll take care of you if you take care of me." Now she made it sound like a sugar-mama deal. Just what Raquel *didn't* want. *If I think of them as my sugar babies, then I really am the lowest of the low.* "What do you say? I'll do what*ever* you desire."

Raquel wasn't sure how to react. On one hand, being spurned by Jackie put her on the rebound. A young woman hitting on her for a change? Paradise! On the other hand, Lisa came off *very* strong. Stronger than most cougars did when they were on the prowl. Raquel wasn't sure she wanted what Lisa truly offered.

Maybe.

Raquel asked that they have one more drink before making a decision. She offered to buy Lisa one, but was rebuffed when the young woman instead paid for both drinks. *That's my job.* The attraction of an older woman was supposed to be taking care of the younger one. That meant buying things. That was one of the funnest parts! Raquel genuinely enjoyed seeing the looks on her new friends' faces when she offered to buy them food, accessories, party dresses, shoes, a makeover, or even a video game or book series if that's what they really wanted. Seeing them happy made Raquel happy. She supposed this was what made Lisa happy. That and sex.

It wouldn't be Raquel's first time having casual sex with a woman she just met. Seemed like every other partner she ever had was that setup. They would meet, have a few words, have sex, then be on their way. So what was so different about Lisa? Was it really because she was the forward one? Raquel stopped sipping her drink when Lisa rubbed her thigh again. Usually, when young women did that, it was in response to Raquel's flirtations. Their roles were completely reversed.

"Are you ready to go upstairs yet?" Damn, Lisa was not a subtle girl. Was this how Raquel sounded? No way. She was coy, flirtatious. This was almost as if a man was hitting on Raquel with no shame.

"You're really pushing this," Raquel said. "I don't understand why you've picked me."

"I told you already. I like older women. They get me so..." Lisa sucked in her breath. "Hot. I can't help myself. Your aura... mystique... power... everything. It makes my body ache in ways you can't even imagine."

Yes, she could. It was probably the same ache she felt when she hit on a woman.

"I don't want to dominate you, if that's what's holding you back," Lisa continued, finally giving Raquel space. "I want to share the power. You do me and I'll do you... doesn't have to be in that order..."

By the time their second round of drinks were done, Raquel conceded. She would go to Lisa's room, but she told herself she would leave if she wasn't feeling it. For all she knew, the best remedy for her shitty night was going home and watching real estate shows on TV while downing a quart of ice cream.

Lisa led her out of the bar and into one of the hotel elevators. While they waited to ascend five stories, Raquel went over how off this felt. She wasn't used to it. Not to being hit on first; not to being propositioned so quickly. She was further surprised when the doors opened, and Lisa took her by the hand like a sweet girlfriend.

***

Everything, from reserving the hotel room in her own city to showing up in the bar right around the time Raquel arrived had been planned to the minute.

Of course, Lisa hadn't seen it that way. That would've been *creepy*. As her therapist continued to warn her, she had to check her expectations with reality. *"What if this woman turns you down?"* Sally had asked Lisa more than once. *"Could you handle the rejection?"*

Thing was? Lisa knew Raquel wouldn't reject her. That would've gone against everything she knew about the older woman with a penchant for fresh blood.

She has no idea who I am, does she? Lisa bit her bottom lip as she squeezed Raquel's hand and eyed her in the confines of the quiet elevator. Every lurch of the contraption was another flip in the bottom of Lisa's stomach. *She doesn't see any of* her *in me.* Could it be denial? Denial on Raquel's behalf, or Lisa's?

It didn't matter. Raquel was more beautiful, more magnetizing in person than Lisa could have foreseen. The few glimpses she had of the real estate queen – that wasn't on billboards or the sides of buses, anyway – weren't enough to convey the truly powerful aura of a woman who knew what she was about and how to get what she wanted. Raquel Mendes was a woman unafraid to wear a floppy black hat with her leopard print dress and black pumps. She strutted down the sidewalk with sheer purpose, wherever she went. Other people turned to glance at her perfect derriere and the way she flipped her mass of curly hair and readjusted her designer sunglasses. She oozed sex. She *dripped* seduction. Men were terrified of her – some of them to the point they didn't hesitate to ask her out – and women either wanted to have half her confidence or realized they were gay the moment Raquel walked into a room.

God knew she was the woman to give Lisa her gay awakening. All it took was a few pictures and a YouTube video of her sales pitch at the real estate agency she called her employer.

Lisa had met some of Raquel's former lovers, as well. After all, Lisa the recent grad was in the perfect storm of young co-eds and sexual exploration. *"She is like a lioness tearing you apart for the pack,"* one sorority girl lamented with a sigh. *"I had five orgasms in one night. Why did she have to get* bored *of me? I had yet to get bored of her!"*

"You want someone who knows how to pull hair and give it to you good?" One of Lisa's classmates, a girl who smoked more than she studied, had said. *"Look no farther than our local leopard. That's what they call lesbian cougars, you know."*

"Go after her if you want!" That had come from Lisa's best friend in undergrad. A sweet baby dyke who took being dumped by Raquel as a chance to chop off her hair and invest in plaid shirts and Birkenstocks. *"I*

mean, *if you like being led on by someone who sees you as a tight body before a woman with a brain. What was I thinking? Women like her aren't any better than men the same age. They fuck college students to fuel their egos. It gets more pathetic the older* they *get."*

Leopards. Lisa had almost called Raquel that to her face, but didn't want to insult her. Cougar was a much more universally known word. Besides, some women were sensitive to being associated with a cat boasting *spots.* Like it was a huge insult to grow older and acquire spots on one's own body.

I was so afraid you would recognize me. Lisa gussied up in the elevator mirror while Raquel checked something on her phone. *My nose. The slant of my eyes. Even my figure is easy to remember, isn't it?* All of it was genetic. The only anomaly in her genes was the fierce darkness of her hair. Nobody, from her parents to her distant relatives, had hair like hers. It was enough to make her think she was adopted.

Or her mother had lied about who her father was.

Lisa smoothed out her dress and boosted her breasts up in her bra. This was her best dress. This was her best set of underwear. Almost like she knew she was out to get laid from the moment she left her studio apartment.

You're going to regret it...

She happened to stop combing her hair with her fingers when Raquel glanced at her. Their eyes met in the reflection of the mirror. The elevator dinged and opened its doors to their floor.

Right. Lisa had the key. She hadn't even been in the room yet. That's how quickly she moved when she realized Raquel was going to *this* hotel bar instead of the other one she favored.

It didn't matter how much it cost. Lisa would pay for three rooms, if she had to. She'd buy a blond wig if it meant getting picky Raquel into bed. She *had* to know. Would her fantasies live up to her expectations, or should she have heeded her therapist's warnings to curb said expectations in favor of courting reality?

As soon as she took Raquel's hand and led her out of the elevator, *this* became reality. Expectations? Expectations were ecstasy, as far as this young woman was concerned. She may have been in way over her head, but she would drown before coming up for air.

Chapter 2

Things heated up once they were in Lisa's room.

Raquel didn't have time to enjoy the nice decor of the hotel room before Lisa pushed her against the wall and kissed her. Hard. Like a semi-truck slamming into her face. Raquel whimpered as her back slowly slid down the wall, the young woman in front of her going at her lips as if she would be the last women she ever kissed.

"Jesus..." was all Raquel was able to get out of her mouth before Lisa kissed her again. Before she knew it, a dexterous hand was up her skirt. "Christ!"

Even the Lord couldn't save her now. Lisa tore open the front of Raquel's dress and immediately cupped her breasts in both hands. Raquel didn't know if she felt violated. She didn't even have time to figure that out!

"I'm sorry you got dumped tonight," Lisa said, rolling her thumbs over Raquel's hardening nipples. The older woman moaned as her body succumbed to sex with this stranger. That may or may not have included her thighs spreading apart. "I'll try to make it up to you. Starting with these gorgeous tits of yours."

Safe to say nobody had called Raquel's breasts gorgeous in years. Especially since they weren't as perky as they used to be. Yet Lisa fell over herself to worship every stretch mark and wrinkle adorning the parts of Raquel's skin she couldn't protect with rigorous exercise regimens, anti-aging creams, and sunscreen. *Aging comes for all of us if we live long enough.* Raquel knew that like she knew she was already enjoying this night way more than she should.

Raquel stopped caring. She was with a beautiful woman who thought she was hot, even if she were almost twice her age. Her nipples could harden all they wanted; her pussy could get wet all it wanted. Short of Lisa getting so weird that the horny train came to a complete stop, Raquel was going to ride it until she eventually taught this whippersnapper how to properly graze on another woman's lawn.

First, Lisa would prove herself. She got on her knees and gazed up at Raquel, her big blue eyes covered by a swathe of brown hair. Adoration. Attraction. *Arousal.* This was the face of a girl ready to serve. Lisa was eager, but she still wanted Raquel's approval.

She was going to get it by pulling down silk underwear.

"Ah!" Raquel looked up to see her reflection in a mirror, splayed against the wall with her curly hair covering everything it dared, from her face to her chest. Oh, and her legs sticking out with a hot girl's head between them. Every time Lisa flicked her tongue against Raquel's pussy, the young woman's head bobbed back and forth in the mirror. It could have been hilarious, maybe, except Raquel was overwhelmed by the sensations rocketing up her body and hitting her brain at a million miles an hour.

Raquel grabbed a chunk of Lisa's hair. A wail tore from her throat. She was at this woman's whim, and the better it felt, the more she was inclined to forget how awkwardly it began.

Or that Lisa was back on her feet, taking Raquel by the arm and hauling her to the bed only a few feet away.

Raquel fell to it with a mighty surge of her weight that shook the entire headboard. Lisa was soon between her legs again, pulling them apart and lifting her skirt high around the waist.

"It's so beautiful." Lisa kicked her legs out behind her as she knelt down and tossed her hair out of the way. Her mouth was back on Raquel's nether lips without further comment.

One of the downsides of dating younger women was that most of them didn't have much experience. This meant that they could be a bit... lacking... in certain departments. Oh, they tried hard enough, for sure. They were always eager to please, and sometimes got lucky by being complete naturals. Yet most of them left Raquel wanting. She got her kicks when she indulged in their expectant bodies.

Then there was Lisa, whose tongue packed a punch – and whose fingers made their way inside of Raquel, as if that was where they were meant to be.

It fueled Raquel's ego. How could it not? A hot, young thing like Lisa literally eating her up *and* ecstatic about it? Shit, she knew she was hot! Also helped that the energetic young girl was pretty handy with her fingers... and tongue... and...

"Fuck, I'm coming." Raquel leaned back and closed her eyes. Did not take long for her body to get with the program.

She was sad when Lisa pulled out of her five seconds into it, delaying gratification before it finally hit Raquel where it mattered most. But at her age, a five-second orgasm was enough to sate her for a while. She wasn't young like Lisa, who could probably go until the sun came up. *That's part of the fun. I'll never get enough of it.* Throw in some toys – particularly, the kind that vibrated – and they were in business. That had been one of her plans for Jackie that night.

"You're like a queen, you know that?" Lisa lay next to Raquel. "You are so mature and confident. It turns me on like you don't even know. She rolled onto her stomach. "I want you to indulge me like the spoiled girl that I am."

Raquel sat up, eyes lingering on the frame of this nubile princess. Lisa still wore her blue dress, the skirt feathered around her ass as it rode up and exposed her firm cheeks. Her legs were as smooth as silk. It almost wasn't fair to know that this girl's youth was so fleeting… but princesses turned into queens one day, and Raquel was apparently the Queen of the city.

"If I am a queen," she said, massaging one of those hard cheeks with her waiting hand. "Then that makes you one of my harem girls."

"I don't mind. As long as I get a piece of you."

"Mm, but I might get bored with you."

"You won't tonight."

Raquel got up on her knees. Arousal swarmed inside her again as she gazed upon this princess, who had no idea what lay ahead of her in life. "Before I let any offering into my harem, I must inspect the goods first." She pushed the blue skirt up higher. *Of course she's not wearing any underwear. Of course not.* Raquel gave that unblemished flesh a spank. Lisa yelped in pleasure, body jerking forward. "I have high standards. Roll over. Please me, and I please you."

Lisa responded with alacrity. She flipped herself over and pushed her chest into the air, enticing Raquel with more than her body.

"Good girl," Raquel cooed, aware that Lisa was shaking in pent-up excitement. Raquel gently lowered the bust of her lover's dress. When did God give young women the right to be so firm? When she released Lisa's breasts, they bounced right back to where they were. Her areolas were a perfect shade of pink and topped her tits as if they were cherries on birthday cupcakes. *It's impossible to be jealous when given the gift of having these in my face.* Youth may be fleeting, but there was a reason so many people, young and old, flocked to the flowers on display in a shop. Picked fresh! Still ripe! *Get them now before they wilt!* "Look at you," Raquel said, keeping those toxic thoughts at bay. "So perfect. Are you trying to trick me?" By now, the wrap dress had completely pulled open, showing how flat Lisa's stomach was. Raquel could only dream of having a body like this again. *I bet she doesn't even watch what she eats or go to the gym that often. I miss my old metabolism.* "Isn't it too much pressure being so perfect? You beg to be tarnished."

"Please..." Lisa dragged Raquel's hands back up to her breasts. "Do it. Tear me apart and ruin me."

You have no idea what you're saying. It was all fun and games now. Young women always wanted to be taken to their limits. Maybe they'd like it. Maybe they'd never do it again. Getting to be the woman to do it was an honor.

"Come on now," Raquel goaded. "Ass in the air."

Lisa rolled onto her stomach again and pulled her legs beneath her.

"You are so lovely." Raquel couldn't stop caressing her, fingers treading dangerously close to Lisa's depths. "I bet the rest of you is even better." She leaned forward and peered between Lisa's legs before sliding one finger against those lovely petals. Someone squirmed beneath Raquel's touch. "So this is what you offer the queen of the jungle?'

She forked her fingers around both lips and pulled them apart, whistling in appreciation. Lisa got so excited that not even a dam could hold back the mighty flows of her arousal.

"*Very* nice." Raquel tormented her with one finger. *Wish I could clamp like that on command.* She pulled her finger out and spanked Lisa's pussy. The yelp echoing in the hotel room was made of finer things than Chantilly lace and diamond rings.

"Will you fuck me already?" Lisa whimpered. "Do whatever you want to me!"

Raquel was used to hearing cries and demands come from her young one-night-stands, but something about the way Lisa turned her head and looked her in the eye when she said that... it came from a different place, didn't it? *Something's going on in this girl's head.* The human inside of Raquel said that she cared. The ravenous woman who was only in it for the hot one-night-stand? Eh, that shit was for Lisa to deal with when this was over. For all Raquel knew, crazed hookups like this one was how Lisa processed the darker parts of her life. *We've all been there.* They manifested in different ways, but they had *all* been there.

"Whatever I want, huh?" Raquel tasted the young woman's essence, still warm on the tip of her finger. She was sweet. Not so sweet that Raquel questioned what a girl like her was doing in a place like this, but sweet enough to make her say, "What is it that *you* want?"

Lisa bit her bottom lip and gently lowered her hips to the bed. She gestured to a bag nearby. "If you really want to know... look no further."

Something by the nightstand? It looked like a carry-on full of pills and toothpaste. Raquel crawled over, looked in, and smiled from ear to ear.

"This is definitely *something*," she said, pulling out the biggest thing in the bag. Right next to the lube and condoms. *Who were you planning on using this with, sweetie? Because hot damn.* Her hand could barely wrap around it. "You certainly have a healthy appetite."

"Yes, ma'am."

Raquel almost choked. *Ma'am?* Great. That was the danger of finding a young woman who was into the older ladies. People spent so much time worrying about the older generations fetishizing the younger, that they failed to consider how it felt getting called *ma'am* during a hookup! *For that, I'll give you* exactly *what you want.* Lisa wasn't going to walk right for a week. Hey, she had asked for it! Raquel would start by antagonizing Lisa with the slow ascent of black straps up her legs. "Brace yourself, then," she said. "I'm about to test how tight that pussy of yours really is."

She situated herself behind Lisa and pulled her hips back. The girl groaned in anticipation. *Say goodbye to walking with your thighs close together, hon.*

"Oh!" That was the last sound Lisa made before Raquel gave it to her.

She cried, pleasurably, but her voice strained to convey how much it pleasured and tormented her at the same time. Raquel had dealt with some tight corners before, but she had underestimated the girth against her pelvis and the sweet elasticity of one young woman she barely knew. She didn't believe for a second that Lisa was new to this, but whenever this monster was last inside of her, it sure as hell wasn't recently.

"You're *such* a trooper," Raquel said with the sarcastic tone so many women begged her to her use. *Don't know why. Besides it being so... me.* She pushed into Lisa, attempting to take it slow and steady. *This is why you don't do these things with new friends, but how do I say no to someone as cute and fun as her begging for it?* Raquel felt like she wielded a battering ram, and Lisa's sweet body was the castle ready for plundering. She had waded through the soaking wet moats. What was a little battering the ol' walls now?

"When I'm done with you," she muttered, "I'll be able to see the other side of the world through your cunt." She pushed harder, meeting the constant resistance Lisa subconsciously put up with her own body.

She was young. She'd bounce back by the morning.

A few more times, and Raquel discovered how easy it became. Time to up the ante. There were other things to do with their short night.

A groan erupted in the room as Raquel slammed into Lisa without a shred of mercy. It didn't take long for Lisa to thrust back against her. Her cries of desperate need were clear. Her movements that matched Raquel's were precise. *I knew it. You've done this before.* How many women did Lisa pick up for this pleasure? What about it got her off the most? The act of doing it with a stranger, or the act itself? What an honor to be the choice tonight.

"If I'm a queen," Raquel began, her sweaty hands losing purchase on the slick skin of Lisa's hips, "do you know what that makes you?"

That sound coming out of Lisa's mouth was a garbled mess of inquiry and pleasure. *Buh-bye.* She'd be popping off to the moon sooner rather than later. Time for Raquel to get the last of her jollies before Lisa was so spent she collapsed into a sleepy stupor the moment she came.

"A s..." The metaphor was on the tip of her tongue, but a woman only had so much brain power when she was on the other end of a behemoth. Her brain could either channel her excitement, or it could act like a literary piece of shit comparing sex to feudal times. *I'm a queen. You're a serf. You know how this works, love.* It started with a big ego and ended with one woman bracing herself against a hotel bed with a strap-on the size of said ego between her legs.

Did the word *serf* come out of Raquel's mouth, though? Fuck, no! Freud was in the house, and he was making damn well sure that every word slipping from Raquel's lips said what everyone was really thinking.

"A slave."

The loudest moan yet sent Lisa into a spiral. She shoved her hands beneath the pillows and slammed her face into the curl of the comforter. That only made it easier to fuck her.

She liked being called that? She liked being reminded that she was a serf to be used for her youth. Raquel was a queen. A mature queen who knew what she liked and wasn't afraid to get it – and she liked twenty-somethings that didn't know any better than to fuck strange women. This animalistic power filling Raquel's veins as she grabbed Lisa's body and fucked her with every spare bit of might was fueled by the frustration she had felt all her life. Ever since her first real love dumped her for someone else.

"Oh, God!" Lisa clawed the bedsheets, her legs falling limp but the rest of her body as ready as ever.

About damn time she came.

A scream rocked the bed. Raquel braced herself and waited for Lisa to ride out her orgasm. The whole time, she thought of nothing but that good-for-nothing ex that ruined her life over twenty-five-years before.

Eat shit, Marian. Look at me now. Raquel had a fist full of hair in her possession and a screaming, squirming co-ed writhing beneath her. Just another Saturday night in the life of Raquel Mendes. *Fucking sorority girls who seduce me, for fuck's sake.*

Lisa was far from the unfussed woman she had been when they got started. Raquel sat back and reveled in the way that sweaty body crumped against the bed, legs still spread. *Sure could use a cigarette now.* Raquel quit smoking ten years ago. Oh, well. There were other sweet scents to inhale.

"Oh, my God," Lisa whimpered. "Now, shall we do what you want?"

Raquel's eyes widened. "What *I* want? You think I didn't like doing that?" She patted Lisa's naked leg. Her skin rippled from knee to thigh. Only then did Raquel see the stretchmarks this young woman had already accumulated in her short life. *Nothing compared to mine.* With more to come. Damn. Raquel really needed a cigarette now.

Lisa batted her eyelashes. Her breath was quick to come back to her chest, and her legs kicked up into the air, showing off her round ass and the sultry way she rocked back and forth on her stomach. "If you could do *anything,* what would it be? Don't hold back. I like to keep it dirty."

I bet you do. Raquel leaned back on her hands and contemplated the far reaches of her erotic imagination. They didn't go very far. Not after a five-minute romp like *that.* "Roll you over and fuck you again." She liked to keep things simple.

"Then what are you waiting for? A signed invitation?" Lisa propped herself up on her elbows. Her tangled hair highlighted the blush on her cheeks. *Me. I put that blush there.* "Come do it again. We're both not getting any younger."

She really knew how to push those buttons, huh? *You're not only a pro at taking it, huh? You're a pro with older women.*

Fine.

Raquel flipped Lisa over and pulled her legs apart. There were no words to say. Why bother? This was the final hurrah of a hookup that would never touch their lives again. The more Raquel realized that this girl was in *deep,* the less she wanted to see her again.

Didn't mean she wouldn't have her fun now, though. Nor did it mean she would hold back on giving Lisa what she oh-so-obviously wanted.

Once she was inside her again, Raquel burrowed her face in those perky tits while she fucked a new hole between the girl's legs.

Orgasm tore through her like she tore through Lisa. This was it. This was what a leopard on the prowl hunted. She devoured her prey and left nothing behind. The queen of the jungle was no different from the queen on her throne who took what she wanted and told everyone else to go fuck themselves.

She waited a long while after their mutual orgasm ended before pulling out again. Raquel was not disappointed when she lifted her hips and saw what she had wrought between Lisa's legs.

It was beautifully erotic. An ode to what happened to every woman who went in too deep and came out someone new on the other side. Lisa was done. She had given Raquel what she needed and was no longer required for a night of revelry. Yet she would never be the same. Her tastes had been elevated. Lisa was done by a queen, and would no longer be worthy of the peasantry.

Yet she was already like that when Raquel met her, wasn't she?

Raquel had her fill of this majestic offering. She cleaned herself up, but Lisa remained on the bed, lying on her side and staring at the woman coming in and out of the hotel bathroom as if she had rented that room herself. Raquel almost asked if Lisa were in town for some conference or to visit family, but refrained. *I don't need to know anything about you.* Best to keep this clean.

Lisa didn't ask for anything else, and Raquel was content to get back to her regular life until it was time to hunt again. *No woman will ever have the chance to dump me again.* Her dates were her willing prey, and she was determined to devour them all.

Chapter 3

Lisa entered her studio apartment only a few miles away from the hotel room. There was no use staying in a rented room when she was the only one in there.

Everything had seemed like a good idea at the time, hadn't it?

She peeled herself off her door and stepped into the small room she called her own. The low hum and dull light of her laptop invited her to sit down at her desk and stare mindlessly at Reddit, but the last thing her body wanted her to do was *sit*. Every inch of her was sore. That's what she got when she invited an experienced woman like Raquel to come up to her room and have her way with a willing woman.

A dream come true. It had been a *dream come true*.

Eventually, Lisa did sit, but it wasn't in her old, cheap chair before her desk. She sat on the edge of her bed. The one she hadn't bothered to make when she got up that morning. Lisa had been fixated on two things: finishing the article she owed an online publication, and going out to get laid.

Finding Raquel in that hotel bar was the perfect marriage of chance and intention. The moment she saw her sitting at the bar, she knew it was fate. Could Lisa really call it fate when all the cards were set up, ready for the world to deal her that hand, though?

I've wanted this for over five years. She dumped her overnight bag in the middle of the floor and stared at her ceiling. Her thighs ached to stretch open again, but that's what she did while she fondly remembered the way Raquel got on top of her and took control of their "chance" encounter.

How many times had Lisa touched herself to the thought of that woman rubbing her thigh, nibbling her ear, pinching her nipples and fingering her slit? How many times had she stared at that picture, wondering what it was like to be the thrall of the most captivating woman in the world?

She had no idea who I was. That was comforting, right? If Raquel recognized her, the game would be up. The whole night would have played out differently, and Lisa would be lying in her bed, wet with tears, not sex.

No. It was important that Raquel not know who she was. It would have changed everything.

Lisa had done an admirable job keeping the truth at bay, hadn't she? Then again, it was easy enough to play the sultry young seductress when that was her natural inclination around women like Raquel. Women who were strong, forthright, and not afraid to sink their teeth into the tender flesh of those sacrificing themselves at the altar of forbidden desires.

I'm hungry...

Yet Lisa did not move. Her computer fan continued to whirl, and the buzz of cars and life outside her apartment window kept her awake, but her whole body willed her to stay where she was. To allow her hand to roam across her body and seal the memory of that night into the annals of her mind.

How was someone supposed to process the events of that night? How was someone supposed to recover?

I wonder what she's doing right now. Raquel had left the hotel room with little pomp. A curt farewell and a thanks for a good time was all she needed to say before showing herself out. They didn't exchange numbers. She never asked for Lisa's last name or inquired about her life beyond how old she was.

She was probably at home now. Soaking in the bathtub. Sitting in bed before drifting off to sleep, thinking of the stranger she had fucked with every breath fluttering through her body. Drinking wine and flipping through her folders from work. Lisa really didn't know, of course. Her fantasies came from what she learned about Raquel online. She was a successful real estate agent who specialized in single-family homes and luxury condos. Surely, she was constantly surrounded by folders full of information about her current listings and the middle-class families looking for their next homes.

Next time Lisa saw that gorgeous face plastered on a billboard, she would be able to say she was touched by that devilish angel.

At what price?

She forced herself up on her hands. "Ugh," she muttered, attempting to ignore the delightful pain radiating throughout her body. For every inch that was grateful for the intense attention only an hour ago, there was another screaming at her to never do that again. Raquel could call her young all she wanted. Didn't stop Lisa from being *human*.

She dragged herself to her mini-fridge and unearthed a cup of yogurt from its depths. She sat at her laptop with a sigh and closed the ancient tabs she no longer needed. E-mail. Facebook. Wikipedia. A million applications simply using up resources in her computer. Why was she wasteful with everything? Like the cup of yogurt left open on her desk while she scrolled through a chatroom for young women who had certain... proclivities?

"You know that woman I've been crushing on for years?" Lisa typed into the window. Her icon, the depiction of Anne Hathaway (the historical figure, not the actress) popped up when she typed. A number in

the corner of the chatroom informed her that at least five other young women were online and ready to read her story. *"Well, I hooked up with her tonight. It was amazing."*

She sat back and ate some of her yogurt. A few dots appeared on the screen, informing her that someone typed a response.

"WOW!!! Go girl!"

"The real estate lady? Sounds hot. Was it hot?"

Lisa put down the yogurt cup. *"The hottest. The woman was a real cougar, if you know what I mean. She was super into it, like I thought she would be."*

"UGH! SO JEALOUS!"

Lisa promised to give them more updates the next day. It wasn't unusual for that group of women to fuel each other's urges to go out and bed people more than fifteen years older than themselves, depending on how young they were. (Since they were mostly college students, Lisa still fit right in.) One woman was a professional sugar baby and said it was the best job in the world. What was better than not only seducing older men and women, but being *paid* to do it? Others, like Lisa, merely harbored the dream and used their youth and perceived naivete to get themselves dates and hookups that they then reported to the rest of the group. It wasn't any different from other groups of friends who giggled and gossiped about their sex lives. This group of strangers, however, were dedicated to keeping it about May-December romances. Or the occasional May-September, as Lisa preferred to think of her crush on Raquel Mendes.

She lowered her laptop lid and finished her yogurt. After sitting in her chair for a few moments, she plucked a pale orange notebook from the top of her desk and grabbed a pink gel pen from a cup that said, *"Future Sugar Mama."*

Inside was either the most embarrassing moments of her life, or the most amazing. It depended on who asked.

"It happened tonight," she wrote on a fresh page dated with that day. *"My life has been changed, for better or for worse."*

What happened now?

Lisa pulled down a framed photograph from the shelf lining the wall. It depicted herself ten years ago, a scraggly thirteen-year-old with her arm around her mother's waist. They both smiled at the camera before going into Disneyland for the tenth time in as many years. It was a yearly trip, both before and after Lisa's parents divorced.

Lisa had long lost contact with her father. She hadn't spoken to her mother since she died of breast cancer eight years ago.

This picture was priceless. It was the last one they took together before her mother's diagnosis. Every picture they took thereafter was laced in the reality that the most important woman in Lisa's life would be gone before she finished high school.

Lisa stared into her mother's face. Weathered. Tanned. Caked in makeup but still glowing with good humor.

The frame landed on the bed, the picture facing down. Lisa picked up her notebook and the gel pen.

"What have I done?"

Chapter 4

Raquel grabbed one of the cucumber sandwiches on the platter and stuffed it in her mouth while texting her boss at the real estate agency. He wanted to confirm that she dragged her ass to the house on Smith Street an hour earlier than she was originally scheduled to arrive. It didn't help that the interior decorators, led by overpriced queen Paisley Price, were in a frenzy putting together the living room at the very last moment.

Not that this was a terrible sign of things to come. The whole reason they were opening the house to public viewing an hour early was because the interest in it was *that* intense. The agency called Raquel the night before to inform her that at least three families were seriously interested in the property without having taken a formal walkthrough. They all had appointments for personal tours throughout the day. Raquel's job was to stay caffeinated, look good, and not forget that it was the *second* bedroom with the squeaky door hinge. *Don't close the door. Whatever we do, don't close the door!* Nobody wanted to hear that thing scream bloody murder while attempting to convince upper middle-class families to part with eight-hundred grand for a five-bedroom house.

"Did you get the bunk beds in the third bedroom?" Raquel asked, mouth still full of the cucumber sandwich that she called her lunch. "Because one of the families has twins." Sounded like a nightmare to Raquel, but what did she know about child-rearing?

Paisley rested against the marble kitchen counter and indulged in a sandwich alongside Raquel. "Bunk beds in the third bedroom, and a quaint mother-in-law setup in the fourth, like you asked."

"Good! Because I'm sure the Malones are bringing their mom along, and I want her to feel like she will die if her sweet children don't buy this fucking house."

"You think you're gonna get a bidding war today?"

"Maybe not *today*..." Raquel swallowed the last of the sandwich and used both thumbs to mash through an app on her phone. "Definitely this week. One of the families may drop out, but... well, you know. With my winning charms, I should convince some couple I've never even heard of that they need this house for their eternal status."

"You're definitely confident today." Paisley grabbed a cup of water from the ice and lemon dispenser at the end of the counter. *God, I hope there are enough cookies for all the kids that are gonna come through here.* "Did you have a nice weekend?"

Raquel slowly rolled her neck until her eyes settled on Paisley's smarmy grin. "Had a date Friday night. Did absolutely nothing all Saturday, and I wouldn't have it any other way." Sundays, ironically enough, were for work. Open houses killed it on the weekend, and at the price range she commanded, Raquel mostly worked open houses on Sundays, when the primary breadwinners of families definitely had a day off. *No rest for the weary over here.* She worked Sundays so the Monday-Saturday people didn't have to.

"A date, huh? You still seeing that girl from the college?"

Which one? It didn't matter. Whatever girl Paisley had in mind was close enough. "She dumped me that night, if you can believe it. Said I'm too old for her."

"What a bitch."

"They're young," Raquel said with a dramatic sigh. "What do they really know? Besides, the night wasn't totally a bust. Picked up another girl at the bar and, well, you know how it goes."

"Sly dog."

Raquel had thought of Lisa more than once since Friday night. *What can I say? A girl who offers a good lay is always on my mind.* It didn't help that Raquel spent so much of her Saturday lounging around her house, hitting up the café across the street for iced coffee, and grocery shopping with nothing but memories of the beautiful young woman on her mind. It almost made her wish that she had gotten Lisa's number before leaving the hotel room.

Then again, some things were best left as one-night stands. Why ruin a perfect thing with unfortunate truths, such as Lisa's inevitable immaturity or crazy family? *It's bad enough when parents find out their daughters are dating women... when they find out how old I am, the shotguns come out.*

"I've got to do one walkthrough before the first family arrives." Raquel patted the countertop before showing herself into the other room. "Great work on the house, by the way."

Paisley always took her compliments with a smile and a small salute of the fingers. In another life, her cute ass wouldn't be married to some guy from the Yukon, and Raquel would stand a chance at calling the artistic interior decorator her girlfriend. *Think of all the business we would accumulate with our minds going 24/7!*

Raquel fixed up her hair and makeup in the bathroom, determined to be nothing but picture-perfect when the first of many families arrived that morning. She was determined to sell someone their dream home that day and make a commission that was big enough to fund a dream getaway to Hawaii. Bonus if she found someone cute enough to take along with her as the luckiest lesbian sugar baby in America.

What could Raquel say? She lived to spoil.

The first two families came one after another, the one with twins shedding tears when they saw the bunk beds and the one with the mother-in-law tagging exclaiming over the adequate distance between bedrooms. The door handle never once screamed its siren song of doom, and the firepit in the backyard always turned on with a flick of a button. Reversible pillows and colored lighting fixtures Paisley installed allowed Raquel to change the mood and palette of the house to custom tailor to the families strolling through. The same room elicited the same amount of awe from two wives, although the walls looked like different colors and the pillows went from "gray and yellow TV chic" to "funky disco nights in Morocco." Raquel loved her biggest party trick: guessing a woman's style after only one conversation.

"We will *definitely* be putting in an offer," the matriarch of the second family assured Raquel. It wasn't the twins from earlier that morning that wiped out the cookies on the kitchen counter – it was grandma, who thought she was one sneaky fuck when she shoved both snickerdoodles and chocolate chips into her handbag. One at a time, no less! "This is our dream neighborhood, and this house is simply... it's divine, Raquel. We're *so* glad you found it for us!"

"Well, I must let you know that there's quite a bit of interest in this house." She grinned at both husband and wife, holding hands as if they were still on their honeymoon. "If you want to cement your chances, I *highly* recommend shooting for the full asking price. Or a little higher, if you're feeling frisky."

"Oh, we've done our research," the husband said. "I think both you and the seller will be quite pleased with our offer."

Raquel remained all smiles as she escorted them – including the geriatric cookie thief – outside. The warm summer sun made Raquel want to run back inside and take full advantage of the air conditioning, but she didn't flinch as she began to sweat beneath her blazer. The woman walked her mother-in-law to the car and happened to overlook the eye candy making her way down the street.

"Well, hello." The husband lowered his sunglasses and glanced at Raquel before further commenting on the young woman sauntering down the sidewalk. "Neighbor, I take it."

Raquel was ready to mentally admonish this man for looking at anyone but his wife, but she was likewise taken in by the beauty coming closer.

While the twenty-something didn't possess a true supermodel's body, she was still built like a beauty queen taking full advantage of the warm day and her no-fucks-given youth. A hot pink bikini bumped up her breasts and put all other attention on the dip of her pelvis, the cute little discount sneakers lighting up with her steps. No socks detected, but Raquel was less concerned about the gal's blisters and more infatuated with the white knit poncho giving her an air of being covered up for a stroll down a public street. Honestly, it put *more* attention on her bangin' body. The pulled back hair and large earrings dangling down her long neck were like cherries on this feast of a sundae.

"I have no idea who that is," Raquel said with a squeak in her throat. "College co-ed home for the summer, I guess."

"You said it first. Thanks, Raquel. I'll let you know about the offer." The husband flashed her a smile before joining his wife and mother in the SUV. He almost knocked over the OPEN HOUSE sign when he pulled out and rubbernecked in the young woman's direction.

Only then did Raquel recognize her.

"You've gotta be kidding..." The shock of recognizing Lisa would normally kill her libido, but for some god-forsaken reason it sent her into overdrive. *Look at her. Oh, my God. Look at her! She's hotter than Friday night!* Was this really the woman Raquel knocked-out? Or was she seeing things?

Lisa stopped by the mailbox and held up her phone. The poncho went up with her arms, and the first thing Raquel saw was that belly button inviting her to come stick her tongue in it again.

The phone lowered. Lisa looked right at Raquel, but it took a few moments before she lowered her sunglasses and dropped her lower jaw. Was the recognition instantaneous? Or was Raquel so good looking that she made women come to standstills on the street?

"Hey, stranger!" Lisa called, the flirtation already on thick. *I'll fucking say! Look at what she's wearing!* Or not wearing!

Raquel looked both ways before descending the front porch and meeting Lisa by the mailbox. The door to the house was left wide open. All that sweet AC was about to be dust, but nothing could cool Raquel's fiery heart now. "What are you doing here? Don't tell me you live in this neighborhood."

Lisa tugged on her ponytail. The rose tint of her sunglasses illuminated the bright pink of her lip gloss and highlighted the neon quality of her barely-there bikini. At this rate, Lisa would be causing that Sunday's ten-car pileup as soon as traffic started cruising by! "Why? Got a problem with me being in the neighborhood?"

Raquel had to remind herself to not gawk at anyone. "Surprised to see you around here, that's all."

"Small world, isn't it?" Lisa shrugged, boosting up her breasts in that ridiculous bikini bra. They weren't actually that big, were they? Raquel would remember porn star tits! "Thought I saw your face on the bus stop bench around here. Didn't make the connection between you and the sign, though." She referenced the FOR SALE sign hanging by the sidewalk. "I like your last name. Are you Latina?"

Raquel could hardly believe she was asked that. "Uh, I guess. From my father's side." She never really thought about it. She was more likely to obsess over her gender and what a disadvantage it put her in the cutthroat world of upper middle-class real estate in a city that size. Everyone wanted a piece of the pie, and she was the one racing toward it with a pie server.

"Cool." Lisa lowered her sunglasses again. "Having any luck with the open house?" she asked from behind rose-colored lenses. She was like a big pink flower with white dew all over her body. *All right, Jesus, I get it. You like the idea of me and this girl together.* Raquel had never been a God-fearing woman, but she was inclined to take heavenly signs as they came to her. It was all that Catholic-churching when she was a little girl. Signs this, miracles that... didn't mean much to a little lesbian fantasizing about the Rodriguez girl two pews down, but she would never forget how many times Dolores Rodriguez cried out to God and Jesus when Raquel went down on her when they were the tender age of sixteen. When her peers talked about how wild the '90s were, *that* was the first thing Raquel remembered.

Better than thinking of the other thing...

"It's all right. Though you almost gave my last client a nosebleed right in front of his wife *and* his mother."

Lisa giggled, hands on hips and whole body cocked to one side. "What about you? Don't tell me that since the mystery has been solved, you're totally over me."

"What mystery?" Since when was Raquel a detective?

Lisa gestured to her breasts. "What I look like naked."

"I don't know what you've heard about me, but I don't cast women aside after I've slept with them." Ha! If only her exes could hear her now! *To be fair, I don't move on because I think of the women I date as used. They start boring me. That's all.* There were few women who could keep Raquel's interest for more than a few weeks. Most of them weren't as deliciously flirtatious as Lisa already proved herself to be.

"Oh, really?" Lisa crossed her arms, shielding her cleavage, much to Raquel's chagrin. "Prove it."

"Excuse me?"

A breeze stirred up, and while it did nothing to disturb the woman on full display to the neighborhood, it did a bang-up job knocking the OPEN HOUSE sale around. "When do you get a break for lunch? Because I've got some time."

Raquel could hardly believe it. Was this girl really asking her out so blatantly? *Again?* This was how they ended up together last time!

"All right. I'm actually going on lunch in about ten minutes. I only have to lock up the house." Raquel sniffed, willing away the allergens blowing in on the breeze. "Why don't you run back home and put on a few more clothes so we don't make everyone jealous."

Lisa looked at her as if she were some conservative grandma fretting over nothing. "I've got the perfect place for us to go, thanks. A place that will accept me as I am." It couldn't be a coincidence that she slapped her hand against her cleavage. "Besides, I'm more worried about you blowing up a place with your hotness."

Raquel almost stumbled back to the house, where she hurried to grab her bag and lock the door. She realized a moment too late that she had forgotten to take in the OPEN HOUSE sign. Oh, well! Some things were more important. Like hot ass.

This will be what sets me back in my career. Not who I am, but how I act! Raquel acted as cool as a fan as she gestured to her car. The #1 thing she wanted was a woman dressed like Lisa sitting shotgun in the Audi Raquel bought after getting her cut of a million-dollar house.

"It's around the corner, actually." Lisa tucked her hair behind her ear. That simple action was enough to fell Raquel where she stood. *Fuck. Me.* She hadn't gotten this girl's number Friday night? Was that how satisfied she was after that rousing round in bed? "Thought we would walk."

"You working on your tan or something?"

Lisa walked ahead, her ass swaying with gusto while the poncho draped down the back of her body.

She wasn't lying when she said the place she had in mind was around the corner. Five minutes later, they were sitting outside at a neighborhood café near the main boulevard cutting toward downtown. Lisa kicked back in her chair, one leg perfectly slung over the other, her look somehow fitting right in with the other beach-bodies ready to hit the tanning beds, public pools, and trips to the cape as soon as their lunches were over. To some, Raquel was probably overdressed in her half-suit. She removed her blazer as soon as it was apparent the sun might visit them where they sat.

Play it cool, kid. Raquel perused the brunch menu before settling on a salad and iced tea. She told Lisa to get whatever she wanted. That included a watered-down mimosa and a turkey sandwich on ciabatta bread.

"Let me ask you a question," Raquel said, as soon as their orders were taken. "If you live around here, what were you doing in a hotel room the other night?"

A flash of embarrassment sparkled behind those rosy sunglasses. Yet when Lisa recollected herself, she did so with the utmost grace. "Can I tell you a secret?"

"Naturally."

Lisa leaned in across the table. "That wasn't my hotel room."

Raquel had figured as much. "Whose was it?"

"My friend's. She was in town for the convention, but since she has a boyfriend, she stayed the night with him and let me use her room in case I got lucky." That girlish grin was the kind of shit they wrote birthday cards about. "Afraid I have a studio. Not much fun for those of us who like to live it up a little, let alone court women of an older flavor."

"You think I wouldn't be impressed with your place or something?"

Lisa hesitated. "Sometimes a girl wants to keep some things private."

Raquel hadn't been expecting that. Every time Lisa became more transparent, she built herself up again in infinite mystery. "So let me get this straight… your friend loaned you the hotel room meant for her but she never intended to use… in case you got lucky Friday night?"

"Is it so hard to believe?"

"Now I know why you were seriously pushing yourself onto me."

"Did you have a problem with that?"

The waitress returned with their drinks. Lisa and Raquel did not break eye contact. "What if I hadn't been interested in you? Would you have hooked up with the first woman to give you the attention you wanted?"

Lisa batted her eyelashes. "I was a woman on a mission. You know how long it's been since I last got laid before you?"

"Can't be that long." Raquel said that after only considering the way Lisa dressed and carried herself. *Good God. She could have any queer-leaning woman she wants! Even the married ones!* If Lisa were at all interested in guys, then her young sex life was locked and loaded for an all-twenties party. Not even Raquel could take her eyes off the curve of Lisa's sides and the way her cheekbones held up those big sunglasses.

"Probably a lot longer than you usually have to wait." Lisa continued before Raquel could correct her. "You've got that older woman thing down. Bet you've fooled around with some of my classmates. Got a few that are like me, you know. Can't say no to a professional woman as hot as you."

Raquel studied the expression on Lisa's young visage, the one that was indiscernible under a certain light. Was she fucking with Raquel? Playing some silly, immature game they would both regret in a few years? *I've been with a few extroverted girls before, but she's taking the cake.* That's what made someone memorable, though. It wasn't only the body or the way she smelled after all was said and done. It was the feeling she speared into Raquel's abdomen on a daily basis. The one that made her come back for more, because what woman didn't like being slapped with her own sexuality every time she turned around?

"We seem to have extravagant ideas about each other's sex lives."

"Well, after the night we spent together, can we blame ourselves?"

Raquel was caught off guard by her own laughter. "I suppose not."

Lisa's tongue wrapped around the straw of her mimosa, eyes never breaking contact with Raquel's. It was the rare woman who gave her so many shudders in so little time. "I really love the way you look at me. Like you did the other night. Have you been thinking about me?"

Amazing. She didn't put the spotlight on Raquel by proclaiming how much she thought about *her*. Oh, no. Lisa was insistent on putting any and all attention on herself, the veritable woman of the hour. So happened that Raquel loved fawning over women who would let her. Any excuse she had to lay it on thick was welcomed more often than not.

So why did it feel so strange right now?

Perhaps it was how closely they sat, their noses only a few inches away from each other. Raquel could see every freckle on Lisa's face. The ones that formed little constellations in the shapes of diamonds and clubs, a full house in the game of poker. *I used to know someone who had freckles like these.* The little brown blotches were a dime a dozen when it came to women – let alone those prancing around in the sunshine – but Raquel had such a soft spot for them that it was almost painful. No. It *was* painful. Because twenty-five years ago she once loved a woman with so many beautiful freckles that she claimed she could draw every star in the sky.

I often tried.

"What's wrong?" Lisa pulled away, taking her glossy pink lips and the scent of her perfume with her.

"Nothing is wrong." Raquel wiped something from her eye. "Sorry. Terribly allergic."

"Oh, dear."

Raquel nodded. "To answer your question... of course I have thought about you. You think I could find it possible to do anything but remember how you look naked?"

That elicited a surprised giggle from Lisa's lips. "I was thinking the same about you. Honestly, you should start a video blog about staying hot well into your forties. I think a lot of women my age would break YouTube to find out your beauty secrets!"

Raquel cocked her head. "How do you know that I am in my forties?"

"Lucky guess." When that didn't sate Raquel's curiosity, Lisa said, "You look older, but in that mature way, you know? Plus, you've got that successful real estate thing going on, and I'm guessing that comes with a lot of experience and a few years under your belt. The real kicker, though?" She leaned back in her chair, those smooth thighs still crossed and one white sneaker dangling in the air. "You started singing along to a New

Kids on the Block song the other night. I'm not even sure I remember that song well."

"Were you even born when that song came out?"

Lisa shook her head. "I was born in '95."

"Ninety..." Raquel was grateful that her salad had arrived. It saved her from looking like the biggest grandma at the café. "That makes me almost a full twenty years older than you!"

"Is there a problem with that? I thought you liked your lovers young and ready to party."

"I like lovers of all ages." Raquel would back that claim up with her dating history, as well. Just because she mostly dated twenty-somethings didn't erase the older women she dated when she was Lisa's age, or the other women of her generation she got along with fine in the sack. She simply had preferences. *Show me a forty-five-year old who can keep up with me like the college kids do and I'll swoon.*

"Well, you already heard what I had to say on the subject." That sigh blowing from Lisa's lips was faker than the tan on the woman walking by. "I love women mature enough to teach me the ways of love."

"Don't ever put it that way. Even if you're joking."

"Only a little." Lisa picked up a piece of lettuce left on her plate and crunched it between her teeth. "So, tell me. When are we going out again?"

Raquel shoved some of her salad into her mouth. She needed the excuse to contemplate an answer, let alone how she felt about Lisa coming on so strongly. Again! *I don't have to be the one in charge in a relationship, but I need to know if this attitude of hers is genuine or not.* She didn't like fakes. She didn't like women – of any age – who painted veneers on top of their makeup and pretended to be personalities that they were not. She wanted to know who she was dealing with from the beginning. Any woman she was 100% with? She expected the same in return.

"I hope you realize," Raquel said after she swallowed, "that I'm not a girlfriend you can walk all over and play Greedy Sugar Baby with. Outside of the bedroom, anyway."

A full-body shudder zipped down Lisa's spine. It was that kind of honest reaction that made Raquel appreciate where this was going. "So happens that's how I like it. I can't help it if I want to lock this down right now."

"Lock what down?"

"*This.*" Lisa twiddled her fingers in the space between them. "I see a hot, mature woman who is more than available, and I want a piece of the action. I think it's fate that we've bumped into each other again. Forgive me if I'm anxious to see where it goes. Bedrooms or no bedrooms."

Lisa took a bite of her sandwich and lowered it to her plate again. Raquel picked up her napkin and slowly leaned across the small table, the tip of her napkin touching the edge of Lisa's lips. Mayonnaise had made itself at home there. As lovely as it was to see a touch of white to match the poncho on this woman's rockin' body, Raquel was inclined to use any excuse she could find to touch Lisa. Because she couldn't afford to take her back home and fuck her brains out right now. There was money to be made as soon as lunch was over.

Besides... sometimes it was worth it to put off pleasure. It made it even sweeter when it finally came.

"How about you give me your number, and I'll call you sometime next week?"

Was that a look of consternation on Lisa's face? Because Raquel could dig it. "Why not make plans with me right now? The summer is young, and I have nothing going on."

"I don't know what my schedule looks like." That was a lie. Raquel could guarantee that she would spend most of the week taking offers for the house on Smith Street and fielding calls for potential properties her agency wanted her to take on as soon as the current project was closed. Depending on what kind of bidding war erupted, it could eat her whole day. Not that she couldn't make time for a hot date somewhere in there. She knew it would be worth it, too.

But she wanted to play with Lisa a little. Make her *really* want it. Blow the promises of something more into her ear and watch her writhe. This was only possible if the phone numbers went in one direction.

Lisa had already made her romantic intentions clear. The ball was in Raquel's court – right where she liked it.

I don't always have to be in charge, but I have a feeling I should be with this girl. She got out her phone and created a contact for Lisa, who was more than ready to hand her number over. She only pouted a little when she realized she wasn't getting a number back yet. *I want her to know that I'm the one giving the orders until I know where this is going.*

That was part of the fun, after all. That and ogling what a woman like Lisa had to offer beneath her scanty clothing and her promises of more sex than most college co-eds could ever say they had.

Raquel always did love delivering on every young lesbian's fantasies.

Chapter 5

Lisa became one with her therapist's couch. The plush fabric and the way the sunlight hit the windows of the brick building was more comfortable than Lisa remembered from her weekly appointments. Shit, this couch was one of the reasons she kept Sally as her therapist after shopping around for a month. It had come down to Sally and another woman on the other side of town. The other therapist had a leather couch. Soooo not comfy or hip! How was anyone supposed to get comfortable on a leather couch when it was always in the sunlight?

Sally had the high-back chair to make every office intern jealous. Not Lisa, though, who almost made the mistake of falling asleep on the couch the moment her head hit the pillows. "How has your week been, Lisa?" the soft-spoken therapist asked.

Eyes flitting open, Lisa encountered the flood of conflicting emotions enveloping her body. She was elated over meeting Raquel and setting those romantic wheels in motion. She was discouraged, because after giving Raquel her number – and not getting one back – she hadn't heard from her in *days.*

It was Wednesday now. Where were the texts? The voicemails? The invitations to WhatsApp and Snapchat? Damnit! Didn't Raquel have an Instagram so Lisa could slide into her DMs? Some women of the Gen-X world really needed to get with social media. Raquel's only online presence was her business's Facebook page and a professional Twitter account that she – or an assistant, it was hard to tell – posted new listings and house buying tips to. Hardly the appropriate avenues for establishing personal contact. Lisa didn't want to come across as a stalker. She simply wanted to know what was going on!

Yet when she told her therapist about her great fortune that weekend, she kept her smile big and her optimism apparent in her voice. Sally's eyes widened to hear that her client had finally met this woman she had been crushing on for "a while," as Lisa put it during previous appointments.

"You went for it, huh?"

"Hell, yes!" Lisa sat up on the couch, her sweatshirt tugging up her stomach and getting caught beneath her breasts. She absentmindedly pulled the fabric into place. "I was so stoked to see her hanging out by herself in a bar! I thought to myself... well, what do you have to lose, Lisa? Go chat with her!"

"How did that go?"

A touch of blush hit Lisa's cheeks. She looked away before Sally could smile at her with her thirty-something eyes. *In another life, I'd have a crush on you, too.* Didn't help that Sally had a long-term female partner. Or that Sally was more masculine-of-center than a lot of the other queer girls Lisa encountered. *I like my women a bit more power-femme, though.* Like Sally's partner, prominently displayed in a picture frame on the other side of the room. That big, curly hair and smoldering look made Lisa jealous of her therapist – until now.

"We may or may not have hooked up."

Sally was a master of imparting no judgment. Not that Lisa gave a shit what her therapist was thinking right now. *Judge me all you want. I got the one thing I wanted.* Well, the one thing she *wanted* was a wedding ring on her hand, but she was a practical girl when it came to taking things one step at a time. *That's how I got here. That's how I found Raquel on the perfect night to initiate contact. One little step at a time.* Her mother used to say that every step added up to a marathon over time.

"Wow," Sally finally said. "How do you feel about that now?"

"Awesome. You may not believe it, but I actually bumped into her out in the wild on Sunday. I happened to be in a neighborhood where she was working, and she came running out to see me! I could hardly believe it myself." Lisa left out a few pertinent details. Like how she had been following Raquel's Twitter account and saw that she was having an open house not too far from Lisa's apartment. The weather was hot enough to warrant putting on a string-bikini and tossing some sheer material over it. As usual, Raquel's attentions had been on Lisa's assets for most of their lunch date. Lisa was only more than happy to show off her body to a woman who appreciated youth in its greatest glory. "We exchanged numbers and have plans to go out again."

Sally merely nodded as if this were all information she expected to hear. Lisa couldn't tell. Nor did she care. Sally had one job, and that was to keep Lisa focused on the real issues she constantly dealt with. *I got into therapy after my mom died.* A grief therapist had transformed into a general counselor who guided Lisa through college and now watched her take on her post-university life. Sally had been Lisa's therapist since sophomore year, and knew all about her tastes for older women. They had *bonded* over the fact, because Sally had been quick to point out that most young lesbians covet relationships with older, confident, and more established women who could guide them through an unforgiving world – let alone initiate them into the hot world of girl-on-girl sex and impart everything they had learned. Slowly, Lisa had revealed her attractions to a certain woman in the area. One that she knew was gay, but could hardly say was easy to approach with romantic intentions. Sally had never told her client to not pursue her crushes, but she *did* caution Lisa against crossing boundaries and ignoring her gut. Two things Lisa willingly admitted she needed to hear.

"How is work going?"

Sally was also a professional at swerving the conversation before Lisa went down those deep rabbit holes she loved so much. Besides, it was good she had reminded Lisa that she had money to make so she could keep her studio apartment in the town she so badly wanted to live in. Because Lisa had *totally forgotten* about an article she had due by seven!

After her appointment was over, she rushed back to her apartment and grabbed her laptop and USB mouse. There was a café at the end of the street where she sometimes liked to get a small coffee and blast through her assignments, and on sunny days like that one when her life held some hope, she didn't mind parting with a couple of dollars if it meant getting out of her house for a while.

Lisa cobbled together a meager living that kept her roof over her head and her stomach relatively full. Yet she hungered for a little more freedom in where she could go every day. The only reason she could afford the therapist was because she was still on her estranged father's insurance that covered everything but ten dollars a visit. She had no idea what she would do after turning twenty-six. A part of her simply assumed that she would have a full-time job by then, or at least a solid writing career that allowed her to afford insurance from the marketplace. Writing wasn't Lisa's passion, per se, but she was good at it, and her boss at the online periodical that covered topics on Millennial life was quick to hand her bonuses for the amount of clicks she received from social media. Lisa was assigned about two to three articles a week on top of having a regular weekly column about topics that concerned single queer women in their twenties. The current topic she was assigned was about *Summer Blockbuster Films to Watch Out For,* a throw-away article that would get a helping of clicks from regular readers, making a few bucks, then fall into the ether because its shelf life was not only terrible... the topic had been done to death by other online periodicals.

She cracked open her notebook detailing the biggest upcoming movies of that summer and jotted a few keywords. Her editor wanted positive spins only, regardless if more Marvel movies or Pixar hits were her usual cup of tea.

The words *Action, Adventure,* and *Animation* were barely out of her pen when her phone buzzed with an incoming text. Lisa had forgotten what had been on her mind only an hour ago when she picked up her phone and saw an unknown number displayed on her screen.

"*Saturday...*" the preview text said.

It took Lisa a moment to realize who it probably was. As soon as the name RAQUEL echoed in her head, she jammed her thumbs against her pin code and cursed her excitement for making her mess up no fewer than three times.

"*Saturday. Are you available?*"

Lisa stared at her laptop screen. *Don't let her think you're so eager you're living on your phone, waiting for her text!* Five minutes later, however, Lisa couldn't take it anymore. She replied, "*Is this Raquel?*"

"*Of course it is.*"

Of course it was!

"*I'm free Saturday :)*"

"*Good. I'll send you more details later. Sorry I didn't text you sooner. I'm super busy this week closing on a house and getting ready to take on another. The cycle never ends.*"

No, it sure didn't. For when Lisa finished adding Raquel to her contacts and attempted to return to work, she was so overwhelmed with the feelings manifesting in her body that she almost forgot to finish and hand in her article by the time it was due.

She cut it close by about four minutes. Her editor wouldn't be happy about that... but he could kiss her happy ass.

***

"Brenda!" The last of Raquel's coworkers were filing out of the office late Friday evening, most of them muttering that they would love to eat outside at one of the local restaurants since the sun now stayed up so late. "Tell me a good place for a date. One that won't knock me on my ass but keep the atmosphere *up,* if you know what I mean."

She drummed her fingers on her desk while waiting for her friend to respond. Raquel's phone dug beneath her curly hair and pressed hard against her ear. Reception wasn't always the best in the office, but the days were getting hotter, and Raquel was not in the mood to try her luck outside while still wearing her baby pink blazer.

When her friend finally appeared again, it was with a yawn that signified the end of a long work week. Brenda wasn't in real estate, but she was in publicity, and at this time of year things could be as intense as in Raquel's line of work. "Is this for another one of your young gal pals?" Her droll voice was the kind to get a girl scoffed at, but she must have been used to that with Raquel. *Can't you answer one of my questions without throwing in the judgmental attitude?* "Because I always thought the new playset they put up at Jefferson Park looked fun."

"Don't be a bitch because I get dates and you don't."

"Excuse me?" Brenda laughed. "I get dates. Mine simply happen to have fully developed brains that know the stunts I'm trying to pull."

"For your information, my current girlfriend is twenty-three. I think."

"You think."

"She's out of college. Isn't that your big barometer these days?" Brenda used to be as bad as Raquel, albeit she was younger than her friend in her forties. But Brenda had sworn off college-aged girls two years ago after one proved to be so insufferable and immature that it simply wasn't worth the endless energy. Now she mostly dated young professionals who were establishing their adult lives while still courting a certain butterfly called *hope.* "Come on. Help me out here. I've already sealed the deal with this one can go beyond dinner and a nightcap back at my place." Although she would definitely be treating Lisa to both of those things.

"You know what the kids like," Brenda said. "Same shit we were doing when we were their age. Clubbing."

"I said something that won't knock me out." Besides, Raquel then added, she wasn't that interested in clubbing when she was Lisa's age. She had been too depressed to drag her ass out of bed and go dancing, even if her friends promised enough party-drugs to make her forget her woes for the rest of her life.

"It's summer, so everyone is out dancing and drinking mojitos or whatever. I mean, you can take her to a fancy club that has the firepit and all that shit. I think there are a few over on Rochester Boulevard at this time of year. You know, the seasonal ones."

Indeed, Raquel *did* know. The most lucrative condos for young professionals in town were located on Rochester, because kids with daddy's money who could afford a one bedroom were often keen to live near their favorite clubs. Raquel knew much about them so she could sell properties, but she hadn't been to many. *Usually too many guys there.* Last time she went stag, more than one young stud asked if she were looking for a boy toy. As flattered as she was, she had to inform them that they were the kind of stud she did *not* prefer. *Nobody will ever stop Stacey. Damn, that girl could go for days.* That had been back in the '90s, when Raquel finally picked up the pieces of her broken heart and attempted to move on in her dating life.

She soon hung up on Brenda and gathered her things to go home. Maybe she would join some of those coworkers to have dinner at a restaurant, but she was more likely to enjoy her meal alone. A woman rarely had time to savor a sunny day without being hounded by lovers and coworkers.

Besides, was she ever truly alone on a day like this?

As soon as she solidified her plans for Lisa the following day, Raquel walked five blocks away and had dinner at a low-key Thai restaurant that was a hit with locals but blissfully free from tourists. She had a small table outside, where she enjoyed the cool breezes and considered herself lucky that she made enough money to splurge on dinner every night of the week if she so chose. Closing on the big house had ensured she would have plenty to spare for that trip to Hawaii. She only needed a good date to go out with – maybe Lisa would be her bed bunny that summer. Would she say no to *Hawaii?*

Could you have ever envisioned a life like this?

She sent that into the ether. Preferably, up toward Heaven, where certain people may be able to hear her. Even if they had made it clear before they died that they wanted nothing to do with Raquel and her Sapphic ways.

Raquel wasn't surprised when she saw her ex-girlfriend's face in the woman walking by. It was impossible for it to be Marian, of course, since the woman leading her dog on a leash was still in her early twenties and enjoying every benefit of those years. Marian was Raquel's age. In a perfect world, she would be sitting across from her lover at that Thai restaurant where they used to eat when they had a few extra dollars to spare every month.

We had our first date here. Back then, the whole neighborhood looked completely different, and the décor at the restaurant lacked the sophistication it courted now. Most of the apartment buildings were single family homes or brick walkups. They were gone now. Torn down in favor of *progress*. Raquel had sold a few of those properties after getting her license. The first few thousand dollars to hit her bank account – in her life. *We dreamed of owning one of those single family homes.* Gone now. All of them gone.

Marian had been Raquel's girlfriend right out of high school. They met at the local community college and hit it off so hard that even their friends had whiplash from how serious they became in such a short amount of time. Looking back, Raquel saw the signs of a relationship constantly on the brink of dismantling. Back then, though, she was so incredibly in love that she never saw the ultimatum coming.

"It's over. I'm going back to guys."

Raquel had made an ass of herself trying to get Marian back. How was it possible to look at two solid years together and think oh, yeah, let's flush it all down the toilet! It wasn't merely breaking up that broke Raquel's young heart. It had been how Marian did it. For one minute they were holding hands while walking away from this Thai restaurant, and the next, Raquel was watching the love of her life run off with a guy from a trade school.

Everything had come out of left field. The rejection was felt through the city, and not even Raquel recovered in a timely manner.

There had been a few serious girlfriends between Marian and now, but none of them had meant as much as *her*. The woman who first absconded with Raquel's heart and changed her life, for better and worst. She had been the woman to teach Raquel about the amazing emotions fluttering out there in the big world. She had also been the one to teach her that none of it mattered when one's heart had been shattered into a million pieces.

Why do I subject myself to this? The décor changed, the menu shifted, but Raquel always felt the same whenever she came to this restaurant. She often wondered if the old host ever wondered whatever happened to Marian. Or had he seen her come here with her male dates over the years?

Heartbreak would have come for Raquel eventually, but she wished she had more time with Marian. She wished love didn't feel like a betrayal.

Jesus. No wonder she was a fucking mess.

Raquel picked up her phone and did what she always did when the memories came flooding back and she needed a quick pick me up – also known as a way to feel like she had any control in her life. She texted her current lady of the moment.

"Don't suppose you look cute today?"

She downed her cocktail and stared at her phone until she received a response.

"Do a tank top and shorts count as cute?"

"Is there a universe where they don't?"

Two minutes later, Raquel had a picture in her inbox. She smugly sipped her water and pushed food around her plate as she contemplated what would happen should someone walk by and see the nipples poking through Lisa's sheer white tank top.

"That's very cute. Thank you."

When Raquel played games, she never sent pictures, let alone any that showed off a snippet of her goods. She was more inclined to make her dates beg for it while never intending to deliver. Besides, was there ever a time – okay, except for that one – in which she outright asked for nudes or something like what Lisa sent her? No. They always came when she instead asked for a selfie. She didn't doubt that dating men would provide her with an endless list of dick pics. Some women weren't much different.

Yet she never returned the gesture. She preferred to keep her goods locked up tight until date night. Wasn't it better to see them in the flesh, so to speak? Wasn't that what people *really* wanted?

Raquel knew the truth. She was a woman who came of age long before cell phones were as ubiquitous as a pair of shoes on someone's feet. Back when she was Lisa's age and younger, if she wanted an instantaneous picture to share with someone, then she would take a Polaroid. That still required having the other person next to her. A constant human connection.

Hey, Marian... Her thoughts once again traveled to the ex that broke her heart, as they almost always did. *What would we have been like if we had cell phones back then? Would we be like kids today and sending each other nudes?*

She still had a box of Polaroid nudes Marian took once upon a time. They were deep in Raquel's bedroom closet, carefully tucked inside a handmade pouch and placed into a shoebox that once held a pair of vintage Chanel heels. Raquel hadn't looked at them since the turn of the millennium, but she knew they were there, waiting for the day when she lost her grip on reality and fished them out in utter desperation.

That day hadn't come yet. Sometimes, Raquel wondered if all this faffing about with young co-eds was because she was constantly trying to recreate those days with Marian. Or, at least, that sounded like something her therapist Ms. Tithe would say.

Raquel was subsequently reminded that she needed to make an appointment with Dr. Tithe. She had missed out on her usual one that week due to being so busy closing on the house. She should have time the following week,. It wouldn't be a terrible idea to update Ms. Tithe on the goings-on of Raquel's messy life.

Because she had no reason to believe that this stint with Lisa *wouldn't* turn into a big, fat mess like most of her other relationships. Her main goal was to merely ride out the fun while it lasted.

Chapter 6

Brenda had come through with her recommendation. Not only was the club on the end of Rochester Boulevard smart enough to keep their outdoor dance floor contained to the back decks of their renovated building – one that Raquel instantly calculated to be worth a cool million dollars – but they employed smiling, eye-candy-quality bouncers who doubled as hosts for every group of gals coming in for a fun night on the town. The few men allowed paid a premium and were either with their girlfriends, gal pals, or two other young men who were more interested in talking about the latest "game" than hitting on every woman in the room. Raquel helped herself to the tiki bar – chic, yet effortlessly trendy – and ordered a coconut flavored cocktail sure to relax her after spending her whole Saturday afternoon touring the next house her boss assigned her. Not a single guy bothered her, and she couldn't be more pleased.

Well, perhaps she could. Without turning around, she knew the exact moment when Lisa bypassed the bouncers and entered the open-air club.

Half the heads in Raquel's general vicinity turned. Raquel did not bother. *Well, well. She must be here.* A content smirk hit her face before the straw of her drink did. As much as Raquel wished to behold the sight of her beautiful date, she was more inclined to let the moment come on its own. Why rush something she knew would be wonderful, anyway? Raquel had learned over the years that many things were worth waiting for. Like seeing what scandalous outfit her date had decided to wear *this* time.

When Raquel told Lisa where they would be going Saturday night, she had helpfully included the words, *"They may desire you to wear something a little more conservative than what I saw the other day. Although it's still a fun joint, I'm sure."* She had followed that up with assurances that she loved Lisa's style and how she worked it, because she did *not* want to discourage gorgeous girls dressing up like they were hitting up their pool.

"Hey."

A pair of sunglasses and a burgundy-sequined clutch hit the bar top. Raquel slowly put down her drink and turned to the woman who smelled like honeysuckle.

Excellent perfume choice. You'd think I picked it out for her. How did Lisa know that Raquel loved all floral scents, but *especially* honeysuckle? It wasn't exactly as common as rose, jasmine, or even cherry blossoms in the perfume world.

Lisa was as beguiling as anticipated, although Raquel would have never guessed the exact kind of outfit her date would wear that night. While it wasn't a bikini and poolside top – let alone with matching rose-colored sunglasses – it was certainly *revealing* with its plunging neckline and high hem. Lisa rocked a beige halter top that *lifted* and *separated* as well as a bra straight from the lingerie shop could accomplish. Rhinestones underlined her breasts and called attention to them every time she moved enough to reflect the club lights. The black skirt that hugged her thighs and barely covered her ass did nothing to conceal a damn inch of skin before reaching her dance-appropriate sandals that allowed her toes to wiggle in the warm night air. Her brown hair was pulled back into a messy bun, every strand somehow carefully contained by a single white-rhinestone clasp that looked like it came from the end-of-the-season discount bin from the mall.

Women like Lisa always made this tacky style work, and Raquel was grateful for it. Few would guess that she was a jeans and T-shirt girl when she was twenty. Now that she was older, she took care to wear only the most flattering of dresses when out for a hot date night. Her makeup took an hour to apply, and her hair was freshly washed, blown dried, and crimped to perfection. Out of everyone who could never guess how she dressed when she was twenty, half of them couldn't believe that her eyes weren't naturally smoky, her lips a bold red, and her hair exactly like that whenever she rolled out of bed. She liked to keep it that way.

"Well, don't you look delicious?" Raquel hailed the bartender while keeping her giddy grin to herself. *God, I can't wait to dive into that later.* The scent of honeysuckle would have to keep her content for now. Besides, was there anything wrong with some extended foreplay? The throbbing beats of the club as it heated up for the night was only matched by their ability to hold a conversation while sitting by the bar. "I love that perfume you're wearing."

Lisa ordered a drink after Raquel insisted on putting it on her own tab. "Thank you. I got it a few days ago. Haven't splurged on perfume in a while."

"It's almost like you got it for me." Raquel turned her body toward her date, inviting her to check out an older woman's cleavage as shoved into a navy-blue bodycon dress. "Honeysuckle is my favorite."

"Is that what this is?" Lisa was all smiles when she received her drink. She pulled out the lime green umbrella and placed it on a napkin next to her arm. "I honestly had no idea. I knew the sample smelled good when I tried it on."

Raquel wondered if now was a good time to lay down one of her offers. *"I could buy you all the perfume you want, honey."* *"How about I take you on a fun outing to the mall next weekend? We'll get you something to wear when we go to Hawaii. My treat."* The more she thought about it, the more she wanted this young woman naked on the beach. *I hope she's wearing those rose-colored sunglasses.* Lisa hadn't brought them tonight. The pair on the bar looked like they came from the drug store. Perfectly functional, a little fashionable, but beat up and scratched to hell and back. Shame.

"What's your favorite flower?"

Lisa was slightly taken aback by that question. Nothing a sip of her drink couldn't help. "Carnations, I guess. I really like the red ones. The geometric design is the most pleasing."

Geometric design? "I never did ask you what you studied in school."

"Does what one majors in even matter these days?" Laughter hit Raquel before she could contemplate that response. "I studied a little bit of everything, of course. Math, English, Philosophy, Biology, Rhetoric... even shoved some French in there." She made a sour face after sampling another sip of her drink. "I'm a writer now. As much as one can cobble together a living from that."

"A writer?"

"It's the gig economy, you know? Getting employed is hard shit. Besides, isn't it better to make your own schedule so you're your most productive? I was listening to this podcast the other day about these guys working during the dot com boom in the late '90s. They were saying that working from home was so unheard of. Now we all do it, sometimes full time."

Those kinds of statements only served to remind Raquel that Lisa was younger than she seemed. The way she talked about the dot com boom implied she barely remembered it... meanwhile, Raquel had been busy nursing her broken heart. Living her life as a grown adult. Damn. *Great way to make me feel so old.* "What kind of writing? Hopefully you're telling the world that they should be moving here and buying houses and condos from me."

Lisa giggled into the wide rim of her drink. "I write about things Millennials care about. So, no. Not many are looking to buy super expensive houses like you sell."

"Tell me about it. I think the last time I sold anything to a Millennial, it was this dire little studio apartment that had barely been updated to modern standards. But it was in a trendy district, so it still went for a couple hundred grand."

"Hey, I happen to live in a dire little studio apartment around here. Except I pay rent."

Raquel couldn't tell if her young girlfriend was offended or not. Her tone said she was only kidding, but the look on her face implored Raquel to come up with another subject matter. "Renting has gotten crazy around here. I remember when half the apartments on this block used to go for only a few hundred dollars."

"Yes, and now they cost over a thousand. That means you make total bank, right?"

"I don't do too bad for myself, no."

Lisa played with the clasp in her hair. One wrong move, and the whole look would come crashing down. *We can do something like that later.* Raquel was thinking of a little hair pulling, some dirty talk, and three of her fingers in the woman sitting next to her. It would be a night to rival the first time they hooked up. Now, if only she could arrange for Lisa getting away with going naked in this place...

"How does someone get into real estate? You need a special degree for that?"

Raquel snorted right into her drink. The surface rippled from the strength of her breath and brought back with it the strong scent of alcohol. She wondered how potent Lisa's drink was. Hopefully it wasn't too strong to keep her from having a good time. Nothing worse than a twenty-year-old who drank Raquel under the table – and thought herself a grand woman for it.

"No." Raquel had answered this question so many times in her twenty years of real estate that she could recite it like she was at the front of the class. But for Lisa's sake, she would keep her tone cordial and informative. Could she help it if young people always had the same questions? Some of them wanted to know how to get into the biz for themselves – it sounded lucrative, after all. Others simply wanted to know how much money Raquel was making. They scoffed at a commission number that was less than their student loan interest rate, but when Raquel dropped how much the places she sold went for... ah, the math students were quick to widen their eyes in absolute awe. If ten percent of a million was still a hundred grand, then a little less than that was nothing to sneeze at.

Depending on the date, however, it could send entirely the wrong message. Raquel was solidly middle class – a feat, considering how she grew up – but hardly wealthy. She wasn't about to pay off anyone's debt unless she was sure it was a forever type of situation.

"It's a license," Raquel continued. "After I got that, it was digging my knees into the trenches until I was able to work for one of the best agencies in town. I work off commission, but there is still competition within my own agency to get the best listings. I'd say I'm probably number two or three right now."

"Out of how many?"

"Five." Raquel was only one of two women at her agency, but she had yet to call her boss's decisions unfair toward her. The few times she fucked up, she got what she deserved. Now, as for Blake, the little rat who threw a fit every time she got a listing over him...

"Impressive." Lisa's elbow was up on the bar, her eyes twinkling in Raquel's direction. "What was your major in college, then?"

Raquel bristled. "I actually dropped out of community college. Academia isn't my strong suit. I'd rather hustle on the pavement, so to speak."

"Whoa. Everyone I know toughs it out in college, whether they're suited to it or not."

"This might shock you," Raquel began with a smirk that could hardly contain itself, "but there was a time in history when not everyone went to college, let alone finished. You could also get a job right out of college. Decent ones that helped you pay the bills."

"Oooh, was it less expensive back in the Middle Ages, too?"

"Watch it."

Lisa flashed her a grin that suggested she didn't mean anything foul. "My mom dropped out of college, too. She said she got pregnant with me right after she transferred to another city."

"Is that so? I'm guessing she did fine without college, based on how well you seem to have turned out." *Butter her up, Raq. Get her more smitten with you.*

The batting eyelashes gradually slowed on Lisa's face. "She did okay. Married my dad until they couldn't stand each other anymore. Between child support and an office job, she was able to pay for a few things. We ed. Then..." Lisa paused. "She died, so it didn't matter anymore."

"I'm so sorry."

Lisa laughed away the awkward energy infiltrating their corner of the club bar. "*I'm* the sorry one! Definitely didn't mean to dump the dead mom stuff on you on our first real date. Sometimes I don't even realize I'm doing it until it's too late. I hate being such a bummer."

"I'd imagine that your mother being deceased is a pretty big thing you're always thinking about. Especially if you knew her well."

Lisa did not respond, although her visage implored Raquel to keep talking.

"Consider yourself lucky that you ever knew your mother at all. That's all I'll say." What was she thinking, though? *My mother died when I was three, but nobody wants to hear that.* Raquel's father had been largely out of the picture as well. *My aunt and uncle raised me. My grandmother was around, too.* Except nobody truly claimed Raquel Mendes. As long as she minded her manners, ate her vegetables, and got decent grades at school, she was largely allowed to come and go as she pleased while doing whatever she wanted. That led to a crazy time as a teenager, when she felt free to explore her sexuality with absolute abandon. Boys at first, of course, but it was the girls she met in high school that

- 88 -

really made her heart race and her loins thunder in arousal. The serial monogamist inside of her had a dandy time at her large high school in an even larger school district. Seemed like there was always at least one girl ready to experiment with super extroverted Raquel. By the time she graduated and enrolled in the local community college, she had already met Marian. It was only a matter of time before they were shacking up together and cooking each other breakfast in the morning.

Raquel always thought it perfectly natural to go from unbridled sexuality to domesticated bliss with the love of her life. *I was so lucky, meeting my soulmate so early in my life.* It was one of the heterosexual dreams she never thought she would encounter.

The heartbreak that came when Marian dumped her was the biggest wakeup call of Raquel's life. She dropped out of college, quit her part time jobs, and spent almost a year of her life holed up in her grandmother's spare bedroom crying her eyes out.

It felt like a whole lifetime ago.

"You finished with your drink?" Raquel gestured to the empty glass in front of Lisa. "C'mon. Let's go dance." Anything was better than sitting there and stewing in her own past. *Anything.*

Lisa's grin grew wider as she slid off the stool and took Raquel's hand. People parted to allow them through, although a few had to double-take when they realized that it was two feminine women about to take the dancefloor by the horns.

Party girl days, don't fail me now.

Raquel may not drink like she used to, but she could dance. Helped that she wore her pair of flats that allowed her to twirl on the dancefloor, shaking her derriere to the tropical house music blaring through the speakers. Raquel took Lisa into her arms and inhaled that honeysuckle perfume that had been tormenting her ever since her date walked through the door.

"I shouldn't have worn such crazy heels!" Lisa called over the dance music. "You're smart! You wore flats!"

"One of many bouts of wisdom that comes with age!" Raquel held Lisa out at arm's length and gave her a mighty twirl. A pair of female friends dancing together cheered them on. A few men were beginning to surround them, curiosity blowing up their retinas. *Some things never fucking change.* Raquel had been a party trick back in the '90s. Eventually, she caught on that most of the girls coming up to grind on her and kiss her in the middle of these crowds were only doing it to make their boyfriends happy. Although it didn't stop her from getting their numbers half the time.

She didn't worry about that happening with Lisa. It was a new era, and the younger generations were more open-minded than ever. Yet just because she didn't anticipate any hate thrown in their direction, didn't mean she was open to ogling.

"Everyone is looking at you." Raquel defiantly turned them away from the spectators with Lisa still in her gasp. "It's making me jealous." She said that with a sigh. If her plan worked, Lisa would be completely taken in with this hint of possessiveness that marked her as the most desired woman in the room.

Well, Raquel knew that *her* attentions weren't on anyone else in the club.

"I think you mean that everyone is looking at *us*."

"Think what you'd like. I know."

They wrapped their arms around one another and swayed to the downtempo beat of the next song. Lisa's cheeky smile was what brought Raquel's lips closer – the scent of the honeysuckle spritzed on her throat wasn't the only thing capable of knocking Raquel on her ass.

I can't wait to get her out of here. Clubs weren't really Raquel's thing, although they served their purpose. *No, I don't count getting people intoxicated as one of those purposes.* She meant the sexually charged atmosphere crawling up their legs and getting ready to knock them over. Raquel was in the business of sealing deals. That included blowing kisses in women's ears and transforming them into little puddles of lust.

It helped that she remembered how rowdy this girl got when she was in a certain mood. Raquel would die with the memory of Lisa's orgasms burned into the back of her eyelids.

"Oh, my." Lisa bit her lip and pressed her palms against Raquel's chest when a few fingers taunted the hem of her skirt. "You're so frisky!"

"I should be saying the same thing about you." After all, Lisa had quite the grip on her. Raquel would survive about five more minutes before her breasts needed to be released. "Or are we on the same page?"

They elicited applause and whoops from the crowd as they sealed that thought with a tentative kiss that brought giggles out of both of their mouths. Raquel had almost forgotten how much fun flirting and grinding on the dance floor could be.

She hadn't forgotten how much fun it was to grab a girl's ass and give it a hard, firm squeeze, however. She would have to be dead to ever forget that.

"Do you want another drink?" Raquel had steered them to the corner of the dancefloor, where there were fewer pervs and the music wasn't as deafening. "Or should we head home?"

She was met with a pair of bedroom eyes that had almost killed her a week ago. Now, she would be lucky to make it home before she completely lost her mind. "You've got drinks at your place, right?" Lisa asked.

"I've got lots of stuff at my place."

"Including the fuzzy handcuffs?"

"Well, I don't know about *fuzzy*..."

Lisa slipped one arm around Raquel's midsection and winked at her. There was no denying what they were off to do when they marched through the dancefloor, out the door, and down the street toward Raquel's place.

She didn't have a problem with that. The whole neighborhood could know that she was about to get some of *this* for all she cared. As far as Raquel was concerned, that was one of the many benefits that came with age. She lost the ability to be ashamed of anything.

From the looks of things, shame wasn't an issue in Lisa's life, either.

Chapter 7

The most impressive thing about Raquel's place wasn't the view or the fancy concierge desk in the lobby of the building. It was the cool and sophisticated décor that screamed this woman had *taste* and wasn't afraid to spend a little money on what she liked.

"Wow." Lisa helped herself into the maw of Raquel's spacious one-bedroom apartment while the door was locked behind her. Raquel tossed her keys and purse onto a table by the door before approaching her date. They didn't touch, but the tension between them remained palpable. Anything to remind Lisa that their attraction was most definitely mutual. "Look at this place! It's gotta be the nicest apartment in town."

"As someone who sees a lot of residences around here..." Raquel leaned against the island counter in her kitchen. "It's close to being the nicest. Can't quite afford *the* nicest. That's for CEOs and old money assholes."

"You'll be a CEO at the rate you're going." Lisa flitted from the sectional sofa to the large entertainment center backed against the windows. Twilight had descended upon the city, washing it in golden lights that twinkled in half the windows and little red dots that blinked in and out on top of buildings. Airplanes took off and landed at the local airport outside of town. The fact Raquel had a view of *airplanes* without the noise was amazing enough. Lisa soon looked in the other direction and caught sight of a barge on the river. "Did you get this place for a steal because of your job?"

Chuckles followed her into the living room. "Guess you could say that. I get to see advanced listings, which meant I was the first one to tour and put down an offer for this place. Cost a bit more than I would like, but I see it as an investment. Helped that I had landed a big sale a few weeks before."

"Like the house I saw you showing last weekend?"

"Have I told you I made a nice score off that one? Because I did."

"What are you doing to celebrate?" Lisa plopped onto the sofa with her legs flying up into the air. She knew she flashed her thong underwear in Raquel's direction but didn't care. Perhaps she had done it on purpose.

Raquel stood behind the couch, her perfectly coifed hair tantalizing the girl who looked up at her. *Wow, her cleavage is amazing even from this angle.* Lisa couldn't help but grin. She considered herself lucky to get to touch Raquel even *once,* let alone a second time. Yet when she was invited to grope her on the dancefloor, she didn't turn down the opportunity to touch her breasts. Now she beheld them from a most auspicious angle.

"I haven't decided yet," Raquel finally said. "I was thinking about doing a bit of traveling. I hear Hawaii is gorgeous this time of year."

Hawaii... Lisa had never been. Her trips to Disneyland were some of the only vacations she got as a child, and the tradition was so ingrained that she never dared to ask her mother to go somewhere else. Why would she? Disneyland was awesome! *Except I wouldn't want to go there with my older girlfriend.* Hawaii, though... that had romantic sin written in the island sands. A real island, too. Not the kitschy atmosphere back at the club.

"Don't suppose you need someone to go with."

Raquel looked as if she had anticipated that question. "Depends on if you know someone who isn't afraid to get a little tanned. Hawaii is hot. It's a good idea to show a little skin while you're there."

"I know a couple of girls who could use a better tan."

"You do?"

Lisa untied the back of her halter top and let the straps fall down her torso. Unfortunately, the built-in bra wasn't cheap enough to fall with them. Yet it *was* potent enough to boost her breasts up toward her chin, two gloriously pale mounds that screamed they didn't see a ton of sun. "These two girls. They're begging for a nude tan on the beach."

"Not sure I could guarantee a private beach."

"Who said it had to be private?" That was the thing about the right woman – she turned Lisa into an exhibitionist. A little groping at the club hadn't been enough. She always needed more. "I don't mind if somebody sees. Don't you want to show me off?"

Raquel studied her for a few seconds. While Lisa was used to people taking critical looks in her direction, she wasn't used to a woman she wanted so badly considering her options... and some of them might not be in Lisa's favor.

"I love showing off," Raquel said with a light, flirtatious whisper. "Watch what you say, though. I might be tempted to put a tiara on your head and prance you around in a sheer dress and nothing underneath. A naughty princess for the ages."

A full-body shudder took control of Lisa, who welcomed it with alacrity. She turned on the bedroom eyes again. It may have been her hope to get Raquel on top of her. Now.

"You'd love that, huh?" Raquel's delicate fingers dragged across the back of her couch as she stepped away. "Excuse me. I must make a stop to the bathroom before I'm of any mind to offer you a drink."

Lisa didn't care for another drink. The one at the bar had been strong enough to leave her tipsy for the next hour, and while that hour was almost up, she didn't want to be too inebriated to savor another night with Raquel. Besides, it wouldn't be fair unless Raquel joined her, and the last thing Lisa wanted was for them to both be too drunk to remember what happened and what they shared.

It may have helped that she had spent the past few days fantasizing about the possibilities Raquel presented. The day she texted her had been one of the most jubilant days of Lisa's life. *That sounds so hokey, but it's true.* She had never been so... elated. On Cloud Nine. Shopping in the aisles of nirvana and getting ready to use up the last of her free gift card she received for her birthday. Everything, from that night at the hotel until now, had been one blessed dream.

Yet she couldn't let Raquel see it. She couldn't know the truth yet.

If ever.

Lisa was aware of how crazy she looked. Nothing had been an accident. Raquel continued to play right into her hand, but the last thing Lisa wanted was to ruin this good thing. *I've worked too hard to get to this point. I can't forget my goals.* Every time she achieved a goal, the benchmark moved a little farther. Her college advisor had once painted Lisa a picture of a football field – easy enough for her to imagine, because her mother had been a die-hard Atlanta Falcons fan her whole life. *"Imagine your first little goal is alllll the way down at the other team's end zone,"* the professor had said. *"You have to take the whole field one-yard line at a time before you score a touchdown. Sometimes brutes will come up and try to derail you. They'll try to steal your thunder. Sometimes you may drop the ball and fumble your way between the forty and fifty-yard lines. Yet when you make it to your end zone, when your true goal is in sight... go for it. Don't look back. Throw everything you've got into that last surge of energy pushing you through the wall of bodies trying to hold you back."*

Lisa looked around the spacious living room Raquel called hers. It was big enough to be a football field.

I'm almost in my end zone. Some would argue she was already there. She simply needed to throw the ball to the first available player to pass her.

Lisa had a few minutes to spare before Raquel returned. She stood up from the couch and snooped around until she found the bedroom, perfectly kempt with the help of a weekly maid service. According to a small white board by the bedroom door, everything had last been vacuumed and polished two days ago. The only signs of live-in life were a few creases in the bedspread and a head-sized indent in a pillow.

After making sure the bedroom door was left wide open, Lisa helped herself inside and pulled her untied halter top over her head. It hit the floor alongside her skirt one second later.

She was draped across Raquel's bed by the time the owner of that luxurious apartment stepped out of her bathroom and searched for her guest. When she found Lisa, it was with a slight look of shock on her face.

"Excuse you." She crossed her arms with a fake huff that made her breasts lift. Lisa couldn't help but grin at her good fortune. "I don't recall telling you that you were welcomed into my bedroom. Yet."

"What can I say?" With her full body on display, Lisa lay back, both of her nipples jutting into the air. "I don't want to beat around the bush. I'd rather get down to what we want."

"Oh? What's that?"

This time Lisa rolled onto her stomach. Her hair pulled against her scalp as the clasp holding it up in a bun struggled to stay in place. She didn't care. It was more important for Raquel to get a few views of Lisa's ass as framed in her thong. "A little of this. A little of that. All of it hot and climatic."

Raquel's knee hit the edge of her bed.

"Don't let anyone tell you that I didn't offer you a lovely date night, complete with dinner, drinks and dancing. You know, before I fucked you in my bed."

Lisa shrugged. "How could I let anyone tell me that when it's true? You have been a truly gracious hostess, but I'm young and impatient."

"Don't play it up. I'll have to teach you patience."

The grin wasn't about to leave Lisa's lips. "Wouldn't that simply be a terrible thing?"

Yet Raquel wasn't grinning. Everything about her demeanor, from the pull of her brows and the pinch of her lips suggested that she wasn't playing a game with the young femme in her bed.

"Not sure you would like the way I teach young women patience. It can go all night."

She said that, yet the zipper on the back of her dress started to come down. Slowly. Slow enough that it was almost *agonizing*. Was this what she meant about teaching patience? Because Lisa was on the verge of jumping up and insisting that she finish undressing Raquel for her.

"So happens I've got all night." Lisa wrapped her hair around her fingers, grasping the clasp on her scalp and giving it a mighty enough tug to toss it to the floor. Her hair fell across her naked shoulders, but did nothing to enshroud the rest of her body. Raquel's eyes never once moved from what they desired to behold most.

Chapter 8

She wasn't kidding... I'm gonna go mad!

Everything coming from outside and from within was absolute torture. The thoughts plaguing Lisa's brain were made of shrapnel, each piece exploding from her base desires every time she was reminded that patience was a noble virtue. Something she severely lacked.

Poor Lisa had been begging to come for the past twenty minutes. Yet she was forbidden from expressing that sentiment. A stern warning had informed her that any whining would yield the last thing she wanted – utter, absolute rejection for the rest of the night.

Turned out that Lisa was far from the pinnacle of patience. When the first orgasm came to boil in the pits of her body and threatened to burst loose, she made it known with fire on her lips. That fire had been quashed when Raquel pulled away and *tsked*. Now, here they were again, with Raquel's tongue deep inside Lisa's pussy and threatening to make her come at any moment.

Except that was the thing experience brought a woman like Raquel. She knew how to bring another woman to the edge and step back again. It was the kind of torture that made women into stronger beings. Broke them down and built them back up again, like a soldier in dire need of molding. If this was how Raquel treated most of her lovers, then it was no wonder she held such a reputation among chat rooms and college co-eds who were caught in a cougar's paw for one night or more.

I'm not caught. I'm not trapped. I'm living the fucking high life with her! Lisa would lose her mind for a second before coming back to her senses. This wasn't torture. This was amazing! Everything about the moment had been so carefully crafted, from the handcuffs chaining Lisa's hands to the top of the bed and the blindfold forbidding her from seeing anything but the back of her eyelids. Occasionally, her eyelashes fluttered open and brushed against the soft cloth bound around her face. That was usually when Raquel was doing her absolute worst down below.

That masterful tongue bringing so much chaos to one woman *had* to be wearing out soon. Or was it like any other muscle in the body? With enough exercise, could it go on for minutes? Hours? *Days?* Raquel had promised her all night. Would Lisa still be here, in this position, for the next forty-eight hours or more? Was this her destiny? To die at the end of a woman's tongue?

It didn't sound like a terrible death, but Lisa wasn't sure she was ready to expire.

"Oh my *God...*" She was allowed to say anything she wanted, as long as she didn't beg for orgasm. An important lesson was on the line, after all. Patience. Fucking patience. The thing that jaded women as they grew older and realized that life was harder than it appeared when they were so much younger. Lisa was old enough to think herself more than mature. She had learned the hard lessons already. She was ready to take life by the horns and fling it back into its pen. Yes?

God. She was so wrong. She knew nothing. *Nothing.*

"You're doing so well for someone new to this." Raquel's voice sounded like it was a million miles away. That's what happened when Lisa couldn't see her – and when she was so far gone into her own mind that she withdrew from the world. The only sensations that mattered were the ones coming from between her thighs. That tongue. Those fingers. Every press of one of her buttons brought her closer to the one thing she wasn't yet allowed. "You've almost got me fooled. Making me think that you really have done this before. Except you have one tell. Do you know what it is?"

"What?" Breathless. That was the only way Lisa could describe what happened to her voice when she was in this glorious state.

"The way you squirm. You're trying so hard to be good. It's admirable."

"I don't want to disappoint you."

"Please. I've got my face between your legs and you taste as good as you look. What could I possibly be disappointed about?"

Lisa bit her lip. "Maybe next time I'll learn your tricks and won't be as affected by them. Maybe you're only interested in the novelty I bring you."

"Listen to you! If you're capable of these kinds of thoughts right now, I'm not doing my job right."

That was the last thing Raquel said before she returned to torturing her guest. *It's not torture. No, no, the only one who thinks it's torture is the part of me that wants to come so badly I'm about to choke.* Raquel didn't torture her lovers. She bathed them in adoration. Doused them in desirous notions that they truly deserved all the attention they received. *I'm special. If I'm getting this right now, I must be special!* Lisa had imagined all sorts of things when she fantasized about making more love to this woman. Feeling so special that she might as well be marrying Raquel that time next week? Impossible.

Still, she was only human. How much longer could she endure this without disappointing the woman who wanted her so badly?

Perhaps that was part of the game. Nobody was perfect the first time they attempted stunts like these.

At some point, Lisa was doomed to fail. She would come, and that would be it.

Hell, she was sure that's what Raquel really wanted when she relentlessly pursued Lisa's clit into the depths of her folds. It was now or never.

Pleasure seized her as if she no longer had anything to lose besides that part of her that understood what it meant to make endless love. Lisa yanked against the handcuffs holding her to the top of Raquel's bed and mercilessly ground her mound against her lover's mouth. She didn't know if she was grateful for being pinned to the bed, unable to traverse where she pleased while enthralled to the endless bouts of pleasure hitting her, or if she resented the prison trapping her in its bonds. No matter what she did, however, Lisa was at the whim of one person. The only person who had ever done this to her.

She came to her senses moments later. Only then did she realize how her arms ached and her body begged for rest.

"Well," she whistled through her clenching teeth, "that was bound to happen."

Raquel's cheeks remained planted between Lisa's thighs. When she glanced up, her heavy-lidded eyes screaming that she had enjoyed every minute of that, she said, "No reason to sound so fatalistic about it."

She sat back on her legs, her dress straps falling down her arms and the bust loosening around her breasts. Raquel was in no position to possess humility right now. She had spent twenty-five minutes tormenting the woman she handcuffed to the top of her bed, intending to do whatever she pleased until it no longer amused her.

Here was hoping she remained amused for a while.

"Could you *please* uncuff me?" Lisa asked. "I think my shoulder is attempting to come out of its socket."

"Having to reset it wouldn't be very sexy, no." Raquel slipped off her bed and rounded the corner, dress eventually pooling at her feet before she had the chance to unlock the handcuffs and free Lisa. While nothing truly compared to the orgasm she had only a moment ago, Lisa had to admit that moving and stretching her arms again was the cherry on this lovely sundae. "Better?" Raquel's voice was both a million miles away and right in Lisa's ear.

Lisa rolled onto her side with a happy sigh on her lips. "I knew it was a good idea to take off my clothes and help myself. You were definitely going to deliver."

"I did, huh?"

Why did she have to sound saltier than the sea? Lisa would have to start batting her eyelashes again to ensure her older girlfriend remained in a pleasant state of mind. "I'm not afraid to give back, you know."

"No." Raquel sat on the edge of her bed, naked and as beautiful as the day Lisa first saw her. "You certainly don't seem the type to be afraid of giving back."

The endorphins surged through Lisa's body, coddling her like a child tucked away in its comfortable crib. Yet before she got too carried away with those sweet thoughts, she reminded herself of where she was and what they were about to do again.

"Dealt with your fair share of pillow princesses, huh?"

Raquel rolled toward her girlfriend and propped herself up on her elbow. "The type does seem to dominate the dating scene."

"Selfish girls who only want to be pleasured without understanding the true meaning of sticking their tongue in an experienced woman's pussy." Lisa drew a ticklish line down Raquel's cleavage, careful to avoid her breasts while hurtling toward the little fuzzy trail jutting down from her navel. Teeny shivers touched her fingertip every time she touched a new place on Raquel's body. "*Tsk.* I bet it's only gotten worse in recent years, too."

"The age of young women ripping off their clothes and sticking everything they get their hands on into my pussy does seem to be over in my experience, yes." Raquel leaned back, a thoughtful countenance emerging in the soft bedroom light. She suddenly looked like an angel taking a heavenly smoke break from guarding the gates to eternity. *Do angels have dark hair?* Lisa had seen plenty of paintings of angels while growing up in whatever church her mother fancied in the moment, but she never recalled any brunette warriors of the Lord. All she remembered was that their beauty was deadly. Like a poisonous kiss to the lips.

Raquel chuckled, knocking Lisa out of her reverie.

"Until tonight, apparently. Never thought I'd see the day again when someone your age took on such an aggressive role."

"Maybe you're looking in the wrong places. Or maybe I go to school with a bunch of submissive bitches who don't know how to be polite in bed. Speaking of which..." Lisa's finger lingered where she was most likely to encounter evidence of Raquel's unabated arousal. "When do I get to show you how polite I am?"

Raquel gazed down upon her as if she were the most curious kid on the block. *A new neighbor with a totally different style and attitude. One day your world is kosher, and the next? Everything you thought you knew is a lie, and you don't know how to reconcile your past with your present.* Lisa slowly rolled her tongue across her bottom lip and suppressed another giggle.

"I don't think it's that times have really changed," Raquel continued to muse. "I think I have a very specific type. I like a girl I can boss around. I've also learned that lots of girls like being bossed around in bed."

"I admit, it turns me on."

"So you don't want to boss me around?"

Lisa pushed herself up on the wobbly arms. Her hair was completely free, covering everything it touched with the softness of her feminine body. "Would a peasant dare to march into a queen's palace and try to boss *her* around?"

"Ah, so you remember."

"It perfectly summed up everything I love about relationships like ours." Lisa was perhaps too quick to use words like *ours,* and giving collective ownership to anything they shared in the moment. Yet Raquel remained unfazed. "I'm not new to sex, but I am new to finally expressing myself in ways I've been inclined to indulge since I was younger." Lisa attributed many of her unlocked fantasies to what she discovered on the internet as a budding, pubescent teenager. If her mother knew what kind of fanfiction she was reading, Lisa would have never heard the end of it. *Realizing that I could find older women to do those things to me opened my eyes unlike anything else.* Lisa was far from the only woman to harbor those kinds of fantasies. Yet while many of her heterosexual friends found sugar daddies and older boyfriends lining up to take "care" of them while they traversed the minefield that was college and young adulthood, lesbians like Lisa pined for the needle in the haystack. It was hard enough finding other women who were no-nonsense enough to come out and say, "*Hey, I think you're hot. Wanna go back to my place and fuck?"* Finding an older and experienced woman who got off on giving girls like Lisa what-for included prayers every night before she went to bed. *"Please, God, send me a cougar…"*

Apex predators consumed little fawns like Lisa, but sometimes, the doe wasn't afraid to give the cougar a taste of its own medicine. One solid hoof to the face before going down.

Raquel pushed back a coif of Lisa's hair before gently sending her down onto the bed. "If there's anything I like…" That sultry voice was the shit that made Lisa quiver and close her eyes in awe. "It's feeling like a queen."

"What can I say?" Lisa grinned against her lover's lips as they consumed her face once more. "I know a woman worthy of my adoration when I see her." Felt her. Tasted her on ravishing lips. Smelled her shampoo and knew that they were a good match long before either one came into each other's view.

Raquel nestled her nose into the crook of Lisa's neck and blew her breath right into her lover's ear. "Prove it."

Lisa had ached to do that for the past hour. While Raquel had gone to town doing what she did best between Lisa's legs, the younger woman had fantasized about turning the tides and prostrating herself to the bejeweled throne that was this bed. The time had finally come, hadn't it? Lisa was finally granted permission to show Raquel everything she adored about her, from the cheeky grin crowning her countenance to the quirks of her body that made her uniquely *her*.

Raquel was hale and fit for her age, but she still showed visible signs of an aged woman who was no longer twenty – or, at least, few people would mistake her for a young co-ed. Her midsection and the backs of her thighs were covered in the fine stripes of a tiger ready to pounce. Her smoky eye makeup was eventually removed to reveal a crow's small foot on each side. Her stomach had ridden the roller coaster of going up and down twenty pounds for as many years. Parts of her were tanned while others had given up ever seeing the sun again. Yet Raquel was not ashamed of any part of her body, nor of any signs of aging that may bring the derision of those who resented the fact that every woman on Earth grew older. She took care of herself. She treated her body like a temple. It was only right that people respect the goddess within.

She's the perfect example of a woman I both want to be... and want to do. The moment Lisa was given the go-ahead, she jumped on top of Raquel to cover her with kisses and the kind of affirmation only queens enjoyed.

The greatest sound Lisa ever heard was the one Raquel released when she came. Sweet, sweating skin and shuddering sinew was what likewise brought Lisa back into the headspace that allowed her to be her most natural self. In this bed, she didn't have to think about their age difference, the fact that they barely knew each other, or what she had done to get to this moment.

Somewhere, her mother was appalled. Lisa couldn't give a single shit. Not when the woman she wanted most sang her praises.

This is it. This was everything Lisa had ever wanted. The sensations. The feelings. The welling emotions that told her what she had done – she had accomplished everything she set out to do five years ago when she left her hometown.

Now that Lisa had achieved her dream, however, she would have to find a way to keep Raquel from ever discovering the secret buried deep within the heart of a twenty-three-year-old woman.

Because Lisa wasn't about to give this up. She would rather die than ever bear her biggest shame again.

Chapter 9

"This girl seems to be pretty special, huh?"

Raquel turned away from the window overlooking the city. It was a drastically different view from the one she had at her apartment. *The one Lisa couldn't get over.* While Raquel possessed a tranquil view that was nothing but metropolitan beauty in the evening, her therapist had a grand view of the city's business core. With a touch of the button, Ms. Tithe could close the blinds and give her clients the serenity they needed to sit down and have a heart-to-heart chat.

Raquel preferred the view, like she preferred standing and pacing during her appointments. Sitting on the couch or in a chair made her restless. Movement got the blood going and her brain spinning with the thoughts that brought her to this place to begin with. She had been seeing Ms. Tithe for two years. Not her first horse at the therapy rodeo, but Ms. Tithe came highly recommended after Raquel's previous counselor moved out of town. *"You're doing so well on your road to recovery,"* the old woman had said before closing up her practice. *"I'd hate to see you lose all the progress you've made simply because I've left."* Recovery. At least Ms. Tithe didn't make Raquel sound like she was an addict or coming out of a deep depression. *That was my twenties, thank you.*

"It's too soon to tell." Raquel turned away from window and instead set her attentions on the certificates and diplomas hanging on the wall. She looked at them every other week, or at least when work didn't keep her away from talk therapy. *Sometimes I simply don't want to come.* Raquel had paid her fair share of cancelation fees because she decided at the last minute she didn't want to see Ms. Tithe. Today wasn't one of those days.

Perhaps it was because she was in such a good mood.

"Are you going to see her again?" Ms. Tithe asked.

"I'd like to. Probably." Raquel shrugged. "I'm dubiously optimistic. She's fun to go out with and seems to be into me. I'll spare you the details of our night together, but it made me want to do it again."

Ms. Tithe politely nodded. "It would be good for you to have a steady date again."

"Again..." Raquel almost laughed. "I haven't had a 'real' girlfriend since Marian. I've told you that."

"Like I said, it would be good for you to have it *again*. It's been almost twenty-five years, hasn't it?"

Raquel remained silent.

"We've explored the pain Marian left behind when she ended your relationship." Ms. Tithe forgot to mention the circumstances of that relationship ending. *She left me for a man. Said she wanted nothing to do with me anymore. She got Jesus or something.* Raquel blinked away the single tear attempting to form in the corner of her eye. She had cried enough in Ms. Tithe's office. "We've talked about your attractions toward women from younger generations. Perhaps it's time we explore what might happen should you get more serious with this girl."

"What do you think will happen?" Raquel almost snapped that.

"I don't know, Raquel." Ms. Tithe steepled her fingers before her face, elbows digging into the arms of her large, plush tub chair. "What do you think might happen if she becomes your serious girlfriend for more than a few weeks or months?"

She swallowed. "Sounds like you're fishing for me to admit a connection between Marian and my dating preferences."

"There's only a connection if you think there's one."

God, these people and their mind games. Raquel was onto them from her very first therapist. It wasn't that she disagreed with the practice, but what client wanted to realize that they were the ones spinning webs and making connections in their traumatized brains?

"You think I haven't thought about it before?" Raquel stopped staring at Ms. Tithe's certifications and moved on to the knick-knacks lining a mantle place. She ran her fingers along the stonework and admired the opaque urn Ms. Tithe stored her cat's ashes in. *BOOTSIE* had lived a long and happy life, according to the Polaroid picture of a fat orange cat in a windowsill. *Every time I see a Polaroid, I think of Marian.* The nudes in the bottom of her designer shoebox, tucked in the back of her closet... Raquel wondered if they were still okay. Not that she was about to check up on them anytime soon.

"Tell me what you've thought about, Raquel."

Every time Ms. Tithe said her name, Raquel assumed that a coin was dropped into a box somewhere. Like a swear jar, but with clients' names. "My tastes in women were stunted when the love of my life dumped me," Raquel began. "I've always been trying to date her again. It's like I think I can recreate that carefree relationship if I continue to date women in that age range."

"So it's not about them being *younger* as much as it's about that age range?"

"I guess. Doesn't sound much better, honestly."

"On the contrary, I think this is a pretty good breakthrough. You should be proud of yourself for being introspective enough to ask your subconscious the hard questions."

"Uh huh."

Ms. Tithe lowered her arms, her pen thumping against her notepad. A tablet was shut off on the coffee table in front of her. Analog. Digital. Which one did Ms. Tithe prefer around her Gen X client, and which one did she prefer with her younger ones? Did one reflect the other? iPads were the shit of sci-fi when Raquel was in high school. *Star Trek. That's the only place I saw crap like that.*

Marian loved Star Trek.

"How does your own age come into play with your dating life?"

Raquel glanced over her shoulder. "I'm aware of how old I am and what my dates want from me. They want to be spoiled. Sexually. Financially." She ran her fingers beneath the picture of Bootsie the big orange cat. "I'm inclined to do both for them. It makes me happy. When I was their age, I wish I had been so spoiled. I spent most of my early twenties depressed and withdrawn."

"When did you get back into dating after your breakup?"

"Right away, but it didn't mean anything." Women were a blur up until the age of twenty-seven. Raquel thought nothing of continuing to date women a few years younger than her. It didn't look weird. The balance was still there. It wasn't until she hit thirty that she realized she had no desire to date women closer to her age, let alone older. Now that she was in her forties, she embraced it. Whether people called her a cougar or a cradle-robber, it didn't matter. Everyone judged, and she kept on keeping on. "It's been a slow slog coming out of that haze. Maybe that's why I cling to things that are familiar."

"Do you think you're trying to recreate your relationship with Marian?"

"No." Perhaps Raquel had been too quick to say that. Made it sound like she hadn't thought hard enough about it. "I mean, I know I'll never get Marian back. I know no relationship will ever be like that. I told you that I'm aware of how old I am when I'm with younger women. Although..." What was it about younger women that enchanted her so much? Raquel was often *dis*enchanted with the naivete and emotional immaturity. There was also something to be said for a steady girlfriend who could take care of herself and didn't count on Raquel for every little thing. She loved spoiling her girlfriends. She didn't love being the stand-in mom. "There was something extra magical about that time. Everything was new. We were each other's first big loves, and I foolishly believed that it would last forever. Doesn't every girl want to believe that?"

"It's quite common," Ms. Tithe said. "I was also in love at that age. I definitely wanted it to last forever."

"Did it, though?"

The therapist pursed her lips. "No. We parted ways after graduating."

"At least you got to live under the spell longer than me. Maybe there was less pressure to light everything on fire in a heterosexual relationship, though."

"Perhaps what you're attempting to recreate isn't the exact relationship you had with Marian, but the feeling of newness and exploration in a first-time relationship. The women you date are young enough that you might be the first big fling of their lives."

"You might be surprised. These days, lots of girls are having lesbian relationships long before I meet them."

"Even so, how a woman processes relationships in her early twenties is much different than when she's reached middle age."

Middle. Age. Raquel had to suppress a shudder. As far as she was concerned, she was a vibrant woman of indiscernible age. She decided to forego explaining to her therapist that dating women younger than her also helped her feel young. Maybe, when the wrinkles settled in and she forgot where she parked her car, she would finally embrace the next phase of her life.

Until then, she was eternally thirty-five.

"How do you feel with the person you're currently seeing?"

Raquel returned to the couch she refused to sit on. Her hand grazed against the back, her eyes pointed forward while one ankle crossed over the other. Ms. Tithe continued to stare at her, anticipating an answer. "Really good," Raquel finally said. "She seems to know what she wants. She's also out of college, so I guess it's good for me."

Ms. Tithe could barely contain the little smirk appearing on her face. "Does she seem more mature than some of the other young women you've dated?"

Raquel had to think about that. Lisa was as prone to impulsive tendencies as anyone else under twenty-five, but she was almost... self-aware. Every time she got up to do something, she looked back to Raquel to see how she would react. Hell, that past Sunday morning began with Raquel waking up to Lisa in the kitchen cooking some breakfast – in nothing but her underwear. The bra may or may not have "accidentally" popped off while she stood in front of the microwave. Raquel had still been rubbing sleep out of her eyes when she beheld that sight.

"She's like a kitten," Raquel said. "Cute, fluffy, playful... very adamant that she keep your attention, but also still learning when to put the claws away. Sometimes a kitten plays too rough, you know?"

She had a feeling that the woman with her dead cat on the mantle place would understand the metaphor. Indeed, Ms. Tithe nodded along, hand writing a note with a quick flourish. "You have to be careful with kittens, though. Sometimes they come across as more work than they're worth. You have to keep in mind that they eventually grow into adult felines."

"Yes." Raquel stared at her reflection in a mirror hanging on the other side of the room. "They sure do. Some of them even grow up to be mountain lions."

Ms. Tithe clearly caught on to the joke, but did not mention anything about it.

Raquel finished her hour with only one thought in her mind. *Lisa.* The vixen that had stolen her attention with one chat at a bar on a lonely Friday night. Raquel wasn't a woman who believed in signs, yet how could she deny the feeling in her gut when one date dumped her and another perfect one appeared out of nowhere? Maybe there was a guardian angel watching out over her. Maybe she had finally cashed in enough chips from Dating Roulette to earn her one of many grand prizes.

She soon reminded herself that such thoughts were silly, and she was better off playing the lottery.

The warm day greeted her when she stepped outside of the high-rise building. A message was waiting for her on her phone. It was from her travel agent.

"Yes, hello, Raquel!" The peppy woman was almost like nails on a chalkboard in Raquel's ear. "I'm calling about the final reservations for your Hawaiian trip. As soon as possible, I need you to get back to me with the name of your companion so I can finish making the reservations. I'll only be able to hold everything for another hour, so please let me know!"

Before Raquel could do that, however, she needed to call someone else first. Now would be a good time to learn Lisa's last name.

Chapter 10

It had been way too long since Raquel last stepped on Hawaiian soil. *At least two years. How unfortunate.* She used to make a habit of going at least once a year since discovering the perfect beauty of this tropical oasis in the middle of the Pacific Ocean. The fact she didn't need her passport was a mere bonus. She had learned that lesson after discovering that half the women she dated had yet to get their first passports.

The weather was warmer than back home, but a healthy breeze kept her skin cool. The lack of humidity was also a bonus, since that was only ramping up in her high-rise city. Forecasts claimed it might be the hottest summer yet.

But for now, Raquel could enjoy what many people around the world declared to be *perfect* temperatures. Comfort didn't begin to describe what she experienced when she walked around the beachfront in nothing but her sapphire blue bikini and the breezy white cotton kimono that kept her stylish yet ready to hop into the pool at any moment.

She stopped in front of an outdoor bar a few feet away from the resort pool. Tourists milled about, chatting with other guests and the friends they came with. A bachelorette party was amping up for a full day of sunbathing, facials at the hotel spa, and shopping in the nearby town. Families urged their children to mind their manners – or completely gave up on ever corralling the little hellions that only served to remind Raquel why she didn't want anything to do with motherhood. Luckily, it was easy to ignore the cacophony of voices, splashing, and rustlings of the palm trees high above her head.

The only bartender on duty was busy with other guests. Raquel didn't mind. She helped herself to one of the stools and closed her eyes. The breeze continued to kiss her cheek while her toes wiggled in her sandals. In a perfect world, she would be down on the beach letting the warm sands wash across her pink toes.

"You look like you could use some company."

Raquel opened her eyes to find a young man, perhaps twenty-five or older, sitting on the stool next to her. He wore a tank top over his tanned body, but he still left little to the imagination.

"Do I?" Raquel sat up straight, her buffed nails lightly scratching her cheek. She didn't know how much of her demeanor this man could see behind her big, round sunglasses, but she hoped he could sense her amusement that a young guy was paying any sort of attention to her. "That's funny. I was thinking that I love how peaceful the solitude here is."

The guy was persistent with his charming smile and the careful way he flexed his muscles, making sure Raquel beheld every little ripple of his body. *Impressive. It does nothing for me.* Raquel could appreciate a finely chiseled man, but he was better off hitting on the male bartender than trying to get into her pants. Flattering, though. Now, if he could keep the flirting to the sweet side and *not* transform into a creep, Raquel could consider her day more than fine.

"Everyone could always use company in a place like Hawai'i." He pretentiously made sure he enunciated the vowels on the end. He wasn't fooling Raquel, however. She knew he wasn't a native. "Or are you trying to get away from your husband?"

Raquel's eyes hadn't been so wide since the time a house buyer went a hundred grand over the asking price. "My husband?" She checked her left hand. Nope. She didn't see a wedding ring there. Besides, how rich was it that this guy thought she was *straight!* Raquel hadn't dealt with something of this caliber since she last went to a club with a gal pal instead of a hot and heavy girlfriend. "What makes you think I've got one of those?"

She didn't know how he managed it, but the guy's smile grew wider. "Gotcha," he said with a hearty chuckle. "That's my favorite way to find out if a lady is single."

What a charmer. Raquel didn't know if it was time to jet or if this guy would show himself out. It could go either way. "You could've asked."

"Nah. Too forward."

I'll say. Raquel didn't like playing these games with guys. When she wasn't weirded out by their tactics, she was bored out of her mind. At least women brought with them a little mystery. Some pizzazz. The gracious, slender lines that made up their curves and the elaborate styles they adopted to express themselves and to catch appropriate attention. *This guy can't hold a single candle to them.* Did he yet know that he was barking up the totally wrong tree?

"Let me guess," she said. "You're super single. Or at least that's what you'll tell me before we go out on a date."

"This isn't Vegas." One of his bulging biceps touched the counter. Was she supposed to be impressed? Bodybuilders in Hawaii? Who knew! "What happens here doesn't have to stay here. Er, I mean..." Now the grin was just cheesy. "Don't have to leave who you are behind."

Maybe you should, kid. The only thing keeping Raquel from rolling her eyes was the fact that the weather was too nice to let this get to her. "So happens that I definitely haven't left who I am back home. Now, what can I do for you? I recommend the pineapple typhoon cocktail, if it's a recommendation you're looking for."

"I'll be more than happy to buy you a drink. Maybe we could share one."

"I'm flattered that you're interested in me." God knew Raquel looked *divine* in the outfit she bought for sitting next to the pool on her tropical getaway. "Except I'm afraid I'm taken for the weekend."

"Aw, he really doesn't have to know, though, does he?"

He was pushing it. Her humor, that was. Raquel dangled one leg over the other and let her shaking foot do the talking.

It didn't help that Mr. Big Flirt wasn't letting up. "Let me guess... your husband, or maybe it's your boyfriend, I dunno... he's a hot shot in his office. Makes lots of money and keeps you nice and safe in your big house on a nice street. Maybe you've got kids. Maybe you don't. All I know is that you're not as happy as you could be. You're restless. Something begs you to try out something new. A fantasy that you've been harboring for at least a few years now." The guy leaned back, letting Raquel have a grand view of how tight his shorts were. *Wouldn't pants that tight shrink your dick?* Raquel didn't know the first thing about proper penis management, but that was definitely a hard-on presented in this guy's shorts. No wonder he was so impressed with himself. "I think you need a guy who understands *you* and *your* needs."

"Do you, now?"

"I've got a room. Tell me when, and I'll tell you where to meet me."

"Why? So I can ride you into the sunset and call you my thundering stallion?"

He laughed. "Sounds hot, mama."

Mama! The guy's true intentions were coming out the longer Raquel had the utmost pleasure of talking to him. Not only how horny he was for her, but the fact he was *into how old she was.* If he called her a MILF, he was getting his ass kicked.

"I don't have a husband, sorry." Raquel didn't doubt that this guy got off on cheating wives. He probably imagined the look on their husbands' faces if they happened to walk in and caught him. Oh, and how *grateful* she would be to him! Wasn't that the biggest ego boost of all? "Afraid you'll have to find some other hot wife to bother."

"Hey, it's even better if you're unattached."

"I believe I told you that I'm here with someone."

"Yeah, but I figured you were saying that to blow me off."

She leveled her gaze on him. Finally, the bartender was approaching. "Why not both, honestly?"

"Hey, babe!"

Raquel wasn't only saved by the bartender giving them the side-eye. (Or was that a look reserved for a patron who made a habit of hitting on older women at his bar?) She was liberated by the beautiful woman bounding up to her in nothing but a hot pink leopard print bikini, complete with rhinestone chains across her cleavage and the top of her ass crack. *Jesus, I remember when I had a body like that.* Lisa had some cellulite, of course, but it blended in perfectly with her youthful skin and her body's ability to bounce between pounds without a thought. It helped that she opted to eat healthy anywhere they went.

Right. There was some asshole raining on this romantic getaway weekend.

"You're in time." Raquel looped her arm around her girlfriend's waist and brought her into a carnivorous hold. Devouring her was imminent. They had spent one night in Hawaii so far, but jet-lag and a desire to get up early meant they fell asleep before the fun could get beyond any heavy petting. But Raquel could say she fell asleep with her hand on Lisa's naked breast, and that was something! "As you can see, I've made a new friend."

Lisa gave him a dubious look. Gone was the wholesome mirth she exhibited when she found her girlfriend at the bar. Now? She had that same faraway glint in her eyes that Raquel recognized from her talks with Ms. Tithe. *She says I get the same look when I'm thinking about men.* The tired, get-outta-here bluntness of a lesbian who was tired of being forced to think about heterosexual relations.

Nice. At least Raquel knew where her latest and greatest girlfriend stood on such an important matter.

A lightbulb went off above the guy's head. It probably helped that Raquel was squeezing Lisa's ass and had both tits in her face. "Sorry," Raquel said. "I didn't catch your name."

"John."

"This is John, honey." Raquel rubbed the small of Lisa's naked back. *This is my favorite curve on the body. Mm-hmm. Soak it in, John.* "He's been hitting on me for the past few minutes. Thinks he's gonna get with this, as long as I don't tell my husband."

The bartender, who now stood directly in front of them, shook his head. "Man, John, how many times have I told you to stop hitting on older women at my bar? It's embarrassing every time they turn you down."

John's cheeks blazed red. "Shut up, man."

"We'll have two of the pineapple typhoons," Raquel requested of the bartender. She wanted him out of earshot before she said to John, "As you can see, I really am taken. We're also not interested in any threesomes."

John held up his hands in defeat and walked away. The silence he left behind was deafening until Lisa broke it with a giggle.

"You really are popular, huh?" she asked.

"The most popular, apparently." Raquel played with the ends of Lisa's hair, currently pulled back into the same cute ponytail she wore when they reunited on Smith Street. The rose-colored sunglasses were back for this vacation, too. The bathing suit was brand-new, though. Raquel had insisted on taking her bikini shopping before they got on a plane for Hawaii. "It's been a long time since I had a guy hit on me like that. I need to recalibrate my Fuck Off face. It works so well back home, but I guess in Hawaii, people are less bothered by it."

The bartender returned with their matching drinks. Raquel bade him to put it on her room tab while Lisa helped herself to the first sip. "People are a lot more chill in Hawaii. I've noticed that since we first came here."

"Now you know why everyone wants to come here. It's not only the beautiful weather and beautiful women tantalizing your field of view wherever you go."

"I haven't noticed any other beautiful women except you." Lisa said that with a faux-serious tone, but Raquel still appreciated the flirtation.

"Funny. I was thinking the same thing about you."

The moment they started putting their hands on each other, half the resort turned their attentions to them. Between the scandalized wives and their curious husbands, there were a myriad of young, suntanning women who occasionally lifted their sunglasses to get a load of the lesbian lovebirds at the bar and the guys who snickered to one another that this was the best day of their lives. Nobody bothered Raquel and her young girlfriend, however. Everyone was so involved in their own fantasies that they would rather keep their comments to themselves.

It served Raquel perfectly. The mild exhibitionist in her played with the tie of her girlfriend's bikini top, daring it to come undone and show the whole resort what her mother gave her. Knowing how much jealousy was already shot in her direction only made Raquel ornerier.

She supposed some of that jealousy was for Lisa as well. After all, men like John clearly had a thing for older women.

Raquel had promised to take Lisa into town for a day of edible delicacies and fancying every item in touristy display windows, and she intended on making good on that promise. Yet why did Lisa have to be so *tantalizing?* Even when she threw a sheer top and a pair of denim shorts over her bikini, she was still too hot for the public. Oh, half the women running around town showed as much if not more skin than Lisa, but it wasn't like they had the same aura. Lisa screamed sex and seduction. She offered come-hither looks with a side of swaying hips. The way she pulled her hair up when she was bored, piling it on top of her head to show off the svelte build of her shoulder blades was enough to drive Raquel wild. It wasn't enough that they occasionally held hands while looking in shop windows and occasionally dipping inside to sample the wares. She wanted to put her hands all over Lisa. Grab her. Haul her into changing rooms and cover her in covetous kisses. Gently tug that ponytail like the friendliest leash to ever attach itself to another woman. When Lisa's hips weren't swaying in her short-shorts, her arms stretched high above her head and exposed the white of her stomach.

It was torture. Sweet, utter torture.

"I dare you to try on that dress." Raquel said that in an airy shop that sold items that were dangerously close to lingerie. Yet if there was one thing they both learned in that land, it was that a woman could get away with *much* more skin than back home. Not just practically – but morally, as well. "If it looks good on you, I'm buying it."

Lisa lifted her sunglasses and drank in the sheer maxi dress covered in palm tree motifs. "I'd have to wear a whole outfit beneath it to not get arrested."

"Good. We're on the same page."

Tsking, Lisa dropped her girlfriend's hand and approached the shopkeeper about trying on the outfit on display on a slender mannequin.

Raquel really should have thought ahead better. What did she think was going to happen when she stepped into Lisa's dressing room and saw her wearing nothing but her bikini and the sheer maxi dress on top?

Or so it first appeared. A minute later, Lisa spun around, revealing that she had conveniently forgotten to snap the back of her bikini. It may or may not have fallen to the ground the moment she twirled.

"I'm buying it," Raquel quickly announced. "You're wearing it on every date we go on from here on out."

She would hold Lisa to it, too.

***

They finally returned to their suite an hour later. Lisa talked about getting dinner at the resort restaurant on the beach, but all Raquel could think about was taking out the sexual energy that had been mounting her for the past several hours.

"Thanks for the presents." Lisa sealed her gratitude with a sweet smile that followed her into the bathroom. She came out again a minute later, shorts off and walking around in her pink leopard print bikini and the sheer shirt she had brought with her from the mainland. The dress was gingerly tucked into the bottom of a matte shopping bag. "You didn't get anything for yourself, though."

Raquel closed the curtains on their ocean view and turned to her girlfriend with nothing but lust in her eyes. "Oh, I *did* get myself something, though." Before

Lisa could ask her what, Raquel approached her with open hands and a mouth that begged to be kissed. "You. In that dress. A whole day with you."

Lisa grinned. She did that thing where she stacked her hair on top of her head, hands twisting through every strand as the rest of her did a little dance of appreciation. It was like every one of Raquel's heavy-handed compliments completely undid her from the inside out.

"You think this trip is for you, honey?" Raquel restrained herself from grabbing the girl in front of her. While Lisa would probably be down for woman handling, Raquel liked to think she had more class than that. *I'll save the grabbing and kissing for later in this relationship.* At some point, she would reach critical mass. Poor Lisa wouldn't know what to do with herself when that time came. Raquel wouldn't let her out of bed for a whole week.

Bet she'll love it.

"This trip is for me. I had always planned on taking one the moment I closed on that house." Raquel stopped in front of Lisa and lightly plucked the hem of her sheer top. It soon popped over her head. *Holy shit. Look at her cleavage in this thing.* Raquel had seen her girlfriend's tits no fewer than twice on that trip so far, but there was nothing like seeing them lifted and separated in a *bikini* top. Any girl would look like Aphrodite emerging from the foam in this getup. "It didn't matter who I brought with me, but I chose *you* to come along with me on this tropical adventure. You know why?"

Lisa snorted. Not like she couldn't tell what Raquel had been staring at for the past thirty seconds. "Because you think I'm hot, and a hot girlfriend is the kind you take with you to Hawaii."

"Oh, you're hot. Without a doubt." Raquel reached behind Lisa and unhooked the bikini top. Lisa did nothing to cover herself up when the hot pink fabric inevitably fell to the hotel room floor. "Jesus. Did your mother make you this way, or have you spent half your life meticulously crafting this body?"

For a moment, Lisa's soul left her body. Not in ecstasy, but in the reminder of something Raquel was not privy to knowing. Had she done something wrong?

Then, Lisa said, her soul back in her eyes, "I try to take care of myself. Before my mother died, she said I should eat my vegetables and lay off the processed sugars."

"Your mother was a wise woman. We should all heed that advice." Right. Lisa's mother had passed away a few years ago. Probably not wise to bring her up, let alone when Raquel was about to get hot with a dead woman's daughter.

"I mean, you've got a great body, too." Lisa slowly rocked her arms back and forth, making sure Raquel got a grand view of how her chest moved. *Were my tits like that when I was her age? Or is she special?* "I've been meaning to ask what your secret is."

Raquel lowered her lips to her girlfriend's ear. The inhale of Lisa's next breath was the stuff fantasies were made of. "The life force of young women like you. I've been sucking you dry since the moment you approached me in the bar."

"Oh, my." Lisa clasped her fingers over her mouth. "No wonder I feel so lightheaded whenever I'm around you."

That sound eking from Raquel's lips was the last of her sanity leaving her body. She threw herself upon Lisa, covering her chest in heavy kisses that would quickly turn into more.

They made their way to the California king bed not too far away, Lisa hitting the comforter first. That was all part of Raquel's plan, so she could watch the way Lisa's body reacted to the force coming for her.

In many ways, what Raquel had said was true. She really did feel like she was sucking the youth and vitality from the women she slept with. Not with the intention of draining them dry and moving on to the next one, but making everything they did feel more urgent... and maybe a little dirty.

It makes you mine, doesn't it? Lisa was the kind of girl who attracted a lot of attention wherever she went. She drank up the attention, too. While Raquel had dated plenty of women like Lisa before, there was something different about the way she went out of her way to get Raquel's attention – and keep it. This wasn't a one-night stand to either of them. This may also not be forever, but for now, Raquel was confident in thinking that they could have a good long run as a couple. *I'll spoil you silly. You'll make me feel eternally young.* Lisa would practically live in Raquel's apartment while neglecting her own. They would eat most of their dinners together before retiring to bed extra early – how else would Raquel make room for all the sex they were destined to have, *and* still get enough sleep for work? Maybe Lisa could exist on five hours of sleep every night, but Raquel needed the full eight.

They might as well get into the habit of going to bed early now. Maybe they had foregone dinner to fool around in their Hawaiian resort suite, but Raquel didn't care. She wanted to feast upon Lisa, as if she were the grand buffet set up for her own personal consumption.

See? Sucking out their vitality. It was a mighty thought to have when she sank her whole mouth upon one of Lisa's breasts and flicked her tongue as quickly as it could go. Lisa squealed in delight, legs thrashing beneath Raquel as she refused to let go of the masterpiece in her possession.

She needed to be on top of Lisa. Inside of her. Tasting her. Committing every inch of her perfect body to memory, in case this was all a dream and Raquel was doomed to wake up with the knowledge that she was seventy years old and her chance at love was behind her.

"Yes, *yes*." Lisa was always so grateful to have Raquel's attentions. That definitely went for fingering her with the fury of Raquel's self-doubts and insecurities. The same ones she had battled since the day the love of her life exited stage right and went straight into the arms of someone who didn't deserve her.

Raquel spent most of her days wondering what happened to Marian. She never bothered to look her up to protect her own sanity... and it wasn't like Raquel *wanted* to think about the ex that shattered her heart... but it didn't take much for her to remember the sweet and silly girl who used to love having sex as much as she loved playing with Raquel's hair.

She didn't think about Marian when she was with Lisa. Not for long. Not when there was someone new and exciting to shower with ardor.

Experiencing Lisa's orgasms alongside her guaranteed that Raquel thought of no one else. She was so captivated by Lisa's arching back, hardened nipples, and the pulse of her body against the fingers inside of her to think of anything else but that exact moment.

The addiction was planted in Raquel that night. She had fended it off until now, but she no longer denied it. Lisa was more than the one of the moment. She was the one who could possibly save Raquel from herself.

She celebrated that realization by plunging another finger into a place they had yet to explore. Lisa had been begging for it, anyway.

Chapter 11

Lisa was the last to awaken the final morning in Hawaii. She faced a bright, beautiful island morning with her eyes gently fluttering open and her worn out body attempting to remember what it was like to stretch from head to little tiny toe.

She was also naked, but that didn't faze her as she exposed herself to the open curtains. The beach beyond the window was empty that early in the morning. Even if a few tourists meandered along the surf with perverted eyes looking in her direction, Lisa was willing to let them get a gander of her nudity. If it was good enough for the discerning Raquel, then it was damn well good enough for the rest of the world.

The other side of the bed was empty. Raquel had proven to be an early riser who wasn't afraid to get a jump on the day, unlike Lisa, who was still recovering from the terrible sleep schedule she kept during college.

Can't blame her for getting up early, though. Morning air was always the freshest. The endless potential of a day ahead got a girl like Lisa out of bed. Raquel's industry also probably required her to be available from the moment most of the world got up in their time zone.

They were in a totally different time zone now. Lisa tried not to think about how much later it was back on the mainland. Besides, she had specifically come along on this trip to think about nothing but Raquel. As far as Lisa was concerned, that was all that mattered.

It didn't take her long to find her girlfriend. The suite wasn't the largest at the resort, but it *was* big enough to boast a kitchen and small living room complete with flat screen TV. The sixty-inch screen was set to rustling palm trees along a Hawaiian shore. *So we can see the beach even if we're turned away from the windows.* Lisa, who had only thrown on the sheer maxi dress to wear to the bathroom and back out again, stood in front of the television and brushed her hair.

"You roll right out of bed looking like a 10 on the Victoria's Secret scale." Raquel was in the kitchen, chopping fruit on the counter. She wore a white V-neck (no bra) and the cotton sleep shorts she was supposed to be wearing on this long weekend getaway. But like Lisa, Raquel kept going to bed naked. It may have been Lisa's first time seeing Raquel dressed in her pajamas.

"Says the woman who should be modeling." Lisa sat on one of the stools. "What's going on here? Breakfast?"

Raquel glanced up from the meticulous chopping her kitchen knife expertly performed. "Thought it might be nice to have some fruit with our breakfast. I went out for a walk before you got up and discovered someone selling these from their farm. I've ordered oatmeal and eggs from the hotel kitchen, but they're not here yet."

"Delicious." So happened that Lisa was also starving. "What are those? Mangos?"

"Yes."

Lisa continued to watch the hypnotic show. *How in the world is she doing it so neatly? Is there something wrong with them?* "I thought mangos were supposed to be really messy and tough to cut." Yes, there was a pool of juice on the cutting board and in the bowl, but Lisa had a distinct memory of her mother making a huge mess in the kitchen whenever she started a diet and wanted to eat nothing but mangos. Eventually, she had her snacks in the backyard. *"Just like the natives do!"* she often called through the back door. Lisa never knew what natives her mother was talking about.

"I've got a gift for dealing with pulp."

She said that in such a deadpan way that Lisa became convinced she missed some important detail somewhere. *Do I suddenly look like some young, dumb rube because I don't know how to cut mangos?*

The corners of Raquel's mouth twitched. Finally, a short snort exploded from her nostrils.

"You should see the look on your face."

Lisa admitted defeat. She wasn't sure what had defeated her, but her defense was that it was still early in the morning and it was a miracle if she could solve simple math equations.

"Do you like mangos?"

Would be awkward if I said no, huh? Lisa squared her shoulders with a grin. "I'm down for eating anything you prepare."

"I'm serious. I realized last night that we don't know all that much about each other. Besides what happens between our legs when we're feeling the moment."

Lisa pushed her hairbrush down the counter and placed both elbows in front of Raquel. "I used to eat them all the time as a kid. My mom loved them. Had a coworker who used to give her free ones. Right up there with free apples and peaches."

"But do *you* like them?" Raquel wiped her hands on a towel and shoved the bowl forward. "I can find out more about your mom later."

Lisa blushed. When someone got her started, it was easy to gush about her mother. "Let's find out." She picked up a juicy slice and let the stone fruit work its magic on her tongue. Sure enough, juice dribbled out of the corner of her mouth. She grabbed a napkin and cleaned herself up before Raquel could laugh at her.

"It's good," Lisa declared through a mouthful of juice. "You made it look so much less juicy than it actually is."

"I have magic dexterity." Raquel twiddled her fingers. "As you must know by now."

Lisa didn't know why she was still blushing. Nothing Raquel said was particularly scandalous, and Lisa did not consider herself someone who was easily embarrassed by sexy talk and the references that made her think about crawling into bed with a woman she fancied. *It's because it's coming from her.* Any other woman could refer to the way she fingered a girl and Lisa would be all over it. Coming from Raquel, however, and it turned her into a silly mess.

"You have the cutest face." Raquel casually said that while cleaning up some of the mess left behind by the mangos. "It's like the perfect mix of youthful glow and good ol' honest humility."

That made Lisa cock her head. "Youthful glow, huh? Do you know when that starts fading away?"

Raquel shrugged. "Depends on the person. Mine started fading around twenty-four, but that's because my twenties sucked."

"I don't think you look that old."

"Compared to you? I'm the crypt-keeper." Raquel picked up a piece of mango and managed to take a few bites without creating the same level of mess as Lisa. "Every time we go out, people know what's up with us."

"What's up with us, exactly?" This might be it. Lisa's chance to figure out what the status of their relationship was after this trip concluded.

Raquel borrowed her girlfriend's napkin to clean up more juice splatters on the counter. "They look at us and know that I'm your sugar mama."

"Are you?"

"Does it matter? It's what people think when they see a young woman like you making out and canoodling with someone older. Especially when you dress like that." Raquel gestured to the sheer maxi dress bedecking Lisa's body.

"Does that bother you?"

"Does it bother *you?*"

Lisa winced. "I asked you first."

Raquel considered that question with averted eyes. "It doesn't bother me. I'm older. I have a stable career. I have money. What am I really losing? Respect?" She finally looked back at Lisa, who cracked the smallest of smiles. "The reason people get really flustered around women like me is because I break their brains. Old men dating younger women? That's old hat. *Everyone* knows what men are really thinking, right?" That must have been a rhetorical question. "Women, though... we're expected to be obsessed with our ovaries and careers, depending on who you ask. It doesn't matter how old we are or if we're gay. A woman my age having fun with women your age... clearly, I'm not looking for a co-parent. It makes people think of sex. Women my age aren't supposed to want sex."

Lisa continued to give her a bemused smile.

"You'll understand when you're older."

They both laughed. Although Raquel had meant it, the way she said it was too reminiscent of how their relationship could have been like if it went in a different direction.

"So you know..." Lisa bit her mango-covered lips before continuing. "I'm not necessarily looking for a sugar mama. I can pay my own bills and don't need allowances and stuff. Honestly, I don't mind being spoiled, but I prefer if things aren't too crazy. Get what I mean?" She thought of her friends in the chatroom who always tried to one-up each other in the *get money, bitch* department. While Lisa was the first to admit that her financial situation wasn't amazing, she would feel even more embarrassed to have someone else pay for everything. *Things will get better for me. I'd rather base a relationship on things like love and respect.* To some of her friends, that was an absurd notion.

Raquel sat back up again. "Just so *you* know, I'm not thinking that much about it. If I wanna spoil my girlfriend and pile a ton of gifts on top of her, I'm going to do it. So, sorry if you go to pay your rent next month and discover it's already been taken care of."

"Really?"

"Well, don't count on it. I'm just saying."

Lisa laughed. "Sorry if that was a weird thing for me to say while we're fooling around for a weekend in *Hawaii*. Like, when you asked me to come with you, I thought I was living in a different universe. Nobody's ever done this for me before. Let alone so soon after meeting them."

"When I want to jet set, I prefer to bring a friend with me. If you catch my drift."

How many times have you done this? Brought a young girlfriend with her on a weekend getaway? "I am pretty lucky to be your girlfriend of the moment, then. Because who knows who you will be taking next time."

Raquel lost her contentment. "Who says it won't be you? Are you planning on moving somewhere in the coming weeks?"

The blush refused to leave Lisa's cheeks. A shame, because she always got unpleasantly red when she blushed for too long. Only a matter of time before she looked like a giant apple.

"Aw, you're so adorable. You think I'm out to drain you of your vitality and move on to the next hapless young woman who is a big enough of a lesbian fool with an older-woman-complex."

"You sound like you've had this argument with yourself many times."

"When you've lived through as much judgment as me, you start to anticipate what other people are probably thinking about you."

"You think people are thinking negatively about you dating younger women? Is it because you've dated so many?"

Raquel's lips twitched. "How many do you think I've dated?" She cut Lisa off so she could answer that for herself. "All right. So I've dated more than a few in my life. This year alone I've probably had four women, including you, whom I would consider *girlfriends*. Yet I'll have you know that I'm not breaking up with them because they get older or I'm totally bored of them. All right, that last one happened a few times. Maybe once this year."

"You don't have to explain yourself to me."

"Don't most cougars see younger people as expendable, though? See, this is why I rarely have other women like me for friends. Most of them are inane and, honestly, some of them are downright terrible."

Lisa considered that for a moment. "So why do you break up with most of your girlfriends?"

The answer was on Raquel's lips, but she was more preoccupied with eating mango slices than saying anything. "Some of them get tired of it and dump me first. Others are simply too immature for a relationship with me. This may shock you, but I actually want *real* relationships on top of hot sex. You wouldn't think it's so hard to find both when you've got a little money and enough confidence to swagger like a real mountain lion, but..."

"I appreciate the swagger." *Am I too immature for her?* Lisa honestly didn't know how immature *or* mature she was. She was at that awkward age where she could look back at her younger self and cringe, but still realized she probably had a lot of growing to do. Raquel, on the other hand, was set in her ways and knew herself pretty well. *What if I grow into someone who isn't compatible with her?* Was that what was happening with Raquel's girlfriends. "But, if it bothers you so much after a while, why don't you, uh, you know..."

"Date women closer to my age?"

Lisa nodded.

"That's the million-dollar question, isn't it?" Raquel stared into the bowl of mangos but did not grab another piece. "Now you know why I'm in therapy."

"I'm in therapy too."

"How about that? We're all in therapy."

They both sat in silence for a short while, Raquel musing something she would not share, while Lisa continued to wonder if this relationship was doomed from the start. *Will I be content if she dumps me because I'm not what she's looking for? She could be lying about wanting a real relationship. Even if she's not, she might not like me that much. Maybe I'm too immature for her. I do walk around with my tits hanging out like I'm nineteen...*

"You ever been in love before?" Raquel suddenly asked.

Lisa slowly swallowed. "A little." She didn't dare say more than that. "Not sure what's love yet."

"Ha. You've got a better head on your shoulders than most people your age I've met. Including me when I was your age. And younger." Raquel's finger rounded the rim of the mango bowl. "I've been in love. Big, fat, stupid love that fucked me up when it ended."

Lisa had to inhale a deep breath while thinking over her words. "Tell me about her."

"You wanna hear something about that?"

More deep breathing. Something reverberated in the back of Lisa's mind, daring her to keep the conversation going while warning her that she might not like what she heard. "Yeah."

Raquel planted her ass firmly on one of the other stools. She looked her age in that moment, a few wrinkles appearing on her face and her body showing off the sag and cellulite that wasn't there whenever Lisa usually looked. *It doesn't bother me. Isn't it kinda empowering to see a sexual beast like her confidently showing her age to the world?* Raquel looked like she took expensive care of herself, but was that for *her,* or to keep the young women interested in her? Wouldn't it only get harder as she got older?

I won't care when you get older if you don't care when I get older...

"I had a girlfriend right out of high school. My age, mind you. We went to the same community college together. Long story short, I was head over heels in love with her. Spent every waking moment with her in some way. Thought she loved me as much. Which is why it was such a shock when she dumped me for some *guy*. I didn't even know she was bi, although we didn't talk about that much back then." Raquel followed that up with, "Not like now! The girls I date have gradually gone from lez to bi. Doesn't matter to me, but it's interesting how times change."

Lisa didn't comment on that. "I'm sorry to hear that. About your ex, that is." *I may or may not know who it is...*

"Yeah, well... I took it really hard. It was the first love of my life, and the first heartbreak of my life. Although it seems like so many other people handle it better than I did. I was around your age when I finally checked out from the heartbreak hotel. Three years. That's how long it took for me to start moving on."

"My mom never really dated again after she split from my dad. Said it hurt too much." Lisa shrugged. "Their marriage was kinda miserable, I guess. Even so, she didn't date until she died. Maybe it's not as rare as you're imagining."

"Not even out having hookups, huh?"

Lisa couldn't help but grimace. "I don't know, and I don't wanna know that about my mom." *Gross.* She would rather face the physical decline her mother suffered once the cancer really took hold. *I never thought I'd be so grossed out again. My mother told me to wait until childbirth. Then nothing would ever gross me out again.*

"Sorry." Raquel eyed the mango slices again. After she offered another one to Lisa, who declined, she picked up a small slice and nibbled it with nimble fingers. Only a tiny bit of juice washed down her chin. Nobody moved to wipe it away from her skin. "So, is this the part where I ask you why you date older women? Because I doubt I'm the only one you've fancied. You practically said so yourself when we met."

Lisa wouldn't deny it. There *had* been other women before Raquel, although none like her. *If she's the queen, then they were mere duchesses.* Lofty women who always thought of how much higher they had to climb – and how close they were to falling from grace at any moment. None of them were as cool, as confident, or as professionally secure as Raquel Mendes, the woman whose face often appeared on billboards and bus stop benches around their city. "*Call Raquel Today to Find the Home of Your Dreams!*" Sometimes she stood with the rest of her "team." Usually, however, she was picked as the face of her company and got a spot all to herself. Lisa often wondered how her coworkers felt about that. Did they care? Or were they happy if a solo Raquel meant more money in their pockets?

"I dated my first older woman when I was twenty, but I told her I was twenty-five and started college later. Who knows if she believed me."

"What did 'older' mean?"

"Eh... forty?"

Raquel said nothing.

"I had been with girls before. Fooled around with a couple classmates in high school and then in college, but it was mostly... you know... *pure*." Lisa didn't mean to say that with disdain. It simply hadn't been what she was looking for in the bedroom. Her body and mind were ready for the time of their lives. Why was it so hard to find a girl on campus who could give it to her the way she liked? To take the lead and initiate her into a world of cosmic, Sapphic bliss? Lisa had been totally spoiled by lesbian romance novels and erotica shorts that got her so hot and bothered she needed the hot next-door-neighbor in her dorm to barge in with a strap-on.

Unfortunately, stuff like that never happened. Not until she started looking for and dating older women.

"I found her online. There was a chat room that was for matching older and younger people together, although it was such a landmine because both men and women were on it."

Raquel nodded along. "I've heard of it. Never used it, though, for that reason."

"It was like picture-less Tinder for older-younger people!" Lisa had tried that, too, but had zero luck. The only dates she got off it were with women closer to her age, and none of them amounted to anything. She was more likely to get bots and men posing as hot women trying to troll her. "I met one woman through a friend I found on there, and she took me out on the nicest date of my life. It was like right out of a romance novel or a movie. Candlelit dinner, dressed nice, *smelled* nice. She was so courteous and laid so many compliments on me that I didn't know what was up or down by the end of the date!"

Raquel looked like she was riveted to Lisa's tale, so it was no surprise when she asked, "Did you sleep with her?"

Lisa's hand ended up on her face. *Too embarrassing! This is my current girlfriend, and she wants to hear about my hookups?* "Not on the first date, no. She took me home in her BMW and kissed my hand before driving off. I thought I was gonna die!"

"Wow. That is some hardcore old school player. May I ask if she was butch or femme?"

"I think she was femme?" Felt weird to say it that way. Lisa wasn't as knowledgeable about those roles. "She wore dresses and had long hair, but her mannerisms were very masculine at times."

"A rare breed. Now you're making me wish she was around when I was your age."

Lisa pulled the bowl of mangos back her way. "For our second date, she took me straight to her house and fed me dinner... in her bed."

"No way."

"Yes, way! She told me to lay down before she brought in this scrumptious platter of finger food. I was so stuffed that night."

"In more ways than one, I'm sure."

Lisa burst out in awkward laughter. *You have no idea!*

"Surprised you didn't lock that one down with marriage."

"In the end, she wasn't the kind of person I was looking for. Besides, I was twenty. I wasn't yet ready to think about the future with somebody. I wanted to date."

"A very twenty-year-old thing to say."

"How about you?" Lisa dared to ask such a question. "Why do you like dating younger women? Do you see yourself maybe marrying a twenty-three-year-old?"

Raquel could have taken that either way. Apparently, she chose to take that as an honest question, for she responded, "My therapist tries to imply that I'm attempting to recreate my heartbreaking relationship from that age. Other cougars make it sound like it's all about sex and being a super important person in someone's life. Weirdos make it sound like I wanna be somebody's *mom.* If that doesn't sound grossly incestual."

"Yeah..."

"In reality, I enjoy spending time with people from a different generation as myself. Maybe I got burned growing up. I always got along more with my baby boomer aunt than I did my fellow Gen Xers. Millennials are a fun bunch. Some of y'all's collective outlook on life is so fascinating. Wait, are you a Millennial?"

"I think so? Everyone calls me one, so I guess I must be."

"I can't ever remember how much time has passed recently. Seems like yesterday Millennials were ruining the Oshkosh industry."

Lisa fell into another fit of giggles. "I *loved* their clothes when I was in kindergarten."

"God, I feel so old."

"You're not old." Lisa propped her chin up on her hand. "You're barely middle age. You've still got so much life ahead of you. People are living to like... *ninety* now! Whoa. Now I feel like a total baby." That was a little under seventy years away. How much would the world have changed by then?

"Yes, my shot metabolism, my wrinkles, and my cynical view of the world are very becoming of young women."

"Hate to break it to you, but I've got some wrinkles on my ass, and lots of us are cynical, sarcastic cunts."

Raquel's eyes widened. "Not as much as you think you are. Trust me. There's such a stark difference in how you view the world between your twenties and your forties."

"Everyone says that."

"Because it's true." Raquel was not laughing with her girlfriend now. "It's easy for you to brush off when you're young. You're convinced your opinions will never change. That you won't continue to grow and mature. It couldn't be farther from the truth. Maybe your views will completely change. Maybe you'll become more radical in your viewpoints than you were while in college. Your priorities will absolutely change. Health creeps up on you. Let me tell you about all the allergies I suddenly developed when I turned thirty."

Why was she telling Lisa this? And why was she getting more adamant as the minutes went by?

"Maybe that's what I like about dating younger women. So much endless potential. Everything keeps going right. You don't have to worry about what you eat as much as you do when you're my age. Between early onset diabetes and metabolism going down the toilet..." Raquel picked up one of the mango slices. It continued to drip juice all over her hand while she spoke. "You don't know what's going to happen. Everything is right ahead of you." Her thumb dug into the flesh of the mango, leaving a large indent that was reminiscent of some of the more sexual things they had done on that trip. *Man, even when she's talking about serious stuff, I have such a one-track mind!* "What job you'll have... where you'll go in the world... who you will marry and the kinds of kids you might have... Jesus. It's so unknown. You're along for the ride. Everything that happens to you is both the craziest and most amazing thing that's happened to you yet. You feel everything so *viscerally.* When you're in love, it's the greatest love to ever infiltrate your system. You can't imagine feeling that way for someone ever again. When they break your heart, it's so depressing and life-ending because it's probably the absolute worst thing you've ever been through before."

"So what happens when you get older?" Lisa asked her.

Raquel looked her squarely in the eye before crushing her hand around the thick, juicy slice of mango. Fruity flesh squeezed between her sticky fingers and dripped from her grip.

Lisa swallowed. Deep beneath that erotic overtone was a warning that flashed bits of Lisa's future before her eyes.

It only intrigued her more.

Chapter 12

Raquel had arranged a meeting with a couple searching for a little bungalow in the trendiest part of town when her boss approached with a glint in his eyes.

That could either be an amazing thing... or a God-awful sign of things to come.

"Mendes!" He slapped one hand on her desk and cocked the other on his hip. While Mr. Filmore wasn't the portliest man in town, his gut lived over his belt and threatened to burst from his dress shirt every time he commanded this position around his employees. Which was often. "You got a minute? Because I have some great news for you."

She closed out of her email client and sat back from her monitor. "Yes?" Was this about the Johnson account? Raquel thought she had nailed it with the last house she showed the family of five, but what if they had gone straight to her boss to request another agent?

Wasn't her fault they were so picky that they found the tiniest faults in everything she showed them...

"It's about the conference in six weeks."

Raquel had to fight the grin trying to commandeer her demeanor. "Oh? The regional conference?" The one she had only ever attended as an assistant to her coworkers? That she didn't attend at all, because there was a younger woman to play assistant now? Didn't matter that the conference was the biggest of the year for their industry. Everyone hobnobbed and swapped trade secrets about how to sell better in areas around America. Of course, what worked in San Jose didn't always translate to Virginia Beach, but Raquel was damned good at taking tips that were useful to her and accommodating them to her career. That was how she had risen through the ranks so quickly. *That and my beautiful smile. Let's be real.* The fact she looked like everyone's fabulously cool aunt helped.

"Got some good news for you." Mr. Filmore was back on his feet, arms crossed on his chest as if he were the coolest clown at the circus. While Raquel didn't hold any derision for her boss, she had to admit that his mannerisms often left something to be desired. How did this guy have a former beauty queen for a wife, again? Oh, right. The money. "Turns out you're still the second highest seller on the team for the past year."

Raquel pretended this meant anything to her. "I'm very good at being #2, if you haven't noticed, sir."

"Ah, but there are times where it's not bad constantly coming in second place, Mendes. Did you know that Fred is going on paternity leave during the time of the conference? Hmm?"

"Is he?" Now *that* surprised Raquel. "Interesting. I knew his wife was having a kid, but not that he was taking paternity leave."

"Apparently, her work only gives her four weeks. Can you believe that? I'm giving Fred a full six, right after his wife goes back to work."

A whole six weeks. You're a saint, Mr. Filmore. One of many reasons Raquel had decided motherhood wasn't for her was the severe hit she'd take to her career if she wanted to have proper bonding time with her child. "You don't say."

"So, since Fred won't be able to come to the conference with me..." Mr. Filmore's grin continued to grow. "It's your chance to shine, kid! 'Course, Fred wasn't impressed when I told him that, but he should've thought of that before putting some infant before his career."

Raquel silently thanked her coworker for taking one for the team. *Her* team. Team Raquel, the only team qualified to dominate upper middle-class housing in their affluent city. *I'm gonna meet so many awesome people. Learn so many great tips. Holy hell, I might finally surpass Fred!* Was it true? Had the day finally arrived?

"Got some other news for ya, too."

Raquel settled farther into her chair. "Go on."

"Bet you are! You should be, because the conference chairs have asked me if you would be interested in being on a panel about women in the industry. Apparently, we're still quite female dominated. I never would've guessed, honestly."

Raquel once more kept her thoughts to herself. When she looked around the office, she saw two other women, and one of them was the office secretary. (And Mr. Filmore's mistress. She had to be, because she was so inept at making copies and creating letterheads that it was the only explanation as to how she was still employed.) While it was true that more women were found in the smaller agencies, they didn't make as much money as Raquel did this far up the food chain. Even then, her male coworkers tended to make more than her. They were given the best assignments. The bastards. "I would love to be on a panel like that, sir. Let them know, and forward me the information when you have a chance."

"I absolutely will! You know..." he said that the moment he turned around. "I always knew you were going to do great things. From the moment you walked into my office for an interview, I thought to myself, *I don't know her name, but I bet it starts with Money.*"

How was Raquel supposed to answer that? Seriously. "You're so kind and supportive of me, Mr.

Filmore. Working for your agency has been an absolute dream come true. I can only imagine what I'll continue to bring to it in the coming years."

"Play your cards right, and you might be running this place someday."

Dare she believe it? She might amass enough capital to buy the agency from Mr. Filmore when he retired in ten more years, but by then she would be in her fifties... what if she wanted to do something else with her life? Maybe open a bookstore. Move to Thailand and be a digital nomad. Become a professional lesbian dominatrix, because she would have to up her persona if she still wanted to land dates at that age.

Her phone buzzed at that moment. Raquel waited for her boss to go back to his office before checking.

"Hey, sexy. What do you think of this?" Raquel opened the text from Lisa to find a gratuitous cleavage shot inside a changing room somewhere. Forever 21? Old Navy? H&M? Raquel had been in quite a few of those changing rooms – including with her girlfriends – but this one was new to her. Besides, she had a feeling the focus of the photo was supposed to be the tits, not where Lisa was shopping with the money her girlfriend gave her two days before. *"Buy something nice for our dinner Saturday night. Because I said so, that's why."* Lisa said she wasn't interested in having an allowance or a "sugar mama," per se, but she had no problem taking a hundred-dollar bill to the mall.

"*I think I've figured it out. It's the left one, isn't it?*"

"*What are you talking about?*"

"*The bigger breast. It's the left one.*"

"*I can't believe you!!! <3 <3 <3*"

"*Or maybe that's forced perspective playing tricks on me. Can't tell from this angle.*"

"*I could show you later. If you think I should get this.*"

"*I think you should get whatever is comfortable, and sexy at the same time. Mostly sexy.*"

"*Aren't you going to tell me where we're going for our anniversary dinner? We didn't put it off because of my period for nothing.*"

"*Technically, we didn't put it off, because I still took you and your Aunt Flo out for dinner.*" These young women always acted like they were the only ones who menstruated, and like it was the most horrible, most disgusting thing a woman ever did. What, did they think Raquel could smell her monthly scent if she sat next to her?

"*Okay, but when is it happening?? You're always making me wait for your texts. Soooo mean.*"

"*I can feel you pouting from across town.*"

"*I'm actually at the mall three blocks from your office. Should we meet up for drinks or dinner after you get off work?*"

"*I'll get back to you about that. Not sure how late I'll be here.*" She would either be up the ass of paperwork or starting her world-changing speech for her panel at the upcoming conference. *Can't believe it's finally happening. Has my time finally come?*

Lisa continued to send messages every time she tried on a new and sexy outfit that threatened to change everyone's lives. Whether it was a halter top that boasted plunging cleavage, or a tube top that was about to let the girls loose from the bottom, Raquel was highly amused every time her phone buzzed with another message. Really, she wasn't supposed to be looking at her phone while working, but as long as the boss wasn't around, Raquel could get away with second degree murder and maybe a little arson. Of course, staring at her phone meant she didn't finish up her work before 5:30, but by then, Mr. Filmore had left the office, and Raquel decided to meet up with her girlfriend before finishing up her work at home.

She still couldn't believe that Lisa had been her girlfriend for the past several weeks. When they got back from Hawaii, convinced that they were addicted to one another, it was like Raquel had found the lover she had been waiting for. *You have to herd a lot of horses before you find the perfect mare, yes?* One of her old friends had put dating in such words. For every wild and free specimen that was otherwise perfect, there was that one frisky filly who wasn't wasted potential. Raquel preferred to *not* think of her dates as animals, but if she was called a cougar everywhere she went...

Halfway to the restaurant, Raquel realized that she was grinning like the goofiest girl to fall in love. Ms. Tithe had also commented that her client was in a chipper mood. When it was revealed that she had been seeing the same young woman for more than a few dates, the therapist had gleaned that Raquel was finally in a situation that suited her well. They forewent talking about the age difference, or the fact that Lisa still wasn't sure what she wanted to do with her life, and focused on how Raquel sent a bouquet to her girlfriend every week and looked forward to more dates. *Three weeks. That's how long it usually takes for a relationship to blow up in my face.* Either she grew weary of her girlfriend's personality (or lack thereof) or she was dumped, because the novelty of dating an older woman had faded.

Three weeks had come and passed with barely a blip of recognition. Raquel was still infatuated, and Lisa said she was game to keep the relationship going. Raquel had never been to her girlfriend's apartment aside from picking her up at the curb, but what was the point of going up to a cramped studio apartment when they could go to her sprawling home with views to die for? Lisa took to leaving some things behind in Raquel's bathroom and bedroom, and aside from organizing them, Raquel had no reason to acknowledge their presence other than as a natural progression of her current romantic relationship.

- 168 -

They were going steady and monogamous. They talked of taking trips as soon as work let up again for Raquel. She took a passing interest in Lisa's writing, going as far as to proofread some of her articles and check out the rest online, but most of their conversations revolved around their whims of the moment and swapping stories about their friends' love lives. Raquel had talked about Marian more than once – way more than she ever did with other girlfriends – but all she knew about Lisa's sexual past was the girl she first fooled around with and the woman she went out with when she first started dating older.

Why do I need to know more about that when she's with me now? For everything they did in the bedroom that appeared familiar to Lisa, there was something that made her sheepishly admit she had never done that before. Raquel lived to see that look of wonderment on her girlfriend's face, both in and out of the bedroom. *I've yet to replicate the face she made when I asked her to go to Hawaii with me, though.* Raquel was already plotting her next surprise destination. How did a cozy cottage in Alaska sound?

Raquel had no way of knowing where this relationship would go and how quickly or slowly they would progress to the next natural stage. It had been so long since she last had a *proper,* long-term relationship, and the first time she had one with such an age difference. Falling in love (if she dared to admit that

Hildred Billings

was what she felt) for the first time since Marian had reminded her that she cared about the emotions more than the sex. A feat, considering she had been nothing but an uncaring yet sexual being since the ripe old cynical age of twenty.

She had to often stop and deeply inhale before going on with her day. Thinking about so many possibilities with Lisa could be dangerous. Like Raquel couldn't risk getting ahead of herself with her career goals, she had to admit that anything could happen with Lisa.

They met outside the restaurant, Lisa carrying two shopping bags while dressed in a black and white striped tank top and denim shorts. The weather was enjoying a cool spell, but only cool enough to send her into socks and sneakers instead of the usual flip-flops she had been married to for most of the summer.

The thing that amazed Raquel the most, however, was how much her girlfriend lit up any room she entered. Raquel held open the door for the woman whose arms were laden with bags, and the moment Lisa bounded into the bright restaurant, everyone turned their heads and the sun shone a little brighter through the skylights. *She's only wearing regular clothes. Her hair is nothing special. We're going to spend most of tonight talking about trivial things.* Yet Lisa looked more excited than a Golden Retriever finally released from her leash. The hostess couldn't help but smile back at her as they approached the table by the wall.

This was one of Raquel's favorite restaurants, and she was pleased when she brought Lisa there the first time and heard a rave review. While it wasn't the fanciest restaurant in the neighborhood, it was cozy, fresh, and far from crowded even on busy nights. They were early enough to beat the rush that came in later. Good, because Raquel wanted to hog her girlfriend's attentions.

"Are you going to show me what you got?" Raquel removed her sunglasses when she sat down in the booth. "Or do I have to wait for it to be a surprise?"

Lisa rolled the tops of the bags down and stuffed them into the far corner of the booth. "No peeking. You'll have to wait for our anniversary dinner."

The waitress brought them water and clean silverware. "What can I get you ladies today?" she asked with a friendly demeanor. "Start you off with something to drink?"

"I'll take a peach cider, please." Raquel had barely begun to peruse the food menu. "How about you?"

Lisa pointed to one of the cocktails on the seasonal menu. "Ooh, I want this."

"Gonna need to see some ID, please."

Nothing was thought of that request as both Lisa and Raquel fished through their wallets for their IDs. The waitress took Lisa's first and stared at it, mentally doing the math while comparing the picture to the in-real-life Lisa.

She left Raquel hanging.

"Well..." Raquel lowered her hand before realizing the waitress did not give two-shits about a forty-year-old's driver's license. "Why did I bother, huh?"

"That's weird." Lisa already had hers put away again. "Thanks for dinner, by the way. And the drink! I walked around so much today that I need to relaaax." She picked up the food menu and *ooh'd* at the appetizers listed on the left-hand side. "You're not gonna get mad if I load up on truffle fries, right?"

"Why would I be mad?" They were hardly expensive. Hell, Raquel was thinking about pairing her cider with some salt as well.

"I'm gonna bloat like I'm PMSing if I eat a plate of those *and* a sandwich for dinner." Lisa shrugged. "I'm guessing we're going back to your place later. Figured you'd want me at my belly-best." Her expression remained unchanged as she perused the menu and sang along to the One Direction song playing over the speakers.

Her belly-best? Bloating? Raquel must have taken crazy pills before she left the office. "What in the world are you talking about? You're cute no matter what you eat."

"Really?"

Sheesh! Was she really so surprised? Hadn't Raquel been adoring and pleasuring that body for the past several weeks, no matter *what* it looked like? *Like she could possibly be too big... ever...* Like Raquel had such lofty ambitions in a girlfriend that she would turn her back the moment a girl hit twenty-five or thirty and discovered youthful metabolism faded away.

"You're gorgeous," was all Raquel said. Until, "I didn't realize you were watching your weight."

Lisa did not respond. She kept her eyes on her menu, fingers tapping against her cheek as the song traveled through its final chorus. Raquel knew nothing about the boys in this group, but she was inclined to think Lisa the better singer. *I'm biased toward female singers.* One of her first lesbian crushes was *Tiffany,* for fuck's sake. *God. The late '80s.* She wondered if Lisa even knew who Tiffany was. Hell, she wondered what Tiffany was doing those days!

The waitress returned after a few more minutes, carrying their drinks. "Ready to order?" That was directed at Lisa.

"Ooh, I'm gonna get the roasted turkey sandwich, no mayo, and a side of truffle fries."

That was jotted down before the waitress turned to Raquel. "And you, Mom?"

"I..."

Silence befell the table.

She didn't. Raquel stared at Lisa, who stifled a laugh behind the back of her hand. *She fucking didn't!*

Raquel had two choices. She could correct the waitress and embarrass everyone, or she could suck in her pride and politely say, "Sorry. I'm gonna get the garlic chicken and substitute the mashed potatoes for a caesar salad with no dressing. Thank you."

The waitress repeated their orders before taking the menus away. Lisa was still nothing but a fit of giggles while Raquel took a generous swig of her drink. The peach cider wasn't tarty enough to bash away the disgust welling up in the back of her throat.

"Wow," Lisa finally said. "You know, for a moment there, I thought she was trying to be hip with the whole internet-mom thing."

Raquel's palm sweated around the bottle in her hand. "The what?"

"You know... kids calling people older than them *Mom* or *Dad* as some respect thing. With a heaping dose of sexual overtones on top of it, because it's the internet and it ruins everything..."

"Can't say I've heard of this phenomenon." Thank God, too. Raquel would punch anyone who tried that shit on her. "Besides, that woman looked to be my age."

Lisa leaned forward, her hands fishing to catch Raquel's. "It's okay, babe. She doesn't know any better, right?"

It's not the first time it's happened to me. If Raquel was on a simple date with a girlfriend, which didn't always include hand holding and canoodling, then the occasional person had to comment on if they were possibly related to one another. "*Your daughter looks like you!" "Are you gonna let your teenaged daughter drink your beer like that?" "You know, I've always had a fantasy about a mom and daughter..."*

People were rude. That was a given. Yet as Raquel grew older, it became more difficult to bear the comments about the apparent age difference between her and her girlfriends.

She had hoped to spend the date flirting with her girlfriend and promising her the moon and stars. *Maybe only the moon. I haven't started making enough money yet to give her the cosmos.* With the unfortunate words of the waitress hanging above them, Raquel dissociated from the first five minutes they had alone and merely stared at her leather phone case.

"You don't look like my mom," Lisa eventually said. "Don't even look old enough to be my mom."

"But I am old enough to be your mother," Raquel shot back. "That's a fact."

"Yeah..." Lisa looked off to the side. "My mom was barely twenty when she had me. I get it."

Raquel didn't comment on that.

"This is gonna sound morbid as fuck..." Great. There went the hopeful, whimsical atmosphere Raquel had been shooting for when she first met up with her girlfriend. "But the only thing that keeps me awake at night about the kind of age-differences I'm attracted to is... geez, you know what? My wife or whatever is probably gonna die long before I do."

Raquel lowered her hands from her head with a scoff. "Jesus, Lisa."

"Well, don't you think about that, too? It's not a pleasant thought, no, but it's a fact. The probability of you outliving me is slim to none. I try not to think about it when I date older women. Even the ones I don't think I'm gonna be with for long. It's too sad to think about. People dating other people their age don't obsess over it. Why should I?"

Raquel remained silent while drinking her cider.

"Then I tell myself that I survived my mom dying when I was still a teenager. So, I can survive losing my partner. Maybe it's for the best if things work out that way. I know how to handle it. I see it coming." Lisa cocked her head at her girlfriend. "Sorry. This is a pretty heavy conversation to have when we're barely going steady."

"It's all right," Raquel muttered. "I think about it, too."

"You do?"

"Yeah. I think about my health and how I'll have to be extra vigilant, not only for myself, but for the woman I'm with. I think about how I'm going to get 'old' long before she does."

"Come on, now..."

"It's true. Not only will I probably die first, but I'll become an old crone while my partner is still looking thirty. That will *really* turn heads. Might also mean the

Forbidden Fruit

end of my relationship. Why would someone enjoying their youth want to be with someone who might hold them back?"

"I can't believe it will be like that for a second!"

Will. She said *will?*

"Come on, babe." Lisa forced a laugh. "Let's talk about anything else. It's supposed to be a nice dinner, right?"

First she made an off-handed comment about trying to stay hot for her sugar mama, and now Raquel was obsessing over staying hot for *her* girlfriend. *Is this it? Is this the fate of our relationship? Always trying to stay hot for the other one?* It was like they admitted that beneath the surface of what they had, everything was about status and sex. Raquel wanted a hot girlfriend to strut around with. Lisa wanted someone to take care of her and make her financial insecurities go away for a little while. That was how Raquel always approached these relationships, although deep down she wished things could be different for *once*. Just once!

"Babe?"

Raquel snapped out of her daze with an apology. "I don't mean to be like this. Guess that lady triggered some shitty thoughts."

Lisa gazed at her for a moment before saying, "For what it's worth, I think our relationship is more than skin deep. That is, if you do."

"What do you mean?"

The way Lisa shrugged made her shoulders pop up against her ears. Her chest bounced within her striped shirt, because what Raquel really needed right now was to have her attention brought to some twenty-something's mammaries. At least it distracted her for a moment.

"I know what our relationship looks like to other people. I'm using you for money, you're using me for sex... that's assuming they don't think you're my mom or cool aunt."

"Thanks for the reminder."

"I don't think of you that way. I like hanging out with you. I love spending the night with you. Sure, it's fun to spend your money and get spoiled like it's my middle name, but... at the end of the day, if you ended up in the hospital, I'd be the first one knocking down the door to make sure you're okay!"

Raquel sat back in her seat. "That's quite the admission."

"Sorry. I don't know why I thought of hosp..." She stopped. "Right. My mom."

Raquel let out the biggest breath she had been holding. "That's a really sweet thing to say." She placed her hand on the table. "I care about you, too."

The grin spreading across Lisa's face seemed genuine as she reached for Raquel's hand. "I'm so relieved. You never really know where you stand with somebody in these kinds of relationships."

"I guess we're both used to being used. That's the name of the game, huh?"

"Yeah..." Lisa squeezed her girlfriend's hand. "I feel like I have my whole life ahead of me, but I don't know what to do with it. Sometimes I feel like I must look so immature and like such a fool to you."

"Hardly. While it's a different world from when I was your age, not much has changed." *Like we knew what we wanted from our lives back then.* Raquel was young enough to remember her peers freaking out in their college classes. Was this really what they wanted to study? What if they couldn't get a job? What if they hated their careers? What if they had made the wrong decision and accumulated all this debt for no reason? *Debts are even higher now...* She didn't envy the Millennials and Gen Z'ers. "Here I was worried I looked like a cynical old haggard bitch to you or something."

"Hardly! I love your devil-may-care attitude! I find it inspiring." Lisa continued to grin. "See? We're okay."

"I guess so."

Lisa backed up against the booth, but kept her hands firmly clasped around Raquel's. "Do you think we'll be more than girlfriends one day?"

"Well, I don't..."

"You think we'll still be together a year from now?"

Raquel chuckled. Young people were so impatient. "Let's take it one week at a time."

"All right."

The waitress soon came with their food. Raquel and Lisa didn't bother to unhook their hands while their dinners were placed before them. The nervous waitress tittered while asking them to tell her if they needed anything. The way Raquel rubbed her girlfriend's finger was unmistakable to the waitress.

Her apparent nervousness was enough for Raquel to forgive her. The extra tip she left may have been a bit much, but she felt better as she wrapped her arm around her girlfriend's waist and led her out of the restaurant after they finished their dinners. They may have turned more than a few heads.

And they may have made short work of their energy reserves when they made it back to Raquel's place. She didn't even need to go to bed early, but thought nothing of it when she came out of the shower and saw Lisa sleeping soundly in bed. All Raquel could think about was curling up next to her and imagining a day when this no longer felt strange and new.

It couldn't come soon enough.

Chapter 13

For their three-month anniversary, they both had a few surprises up their sleeves.

Lisa hopped out of her Uber wearing one of the most modestly scandalous outfits Raquel had ever beheld. The woman was clad in a sheer wrap-dress (not quite as sheer as the maxi dress she wore around Raquel's apartment, but damn close) speckled in black roses with red outlines around the petals. Beneath the barely-there exterior was a black tube top and matching shorts that left absolutely nothing to the imagination about what she had tucked away beneath her underwear. *I knew she had been using my building's gym this summer, but holy shit.* Someone had studied all the best ways to get a firm booty. Raquel cursed her own body for not getting with the program as it aged.

Black hoop earrings and rhinestone-studded sandals rounded out the ensemble. The earrings had been a gift from Raquel one month into their relationship. The sandals looked brand-new, although Lisa later admonished her girlfriend for never noticing the bling on her feet before. Honestly, Raquel felt so frumpy in her little black dress that she had half a mind to tell her girlfriend to take off the wrap-dress and share it for a while. *She always calls me so fashionable, yet look at her! So little effort, and she's ready to walk into a catalog.* Lord, did they still make catalogs?

Lisa confessed that she didn't know what to dress for, since Raquel had been so hush-hush about their plans for the day. Raquel had vied for a few new things to her own dating life, since making it three months with one of her younger girlfriends was something to celebrate. Yet Lisa had no way to anticipate a trip to the planetarium, complete with hands-on cosmic models and a blackhole VR simulator. The highlight was, of course, the light show at the end of the tour. The soundtrack was a popular electronic pop album from the '80s, which was nostalgic to Raquel and trendy to Lisa. The show was sold out, and Raquel thanked her lucky stars (including all the ones she saw during the show) that she bought the tickets a month ago.

"I feel like a kid again!" Lisa said upon exiting the planetarium. She offered her girlfriend a kiss on the cheek and a skip in her step. "We doing anything next?"

Anything next? What, did she think Raquel burnt out all of her ideas in one go?

They had dinner on the river. *Seriously. We're on the river.* A floating dock provided a seasonal dining experience that was more exclusive than the river cruises and required a two-month advanced reservation. Raquel had been that positive about her blossoming relationship with Lisa back when she made the reservations.

It was close enough to the start of autumn that twilight descended at the beginning of their dinner. The purple and oranges in the sky went beautifully with the candlelit meals. The server didn't once call Raquel Lisa's mother. Nor did he let his gaze linger on Lisa's cleavage or Raquel's exposed shoulders. They were left to their own world, where they only had eyes for one another and the bouquet of flowers on every table. They were informed at the end of their meal that they were welcomed to take the flowers with them. Lisa made sure to grab them on their way out.

"I've got a surprise for you," she announced on the sidewalk.

"Oh?" Raquel has been halfway to ordering them a ride back to her place. *I've got more surprises for you at home.* God willing, they would get there sooner rather than later. Raquel was loaded with red wine and needed Lisa naked *now*.

"Yup! It's actually a couple of blocks away from here! Think you can get there without falling in your heels?"

"I'm not that drunk, really."

Lisa took her girlfriend's hand and hauled her toward the nearest intersection. Who needed to walk in her own shoes when she had a girlfriend to lead the way for her?

Raquel was not expecting a gelato shop that was open for only another hour. Lisa stared at the menu hanging up in one of the windows, her hand still firmly entwined with Raquel's. "Yup. This is the place." She opened the door with one hand, two bells jingling as the teenager on duty looked up from his phone and nodded to them in greeting. He also did a double-take at the pair of hotties coming his way.

"Gelato?" Raquel asked.

"Dessert, yes?" Lisa pointed to the flavors on display that month. "I think I'll get one scoop of the merry mint. Do you guys still do sprinkles and Oreo crumble for free?"

"Costs twenty cents a shot now."

"Oh. Okay." Lisa pulled her wallet out of her purse. The only times she did that on her dates was when she needed her ID. "I've got this, babe," she said to Raquel.

"You do?"

"Yup! Go ahead and order whatever you want!"

Raquel was convinced that this was the first time in three months Lisa paid for something. She felt slightly silly ordering one scoop of the strawberry chiffon pie and another scoop of the blueberry fantasy. *Not sure what kind of fantasy blueberries provide, but I know I'm into some fantasies right now.*

They received their desserts and hustled toward the front window, where Lisa hopped up at the counter and grabbed a few napkins from the dispenser. She had the biggest smile on her face as she spun around and leaned her elbows against the table. Both hands were preoccupied holding her sugar cone, whereas Raquel had opted for a dish and spoon.

"I admit, this is a surprise," Raquel said. "I haven't had gelato in a million years."

Lisa closed her eyes in apparent bliss as she took a bite of the minty scoop of gelato in her cone. "This is my favorite place to get ice cream type stuff. My mom and I used to come here whenever we were in the city."

"Is that so?" Raquel kept her gaze on her girlfriend. *Sometimes, you're nothing but a basket full of surprises.* She liked that about Lisa.

"Yeah. My mom and I didn't come to this city often, but when we did, we always came here before driving all the way home. It was always one of my happiest memories. Thought I might like to share some of them with you."

Raquel had half a bite of blueberry gelato in her spoon when she heard that. The ultraviolet lights above her were on a mission to melt the stuff in her spoon, but she hardly noticed. "You were really close to your mom, weren't you?"

Lisa hesitated before answering. She rarely allowed her countenance to reflect any dark thoughts, yet that was what Raquel caught a glimpse of while her young girlfriend stared out the window and beheld a city street getting ready to sleep.

"She was my favorite person in the world. We were all each other really had while I was growing up. My dad is pretty useless. Didn't have any siblings. My mom had cut all ties from her former life, and I honestly don't know much about it. Guess she was mixed up in some stuff she didn't want to tell me about."

That could've meant a number of things, from crime to embarrassing high school bands. Raquel quickly ate her bite of gelato before it disappeared back into her cup. "I'm sorry for your loss." That wasn't the first time Raquel had said that to her girlfriend.

Minty green gelato slowly melted down the side of Lisa's untouched cone. She completely ignored it, favoring her faraway memories as they appeared in the glass before them. The more the gelato covered her sticky thumb, the more Raquel wanted to lick it away for her girlfriend. Yet, somehow, she refrained.

"This week is the anniversary of my mom's death," Lisa said, when she finally came back to her senses. "Sorry. I know you don't wanna hear a bummer like that when we're supposed to be celebrating."

"It's all right." Raquel meant that, too. "I had no idea."

Forbidden Fruit

"Not like I talk about the details much."

"Cancer, right?"

"Uh huh." Lisa swallowed, but it wasn't gelato disappearing down her throat. *How can one woman look so tragically beautiful?* The pain on Lisa's face was at complete odds with the vibrantly flirtatious outfit she wore. Raquel couldn't decide if she wanted to undress Lisa more than she wanted to kiss her oncoming tears away. "One day my mom was fine, and the next, she was making her final arrangements. I was still in high school." Lisa pulled another napkin out of the dispenser and absentmindedly rubbed away a sticky spot on the counter. "I had to go live with my dad and finish my high school diploma in a different city. Part of the reason I came here for school was because of all the happy memories it gave me. I've always tried to return to places that remind me of my mom."

"I can't imagine." Raquel's strained relationship with her family meant they didn't speak often. It didn't help that she never gave up the lesbian life, and even in 2018, her family was adamantly against it. *Whatever. I'll go to their funerals. Guess I'll feel bad when they die...* Maybe. It would be complicated. "Do you think she would be happy with where you are today?"

"You mean right here, with you?"

Raquel couldn't meet her girlfriend's eyes. Turned out that Lisa couldn't either. "Sure. With me. Your older, gay girlfriend."

Lisa acquired a pallor that Raquel occasionally saw on her cheeks. Usually when they discussed something about her mother, or her history with other women. *There's something beneath the surface of this girl. I can't quite place it.*

"Right." Raquel laughed the atmosphere off. "You said she was a bit of a homophobe, so maybe not."

"Yeah. Maybe not."

Raquel hadn't meant to ruin the mood of their dessert. While they ate the last of their gelato and continued to stare out into the night, Raquel thought of her aunt and the way she reacted when she discovered her niece had shacked up with another girl – let alone was sharing a *bed* with her. *It did not end well. I've barely talked to her since.* Other girls got to run to their families when heartbreak was on the horizon. Not Raquel. When Marian left her, she only had herself for consolation. She went home for a while, but it was under the pretense that she left the lesbo life behind her, and never, ever once talked about Marian. It suited Raquel fine. Every time that name left her lips, she was crying about an unfair world once more.

She had left all that behind her when she moved back to the city and started her new life as a womanizing real-estate upstart. *Fifteen years later, and I'm still here, doing the same thing.* Did having the same girlfriend for three months still make her a womanizer, though?

"Moms are complicated, huh?" Lisa said.

"They sure are."

"It's like they love us so much and want us to have the whole world at our disposal, but the things that make us happiest might be the things that make us never talk to our moms again."

"You said it first."

Lisa turned to her girlfriend. "I wish my mom were still alive for many reasons. Most of all, though..." She sheepishly turned away again. The light blush to her cheeks was far more welcomed than that dreadful pallor from a moment ago. "I wish I could tell her that I'm really in love for the first time in my life."

Raquel almost missed that. "Huh?"

A renewed giggle came to Lisa's throat. "Didn't you hear me? I said that I'm in love with somebody."

"Who?"

"You're kidding, right?"

It was Raquel's turn to swallow. "Do you mean with me?"

"Do you see any other hot lesbians in this room?"

Even though that was a rhetorical question, Raquel still looked around the room as if she were going to spot some other hot lady in the vicinity. Only the teenaged boy remained in the small gelato shop, however. A guy with unkempt curly hair and enough pimples to scare away every girl at school.

"Maybe there's one hiding in the back," Raquel said.

Lisa snorted. "You're funny. Hey, if you don't feel the same way about me yet, it's okay. Thought I'd let slip where I stand with you. In case you're worried that I only want you for your hot bod and bank account."

"I don't think that," Raquel whispered.

"Good!"

"I think..." Raquel poked her melting gelato. *I've never had one of my younger dates buy me anything before.* She had received homemade presents, but a date buying her dessert? It was almost unheard of. Not since... well, not since Marian, who always believed in splitting everything down the middle. That included paying for each other's meals, but always making sure they were even. "I think I might be feeling the same way as you."

"Self-love is important," Lisa said with a sigh.

"You know what I mean!" Why was Raquel so flustered? Hadn't she been thinking about how much emotion she was tying into her relationship with this girl? *I barely think of her as a girl. We make a great balancing act, don't we?* Whenever Raquel was feeling a little cynical, Lisa brought the sunshine and wasn't afraid to share it. Whenever Lisa was the one down in the dumps, Raquel took her out for dinner or spoiled her silly. They had different ways to express their support for one another, but the end results were the same. The thought that they could keep this going for years, however, hadn't been a realistic fantasy until that very moment. "Falling in love is a good way to put it. Doesn't have to be absolute right now."

Lisa tilted her head, the rhinestone-studded bun on her scalp threatening to touch her minty gelato. "Think an Uber driver would be mad if we took this into his car? Because I'm thinking we should hurry up and go back to your place. Didn't you say you had some surprises for me there?"

Raquel had almost completely forgotten. She was so caught up in thinking with her heart, that she failed to recall what her loins had been preoccupied with for half the day.

Chapter 14

Lisa wrestled with the depths of her fears. The ones struggling to be heard while she dutifully ignored them, whether she was alone in her bed late at night, or slammed against Raquel's a little before nine.

You're gonna get caught. She thought that every time they came back to Raquel's place, kisses on their lips and frisky fingers on the hunt for a good time. It didn't matter how tipsy they were on wine or how into the moment Lisa became once she realized her fantasies were coming true. *You're gonna get caught* was all she could think, and she wasn't worried about some perv outside the window stealing a peek at them.

She was terrified that Raquel would learn the truth.

Lisa had been waiting. For the perfect moment. For Raquel to thoroughly look her up. For some other force in the universe to dictate when to tell the truth or expose her for the deceptive bitch she was. *If she finds out the truth, I might lose everything.* She might break Raquel's heart. They might sink deep into despair and never recover. While Lisa had never intended for this relationship to last so long, she also never intended to lead Raquel astray and break her heart.

The last thing she wanted to do was break her girlfriend's heart. Hell, Lisa would sacrifice her own heart if it meant protecting a woman old enough to be her mother.

"You're the most tantalizing thing I've ever seen." That soft purr was uttered in Raquel's front hallway, where she had Lisa cornered against an antique end table. While Lisa's knuckles whitened on the edges of the table and her fingers entwined with the metal handle, her girlfriend celebrated their three-month anniversary by drawing a mesmerizing line up Lisa's bare leg.

"Thing?" Lisa squeaked. Three months in, and Raquel still had the power to make her heart flutter and her breath catch beneath her ribs. Her chest rose and fell with those heavy breaths, and the visual was not lost to Raquel, a woman whose lips were a mere three inches away from Lisa's cleavage. "You think I'm a doll or something?"

Her thoughts were so faraway from her that the words came out like an accusation. Raquel's head snapped up, her eyes wide in the dark hallway. "No? Sorry. Think I botched this one up."

"No, no, it's my fault." Lisa laughed the discomfort off. "I don't know why I'm so nervous tonight." She knew why. The longer this relationship went on, the harder it became to tell Raquel the truth. Yet if she did, she risked losing *everything*. She risked breaking hearts. She risked losing out on the biggest dreams she ever had, short of resurrecting her mother.

The smile was back on Raquel's face. "I've got some ideas to help you relax." She came closer again, hands against the wall while the rest of her pressed Lisa against the furniture – and the wall. "Let's start with getting you out of some of these clothes. You can lose the dress or the underclothes. Your choice, darling."

Between the anxiety haunting Lisa's brain and the sexual attraction continuing to explode in the rest of her, she didn't know whether to throw herself into Raquel's arms or die in the puddle she was sure to become. "Which would *you* like?" she asked her girlfriend.

"Well, you know how I am." Raquel untied the sheer dress and parted both sides. If the lights were on, she would have had a grand view of the sweat beading on Lisa's chest. "You know how I get whenever you wear that other dress I got you in Hawaii."

Ravenous? Voracious? Insistent that I not leave your bed until I've come at least five times? That was only one of a million reasons Lisa couldn't bear the thought of coming out with her terrible truth. The thought of losing what would probably be the most passionate relationship of her life was unbearable.

Yet she couldn't help herself. As soon as Raquel kissed her and grabbed the flesh she kept beneath her clothes, Lisa was a goner – ready to give up whatever her girlfriend wanted, and ready to say a giant fuck you to the universe that would keep her away from these sweet and sultry moments.

While Lisa was usually content to play the submissive role in the bedroom, it didn't always work out that way. Sometimes she got on top of her girlfriend and directed who came first before the end of the hour. Sometimes the sex toys went in the other direction – all right, most of the time they ended up there *somehow*. And, sometimes, Lisa took one look at Raquel in one of her tight one-pieces and whispered in her ear that she was about to be crowned the Pillow Princess of the night. Lisa enjoyed having her fingers in her lover as much as she enjoyed being touched. It was all a part of the grand scheme of lovemaking, even if they had become comfortably one-sided through their honeymoon phase and beyond.

That night, however, Lisa completely froze up when she imagined taking any initiative. It was like their first hookup all over again, with the handcuffs she had packed in her bag and the dirty talk that was meant to last her the rest of her life. Raquel still had a filthy mouth in the heat of the moment, but the tone had changed over the course of their relationship. Not that Lisa wanted the (hot) uncertainty of their first night together again. If anything, she had come to cherish the lovingly dirty way Raquel talked to her in bed.

Those kinds of words followed her into the bedroom. Raquel lit a few candles while Lisa pulled off her shorts and removed her tube top before her girlfriend turned around. She wanted her naked beneath her dress? Fine. After that, however, she wasn't taking any more orders. Lisa's objective was to completely surrender herself to whatever Raquel wanted, and that included being called a *tantalizing thing.*

Maybe if I'm a thing, an object, I won't feel how much it hurts. Her heart. She could withstand anything Raquel threw at her, physically, but her heart was a fragile glass figurine, always teetering at the edge of the shelf. One hearty knock and she'd be shattered fragments on the floor.

Raquel rarely wasted time, even if they had all the time in the world to spare. She liked getting down to business. Lisa liked getting to the main event. Together, they would soon be nothing but a grinding lump of limbs and kisses on Raquel's bed. The faster they got to it? The faster Lisa could forget everything eating away at her heart.

One orgasm. *It's slipping away. I don't remember what I wanted to tell her.* Another climax. *Fuck me, what was killing me earlier?* The worst of it had been banished from her body. Lisa lay with her sheer wrap-dress halfway off her body and her hair tangled. Perfect for grabbing, which Raquel intended to do as soon as their thighs entwined together.

Heat. Pressure. They both dominated the mood, but it was the heat that got to Lisa first. Everything, from her scalp to her toes, was on fire with the desire to come again. *I don't know if she has yet. I don't care.* The farther Lisa slipped away and became a *thing* meant for sexual consumption, the less trifling matters such as her girlfriend's satisfaction bothered her. Why would they? If she were an object for Raquel to enjoy, then she was destined to bring her girlfriend pleasure.

So why did how much she loved this woman consume her?

Was it the way she tenderly shared her naughty visions for their night together? How much she spoiled Lisa, both when they were together and when they were anxiously apart? How good it felt to hold her hand when they were in public, and to hold her heart when they were alone? What swindled its way into Lisa's body first? Was she ever prepared to love Raquel as much as she had dreamed?

I'm not good enough for you. She reiterated that thought with her tongue so far down Raquel's throat that they had to come up for air sooner than usual. *I will bring nothing but pain to your life.* How could she be so hard on herself when so much love and pleasure was offered? Was she a different kind of masochist than Raquel liked to joke about? *Why do I have to make everyone's lives harder?*

She was a role model to her online friends, who applauded her scoring the older hottie that they all wished they could attract. Lisa had been sparse on details, beyond talking about how much she had crushed on Raquel until finally hitting on her at a bar – and getting lucky with it. She had also provided a link to her Instagram as proof that she and Raquel were still together three months later, since they had a few couple's photos, including one she had uploaded that night at the gelato shop. *#threemonths* would send her single cougar-chasers into an absolute tizzy. For every girl on there who simply had a sexual fetish and didn't actually want to marry an older woman, there were two more dreaming about having the babies their older girlfriends could now afford but never had the time to have. A few lucky ones actually got married – and only one had divorced so far. What if Lisa became the next fairy-tale story?

What if her friends knew the truth?

"You up for doing something new?" Raquel left a large kiss on Lisa's collar bone after she said that. "Because I've got those goodies I was talking about."

Wasn't Lisa up for anything, especially if it helped her forget what she had to go home and think about?

Goodies meant a number of things. There was the flavored and edible body lotion that was now too late to use. A "personal massager" that was suspiciously shaped like something a woman could comfortably fit inside of her body. And a strangely contoured glass toy that advertised it was meant to go in other places besides the traditional one.

"You wanna do that with me?" Lisa asked, as if she really were so innocent.

Raquel tossed her girlfriend's tangled hair behind her sweat-soaked shoulders. That hand remained locked behind Lisa's neck, bringing her head forward for the kind of kiss that answered questions when words were not necessary. Even so, Raquel said, "Hell, yes. Get on your knees while I grab the lube."

Lisa was too embarrassed – and too stoned on sex, anyway – to confess she had never done it before. She wasn't opposed to doing it, though. When it came to Raquel and the explicit fantasies that cropped up between them, almost *nothing* was sacred. If Raquel wanted Lisa on her knees and begging for a toy up her ass, then she was inclined to obey. The more orgasms she already had in her that night, the easier it was.

And the hotter.

Someone in the cosmos had listened to Lisa's prayers. She could safely say that she forgot everything she had worried about only a few moments before. All it took was one imaginative girlfriend of her dreams, a little liquid courage, and a bed that made the best sounds when it hit the wall every time Raquel thrust.

Lisa made sounds she had never conceptualized before. She even begged for more, because she adored the vacancy in her mind and the weight lifted from her subconsciousness. Her heart continued to scream from the depths of her chest, but it was easy to ignore with everything else echoing in Raquel's bedroom. Like more of that dirty talk that always did Lisa in. And more of that headboard hitting the wall while Lisa's whole body completely gave in to temptation.

"The best part about fucking you..." Raquel's lips trembled against Lisa's ear. So much hair fell around them that even Lisa didn't know whose was whose. Her hands clutched the pillow beneath her while her nipples met the top of the bedspread and hardened for the hundredth time that night. The dress had finally disappeared over the side of the bed. It was only them, their naked flesh, the cascades of long hair, the fluttering of delicate eyelashes against their cheeks, and one glass dildo up Lisa's ass. Practically magic. "Is that you're up for everything I throw at you. You're gonna keep my imagination going for years."

Years! She said years!

Only Lisa would find this moment romantic. That's how sad and depraved she was.

"Guess I must inspire you." That was the first coherent sentence Lisa had uttered in the past hour.

Nothing else beyond *Yes!* and *Right there!* had fallen from her lips, and it was a miracle she still knew how to speak – even with the rambling thoughts flowing through her head. "I better keep inspiring you." Like Raquel inspired Lisa to orgasm yet again. Funny how that happened with a different part of her body stimulated.

"Keep looking at me with those heavy eyelids and I'll be inspired for quite a while yet." Raquel caressed the dip in her girlfriend's back. Perhaps she meant to urge Lisa onto her chest. Maybe she didn't. It didn't matter, when the moment Raquel touched her girlfriend's skin, Lisa went down, face consuming the pillow.

Raquel was always prepared. Oh, not to salvage Lisa's breaths should she asphyxiate herself in the pillow, but to ensure she was properly pleasured in that bedroom. Fucking her in the ass wasn't enough. Clearly, Lisa needed an old-fashioned vibrator on her slit. Probably the same one Raquel had been using for years to pleasure herself to thoughts of women like Lisa. *I'm gonna explode...* Lisa didn't even have to move. Between the vibrations and her girlfriend fucking her with the strength of five people, Lisa was so far gone that she might as well be reborn with a new identity and set of memories.

The physical sensations were so overwhelming that she didn't even realize when it was over, or when she was a single person again, let alone when Raquel keeled over with a sigh that announced she had spent herself on one woman. Neither of them were smokers, but Raquel often indulged in a piece of fruity candy to curb the aftereffects of sex. Lisa had a million questions about that. *Did you used to smoke? What flavor do you like best after sex, and does it depend on how hard you come?* Looked like she was sucking on cherry-flavored candy. An homage to popping Lisa's black cherry.

"FYI," Raquel said after dumping the plastic wrapper in the garbage by her bed. "Your butt is cute."

Lisa pulled the pillow down her body and snorted into the sheets.

"What are you laughing about? It is. You've got the cutest butt I've ever seen. Been daydreaming about fucking your adorable ass since you first bent over in front of me."

"Every time since?" Lisa asked.

"It bounces between your pussy and your ass. I'll figure out a way to get both at once eventually. I'm too tired now."

"Me too."

They lay in silence for a few seconds. Raquel caught her breath while Lisa stared at the headboard, the good feelings of their lovemaking settling into her core and the dopamine releasing from her brain. The same dopamine that married her to the woman beside her.

"Hey..." Lisa finally said, when the pleasure was replaced with an ache that was neither physical nor emotional. "Sometime soon... not tonight, though... I have something I really need to tell you."

Raquel remained quiet while that sank into them both. "Is that so? Should I be scared?"

"I hope not," Lisa said.

"Hmm." Raquel rolled onto her side, hand once more caressing the small of her girlfriend's back. After a shudder rippled through the length of Lisa's body, she closed her eyes and accepted the tenderness only one woman knew how to offer. "Well, whatever it is, I'm sure everything will be fine. Even if it's you telling me you can't afford your apartment anymore and need to move in with me."

Lisa lifted her head. "What?"

"Well... let's not get ahead of ourselves. But if you have something you need to tell me, don't hesitate. I'd rather know upfront so we can plan around something, if necessary."

Does she know? Lisa didn't want to believe it. The thought of Raquel knowing her deepest, darkest secret... she would have brought it up. Surely, she would have. It was so damning, that there was *no way* Raquel could keep the knowledge of it to herself.

Unless... she had known from the very beginning who Lisa was.

"Hey, hon." Raquel's voice went from silly to concerned in fewer than five seconds. "You okay? Didn't hurt you, did I?"

"I'm fine." Lisa folded her hands on the pillow and perched her chin atop her fingers. "Just thinking."

Raquel hesitated for a few moments before getting up. On her way to the bathroom, she said, "For what it's worth, your butt really is cute!"

Lisa couldn't help but laugh into her pillow.

Chapter 15

"What is it that you really want to say to her?" Sally remained sitting in her usual chair while Lisa got up and walked around the office. When she wasn't distracted by the view of the city, she was sniffing through the few personal items the therapist stocked for her clients' amusement. Who knew Sally, who was closer to Raquel's age than Lisa's, was such a big Pokémon fan? *This thing is a Pokémon, right?* Lisa had enough manners to not pick up the cute creature posing on the shelf by the couch. Instead, she wracked her brain trying to remember its name. She used to watch the cartoon when she was a kid. Her mother thought Team Rocket was hilarious. "If your mother were sitting here instead of me, what would you say?"

Lisa turned back to her therapist with renewed thoughts. "I dunno..." She slowly approached the couch and sat down again. Her legs immediately became restless, begging her to get the hell up and burn off the energy. "Every time I try to think about it, my thoughts get all jumbled together."

"Would you like me to pretend to be your mother?"

"Maybe..." Yeah, right. Like Sally could ever hold a candle to Lisa's mother, whether in looks or attitude. *You're too nice to people, for one.* Lisa's mother spent most of her time with her guard up and ready to fling a feisty piece of pie into someone's voice, whether they were a salesman at a department store or her own best friend from work. *I don't know what she went through to make her that way, but she was also sweet to me.* "All right. Maybe it will help."

Sally set aside her devices and sat up tall in her chair. "I'm all ears, Lisa. Tell me what's on your mind."

Although the therapist didn't change her tone or demeanor, Lisa still easily pretended that it was her mother sitting in the chair instead. *She would be heavier. Darker skin. Brown hair like mine. A mole on her upper lip, which she called her supermodel's kiss.* "Mom... I've got something I really wanna tell you. Something good. I really hope you'll be happy for me."

"What is it?"

Lisa inhaled a deep breath and braced her hands against her knees. The knee-high boots Raquel bought her on their last shopping trip provided the perfect texture for Lisa to drum her knuckles upon a moment later. "I'm in love. With someone really wonderful."

Sally waited a beat. "That's great! Tell me all about them!"

"Him," Lisa corrected. "She would say *him*."

"Tell me all about him."

"That's the thing, Mom. It's... it's not a guy. It's a woman I'm in love with. Been in love with her for a long time."

Sally was silent. Then, "Do you need us to continue?"

"No, thank you. I know what my mom would say." Assuming the past few years didn't contain the power to change a woman's personal views, Lisa's mother would be upset. A tad upset. Upset enough to make her daughter cry.

She hadn't even mentioned the part where her love was twenty years older – and someone her mother knew.

"I feel like I'm in such a shit place," Lisa said, when she finally released her pent-up breath. "My mom's dead, so it's not like she could disown me because I turned out gay. I still think about it all the time, though. How mad she would be, and if she knew what kind of women I was into? God. She'd probably think it was her moral obligation to beat the shit out of my girlfriend."

"Your mother sounds like she was very protective."

Was it "protective" to keep her daughter away from the arms of a woman who loved her? Weren't parents supposed to want their kids to be happy? To find love and support? Was it really so terrible if she met a woman from an older generation? Someone with stability? A career? The ability to offer the sweetest of gestures and oldest of financial securities? Lisa knew they looked like a walking stereotype, but she was in love! Raquel was the first woman she ever intimately connected with. The sex, the flirting, the talks of the future... maybe they weren't getting married that time next week, but they were taking their relationship seriously. They were making plans for Thanksgiving and Christmas, since neither of them had any family to hang around. All Lisa had was her estranged father, and Raquel had been vocal about how homophobic *her* family was. It was something for them to bond over!

"She liked to think she was," Lisa finally said. "But she was really fucked up about it. She'd probably rather I be with a shitty guy than with a woman who really loves me and wants to take care of me. As long as I was straight, you know."

"You don't know that for sure, Lisa."

"I think I know better than you."

Sally changed tactics after another few seconds of contemplation. "Sometimes, the way we think of our parents are through *so* many filters that span many, many years, false memories, and little moments that seemed like a big deal at the time, but truly weren't. Your mother died when you were still a teenager. It was natural for her to worry about you and your future. She knew she was about to leave the world when you were still a child. She left this life with unfinished business as a mother. Were she still around today, I'm sure she'd be able to look at you and the world a little differently."

Lisa held her head in her hands. "This doesn't help me with my girlfriend, though. I still haven't told her that thing about my mom."

"Would you like to practice that next?"

"No." Lisa shook her head, still clutched between her hands. "No more practicing."

She wasn't sure what she expected from her visit that day. Sally couldn't really help her face her demons and the decisions she still had yet to make. *I should tell Raquel before we go to her conference in November.* That seemed like a decent deadline. About six weeks away, right before Thanksgiving, when they were planning on staying inside all weekend to eat leftovers and get a jump on the Christmas specials on TV. It would be the nicest Thanksgiving Lisa had since before her mother's diagnosis. There had been no chance for a decent turkey dinner that final year of so-called life.

I took Raquel to my favorite place. Next to Disneyland, that gelato shop was the special place Lisa had shared with her mother. A part of her wondered if Raquel would have guessed her secret there. Maybe she would have seen it in Lisa's eyes. Tasted it in the gelato. Seen it in the reflection of the window. Felt the energy of a ghost haunting their every move.

Passing judgment.

Lisa sometimes played a little too fast and loose with her secrets. Did she want to be in control of how the information got out, or did she want Raquel to do the dirty discovery work for her?

Or did she want to keep her secrets forever? Would she be standing before Raquel's grave one day and confessing what she had harbored for so long?

A part of her figured it would come to that. To ensure she didn't lose everything she had worked so hard to gain. This was the life she wanted to live. While she wasn't scheduled to see Raquel that day, they had a date that weekend. Raquel was knee-deep in selling another house – to pay for Christmas, she promised – and that meant half her week was sold to real estate Satan. They could spare a few moments from Friday night to Saturday morning, but beyond that, Raquel would be touring an executive apartment only a few blocks away from where Lisa was now. *Meanwhile, what am I doing?* Spending her life in therapy and writing throw-away articles that barely paid her bills. Lisa needed to decide what to do with her life, whether it be changing careers or vying for the coveted spot of Mrs. Mendes, Professional Homemaker. *I could totally keep that apartment clean for her... I mean, us.* Lisa would have to learn how to cook, but she was a resourceful Millennial. YouTube could teach her anything.

Her online friends could give her advice. She could save so much more money if she moved in with Raquel, backed off on the soul-sucking article writing, and began dedicating her life to the art of housekeeping. *Lisa Mendes.* She had repeated that name in her head on an endless loop since she first realized Raquel really did like her. *Elizabeth Mendes. Ooh. I like that.* Lisa was a perfectly good name for a middle-aged woman, but Lisa preferred something she could truly grow into. One day, she might be the party-planner for the people in Raquel's industry. Schmoozing. Being charming. Learning how to finalize sales while hanging on her wife's arm like the exquisite piece of arm candy she was. That was something both a Lisa *and* an Elizabeth could achieve.

Maybe Lisa's mother had named her well, after all.

She returned to her apartment a few minutes early, having nothing else to say to Sally. She passed another young woman in the therapist's waiting room and wondered if she was having abandonment issues as well. Sally came highly recommended to people who were grieving. Death of a spouse... parents... kids...

Relationships.

I hope I'm not having to see her a year from now because Raquel dumped my stupid ass. Lisa stopped in front of a café window and dithered about going in to work on her most recent writing assignment. Or she could go home and mope around her apartment.

Yeah, that one sounded good.

It was officially autumn, and while the weather had finally cooled (no more sheer clothing for Lisa, or at least not outside,) the sun continued to brightly shine late in the afternoon. Lisa had a western view that was hell during the height of summer but a blessing later in the year. Like now, when she sat against the wall on her bed and contemplated the few rays spreading across her carpet.

This was her hideaway. Her reprieve. Raquel was banned from crossing its threshold, although Lisa never told her why. *She thinks it's because I'm ashamed of how small it is.* A tiny box with a sliding closet door and a bathroom. A half kitchen in the corner, where the carpet had been cut away to prevent fire hazards. Everything about that efficiency studio was an afterthought. Lisa didn't doubt that it used to be part of a larger dwelling, before a developer built a wall. Or maybe it had been a hotel room fifty years ago.

Except that wasn't why she forbade Raquel from coming up to the door.

Lisa pulled her laptop onto her bed and opened the chatroom.

"There's something I really need to tell my girlfriend," she announced. According to the time stamps, it was five hours after someone named Kayla announced she had two dates with two different people that evening. Since then, the conversation had died.

Dare Lisa bring the mood down after so long? *"Something I haven't even told you guys."*

She checked her email while waiting for responses. When she returned to the chat window, she saw a litany of eager replies.

"Spill the deets, girl!!"

"OMG what is it?"

"You got a kid or something? Seriously, you sound so dramatic right now."

Well, it was rather dramatic.

Instead of working, Lisa spent the rest of her afternoon and evening tirelessly typing into the chat window. Once she began spilling her scandalous guts, she had half the members calling her a liar, shrieking in excitement, and exclaiming that – whether it was all an elaborate lie or the crazy truth – this was the most entertainment they had in months.

When Lisa asked what she should say to Raquel, it was a unanimous decision.

Don't. Say. A. Fucking. WORD.

That only made her more determined to do it. She simply didn't know how to time it... or when would be a good time to drop one of the biggest bombs Raquel had heard since Marian the ex dumped her twenty-three years ago because she was running off with a guy.

That reminded Lisa that she hadn't called her father in a few months. Maybe she should check in. For formality's sake.

***

Raquel helped Paisley unbox the last of the tealight candles, fresh from the manufacturer and ready to make prospective buyers see this apartment as their forever home. (Or at least until they had more than two children, or the mother-in-law tried to move in with them.) Paisley didn't stop to consider how she should arrange them around the luxury apartment. She put the pink ones in the windows, the blue ones on the countertops, and the lavender ones in the bathrooms. The last step was to make the rounds and light every single one until the whole apartment looked like it was ready for a lifetime's worth of seduction.

God knew she couldn't stop joking about it.

"Can't believe you're still seeing that girl!" Paisley called from the half bath. Raquel lined up the brochures and forms on the kitchen's island counter, right in front of the cake display topped in freshly baked donuts from across the street. Raquel put on a glove before rearranging them once again. "Wasn't she supposed to be a summer fling? Or is her ass really that cute?"

"You've seen her." Between the selfies and that one time Raquel stopped by a house staging party with Lisa right behind her, Paisley had seen plenty of the twenty-three-year-old in various stages of summer-condoned undress.

"Right. Adorable ass."

"This is rich coming from a woman who spent a week in Greece riding some college basketball player's dick." Raquel and Paisley were mutual followers of each other's social media accounts. While Raquel was posing with her young girlfriend in tropical Hawaii, Paisley was draped across the broad, muscular chest of a guy she met at a club one month before. She had no room to talk – or to judge – so soon after leaving her husband.

"*What* a dick it was!" Paisley emerged from the bathroom, brushing off lint. "Too bad I had to cut that one off. He had to go back to school in Florida. *Sigh.*"

"I thought you were of the mind that young guys were to be enjoyed, not domesticated."

"Only because you can't domesticate them. What am I? Their mothers? They wish."

Raquel wasn't touching that even with gloves on hand. "Things are going really well with Lisa, I'll have you know. We may have exchanged L words."

"That so?" Was that really genuine surprise on Paisley's manicured brows? "Good for you! Are you sure she's not playing you, though? Sucking up the last of your youth and enjoying every dollar you throw at her?"

Raquel chuckled. "Maybe she is. Still think she's emotionally attached to me."

Paisley eyeballed the donuts beneath the glass lid before turning toward Raquel. "About time you found the college student of your dreams."

"She's actually out of college."

"Whatever. What else do you know about her, though?"

Raquel did a double-take at that. "Excuse me?"

"I mean, it's one thing to have some fun with these kids, hon," Paisley leaned against the counter. "But getting serious with them requires due diligence. You gotta know how their parents will react to your buxom, middle-aged ass, for one. That's the part that always gets me!"

"Her mother passed away a few years ago, and I guess she's estranged from her dad."

"That's all you know about her, huh?"

"Well... I know other things." She knew all about Lisa's coming out experience in high school, and what college had been like. Honestly, besides the death of her mother, was there anything else more important to a twenty-three-year-old? Lisa didn't have any babies running around somewhere. No secret husbands or sugar daddies who *thought* they were her husbands. What else mattered?

Paisley pulled her iPad off the other end of the counter and flipped through an app that reminded her of everything she needed to do before the first few prospective buyers arrived. "So when's the wedding? I hear your clock is ticking."

"Har, har." Raquel wasn't anywhere close to proposing. Maybe in another two years, when she was sure that Lisa was the one she wanted to marry and come home to every day. Things changed. People changed. Raquel knew that twenty-somethings changed more than their teenaged counterparts. For all she knew, Lisa would break her heart by waking up one day and realizing her true calling was to backpack across Asia. *And* she had to do it alone!

Ticking clocks, though... Lisa had mentioned a few times that she wouldn't mind becoming a mother with the right woman. Raquel had only been married to one concept, and that was *not* ever being pregnant or giving birth. But, hey, if her partner decided to do that instead, it might be worth looking into. Raquel would be in her seventies by the time the kid went off to college, but eh, as long as the other parent was hale and healthy...

I can't believe I'm thinking about this. All because I have a girlfriend.

Choosing to marry and possibly have kids with Lisa, though, would require getting to know about her, for sure. They didn't need her parents' permission, and Raquel made enough money to support them both, but Lisa had kept more mum about her past than Raquel had. *It's partially my own fault.* Raquel had a terrible habit of hijacking conversations to talk about her depressing twenties and the childhood that led to her dumping most of her natal family. Whenever she got around to asking Lisa about her life, her girlfriend shrugged and said it wasn't as interesting as Raquel's.

"Well..." Raquel stared at the front door. A sign was folded up against it, a reminder that she needed to go downstairs and put it and the few mylar balloons onto the sidewalk. People struggled to find their homes *after* they were purchased, let alone during the open house. "She has been talking about wanting to tell me something. I guess it must be pretty heavy, because she always looks like a sick little puppy whenever she says it."

"Uh oh. Big secret, huh?"

"Guess so." God only knew what it could be. Raquel was *pretty* sure her girlfriend didn't have secret babies or their daddies out there. Was her father a felon? Did she have so much debt that she feared looking like a gold-digger? Raquel could deal with those things. Hell, she might even be able to deal with a kid given up for adoption or living with grandpa if Lisa was open and honest about it. Communication was key, wasn't it? That's what women her age were always trying to tell the youth. "Her mother died of cancer. Maybe it has something to do with that."

"No way. Don't tell me she has cancer and is getting ready to milk you for the treatments!"

"Your imagination, I swear..." Besides, Raquel saw firsthand that Lisa was still on her father's insurance when she took her to get her tetanus booster. "This is why your husband left you, sweetie. Not because he got too old for you."

"What*ever*." Paisley rapped her knuckles against the counter. "Let's sell this place, huh? You need a fat commission to pay for chemo."

Raquel couldn't help but roll her eyes. Luckily, she had plenty of time to get it out of her system as she rode the elevator down to the ground level and placed the signage on the sidewalk. By the time she reminded the concierge at his desk that an open house was going on upstairs, most of the butterflies had flown away from her stomach.

Most of them.

There was always a *what if* playing at the back of her mind while she gave tours, helped fill out paperwork, and said no to the temptation of the donuts. *Why aren't people eating them?* They had been taunting her all morning, and now that it was afternoon and she had yet to eat lunch? Getting worse. Good thing this open house was over at four and she was due a date with her girlfriend later that evening.

Hell, Raquel was so efficient that she finished up at three thirty. Paisley was long gone, and the last appointment stepped out with forms, brochures, and a smiles on their faces. Raquel did her run-through, making sure everything was clean and orderly, before taking off early. She was eager to see the girlfriend waiting for her to go out on yet another fun date. And, maybe, they would get that thing weighing upon Lisa's shoulders off her chest.

Maybe.

Raquel still had yet to be in Lisa's apartment. Every time she came close, Lisa begged her not to go inside. *"I never have time to clean. It's so small and cramped compared to your place. I've got so much kid-stuff in there still. I don't want you thinking the wrong thing about me."* She didn't get it. While she could remember what it was like to be Lisa's age and embarrassed about straggling the line between kid and adult, she didn't recall it being so bad that she forbade her dates from *ever* coming inside. *We've been dating for three months. What is seriously the big deal?* Raquel wasn't the kind of woman to cross boundaries without invitation, but sometimes she had half a mind to hang around Lisa's door and attempt to catch a glimpse of a boy band poster that hadn't been relevant in years.

The empty lobby was filled with worn-out leather chairs and a few other residents ambling around, whether waiting for rides or trying to bum a dollar off one another. Raquel avoided it by taking the stairs instead of waiting for the elevator. She had texted Lisa that she was coming up to pick her up for their date, but hadn't received a response. She was probably in the shower. There was a reason Lisa always smelled like body wash every time Raquel came to pick her up. *Pretty sure she doesn't naturally smell like flowers.* Oh, honeysuckles. Raquel had yet to figure out where Lisa was getting her perfume, but she loved it.

Even if it did make her think of Marian.

It was a good thing Raquel was physically exerting herself up five flights of stairs, because those thoughts of Marian had the power to consume her mind if she didn't distract herself. How sad was it that she could be in a nice relationship for a few months and *still* think of her heartbreaking ex from twenty years ago? Maybe a woman simply wanted to *live*, damnit!

That's it. No more thinking of Marian. Raquel had that change of heart at the top of the stairs, where she stared down the hallway full of 1990's carpet, blinking lightbulbs, and gnats swarming by the window. No wonder Lisa was embarrassed of this place. Was it her fault, though? She couldn't help what the hallway looked like. That was on the management company.

She knocked on Lisa's door. No answer. Another, louder knock was still unanswered. Raquel checked her texts to find nothing, except one from Paisley that said, *"Go get that young pussy, cougar."*

Another eyeroll. Raquel was glad she got her big breakup out of the way when she was nineteen, because divorcee Paisley was simply embarrassing.

Raquel knocked one more time, this time with the full force of her fist. *In case she's in the shower.* Not that she heard the pipes thumping in the walls.

Yet her heavy knock did have some effect. It slowly pushed open the door, which was not only unlocked, but left ajar for some strange reason.

"Lisa?" Raquel poked her head in. The glow of Christmas lights was all she could see as her eyes adjusted to the small size of the studio apartment. The bathroom door to her left was opened and revealed that nobody was in there. The more Raquel opened the door, the more she wondered why the hell the door had been left ajar if nobody was there.

Wet clothes were piled on the twin bed, bedecked in a fluffy pink comforter that looked like it came from a back to school sale at the local Target or Wal-Mart. The Christmas lights definitely screamed post-holiday clearance and probably weren't allowed by the lease. "Lisa?" Raquel carefully stepped over some underwear left on the floor. "Sorry I'm early..." She knew she was talking to an empty room, but what if her girlfriend was in the closet? Oh, no. The closet door was closed. What in the world was going on?

Where was Lisa? Why was the door unlocked?

What was so bad about this room that Raquel was never allowed in? It looked normal. Pretty clean and uncluttered for a studio apartment that housed one unconventional college student. Hell, even Lisa's laptop had been left behind on her desk by the bed. A light was on atop the nightstand. The curtains were opened, and the mini-fridge happily humming in the corner. Aside from the laundry left astray, Raquel couldn't see a single thing that marked this place the hell in which no girlfriend should enter.

Raquel didn't understand. Not until she decided to wait for Lisa by sitting on the bed and getting a good look at the picture frame on the nightstand.

Is that her mom? It was a photograph from Disneyland. A young, teenaged Lisa, complete with skinny jeans and braces, posed next to a woman who barely looked to be in her thirties. Raquel picked up the frame. She hadn't seen a picture of Lisa's mother before.

She didn't even know her name yet.

She had never thought to ask. Why would she randomly ask her girlfriend what her mother's name was? Like she was trying to hack into her bank account! Besides, Raquel had always been too wrapped up in her own ancient drama, that inquiring about things such as a dead woman's name didn't seem to matter.

Raquel put the frame down. Next to it was an orange journal that said, *THE STUFF,* written in Lisa's handwriting.

Oh, this I gotta see. Just a little snooping. Just a little!

She opened the notebook and immediately saw something straight from middle school. Lisa had written different variations of her name to match up with Raquel's. *LISA MENDES* was drawn with pink hearts around it. *ELIZABETH MENDES* had a striking underline that insinuated Lisa would one day be a proud housewife that knew how to raise funds for the latest cause. (Whatever it was.) Raquel couldn't hate. When she was with Marian, she spent half her time fantasizing of a day when gay marriage was legal and they had to decide who changed their last name. *I always wanted her to take my name, because then she would be Marian Mendes, and I had a thing for alliteration.*

Raquel turned a few pages back.

"*What have I done?*"

What was this? A journal entry?

She didn't dare read her girlfriend's innermost thoughts. At best, she thought this would be a dream journal, maybe a bullet journal to help Lisa stay on task with her writing work. She didn't think it would be nothing but the blood of a young woman who had committed one of the greatest sins she could ever conjure in her inexperienced mind.

"*I love her so much.*" That was one of the last lines Raquel read before she slammed the journal shut and shoved it back onto the nightstand. "*Just like she used to.*"

There was a bad taste in Raquel's mouth. Where the hell was Lisa? She shouldn't be here. This was wrong. Coming in here was a bad idea. She was going to see things she never should have. Things that could possibly end her if she wasn't careful.

Heartbreak was on the horizon. She needed to turn off her instincts and simply go with the flow. Ignore the bad taste in her throat. Ignore the flight or fight response when she saw the words *my mom* in that journal.

Raquel swallowed. Her sweating fingers grabbed the framed photograph and brought it into the light.

Lisa wore those Mickey Mouse ears with her name emblazoned across the front. *LISA.* A common enough name to be on display in Disneyland. Lisa proudly pointed to it while she closed her eyes for the photo, probably taken by a fellow tourist who happened to be passing by at that moment.

Yet Raquel couldn't stop staring at the other woman's face. The one that looked strikingly familiar, yet so unrecognizable.

She placed her fingers directly upon the glass. Fingerprint smudges marred Marian's aged face.

Marian.

Chapter 16

Raquel dropped the frame on the bed. She couldn't breathe.

MARIAN.

She shot off the bed, but no matter where she looked, she faced irrefutable proof that her ex-girlfriend's spirit was in the room. Her picture was in the frame. Another picture hung on the corkboard by Lisa's laptop. Although Raquel had seen the stickers on the back of the purple laptop before, she hadn't thought anything of the one that proudly advertised the city she and Marian used to live in before a certain someone skipped out of town to become a real estate agent. It was a common tourist city in the area. Why would Raquel think about it beyond *I used to live there?* Half the city had lived there at some point!

Besides, it wasn't the sticker that freaked her out the most. It was the website Lisa had left on her screen before she took off to wherever the fuck she was. A chat room, for women who preferred the company of older romantic partners.

Lisa had been in the midst of a private conversation. A blue light flashed to alert her that her online friend had left a few new responses. Raquel couldn't help *but* snoop.

"*So?*" a woman named *Melissa94* had written. "*When are you gonna tell her she's fucking her ex's daughter?*" An emoji depicting a yellow face shoving a finger through its fist followed.

Raquel sank into Lisa's swivel chair, the only seat in the room besides the bed. *I feel really faint.* This was a dream. A really, really fucked up dream preying upon Raquel's innermost insecurities.

"*When you gonna tell her you're the forbidden fruit, girl?*"

Raquel stared at the framed photograph on the nightstand. Lisa had her arms wrapped tightly around Marian, her smile the size of the Mickey Mouse ears on her head. Marian looked directly into the camera, a somber aura claiming the demeanor Raquel used to love so much.

"Raquel!"

She spun around in the chair. There Lisa was, standing in her doorway with a basket full of laundry in her hands.

"What in the world are you *doing* in here?"

That shriek was almost shrill enough to knock Raquel back to her senses. Almost. She was too far gone in the realization that Lisa was Marian's daughter to possibly have any senses right now. *Laundry basket... clothes on the floor... this is a totally freak thing I'm witnessing here.* Raquel was never meant to see this. Or was she? Was a guardian angel looking out for her? Making sure she found out who this girl was before she possibly put a ring on that finger?

"I was early..." Raquel looked between the pallor on Lisa's face and the braces in the picture. *You don't look anything like Marian.* Didn't she, though? A little button nose? High cheekbones? Brown hair that highlighted the flecks in her eyes? Lisa wasn't the spitting image of Marian, but to say she couldn't pass as her daughter was preposterous. *I have no idea who the guy was. It must have been her father...* Maybe his genes were strong enough to prevent Raquel from seeing the truth.

Maybe she simply hadn't wanted to see the truth.

"What in the world is going on?"

Raquel's question silenced the room. Lisa dropped her basket of clean laundry on her bed and clasped her hands over her face, as if she were holding back enough tears to create a torrential rainfall that would wash away the scant items she possessed. When she finally lowered a few of her fingers, she revealed that her skin was as pink as the bedspread she now sat upon.

"I can't believe this..." They both looked at the photograph. Lisa rushed forward and placed it face down. "You weren't supposed to be in here!"

"The door was open!"

"So you helped yourself in?"

Raquel scoffed. "Now I see why you didn't want me in here. You didn't want me to see..." She was somehow calm. As if she weren't traumatized as the moment continued through the seconds. *It's fine. This is fine. Everything is fine.*

"See what, exactly?"

Was Lisa playing a game? Did she think that Raquel hadn't seen the damning evidence? That she now knew the truth, even if it was taking forever to sink into her daft brain?

Because she didn't want to believe it was true?

"That your mother is my ex-girlfriend."

Lisa looked away for a moment. "You mean *was.*"

Raquel flinched. Only because she had no idea that Marian had *died.*

Marian is dead. The woman who broke my heart is dead. Raquel didn't know how she felt about that. Relieved that those memories should no longer haunt her? Upset that someone she had loved beyond belief was now gone?

"What is going on here?" Raquel asked.

Lisa continued to whiplash between pale and pink, as if one moment she was sick and the next so angry that she didn't know what to do. "What's going on is that you came into my apartment without permission."

"I didn't know you weren't in here! I left you a hundred texts... you know what? That's not the point here." Raquel's breaths were increasing, as if her chest thundered with disbelief that they were having this conversation. "The point is that you must have... that you're..." The longer she stared at Lisa's face, the more she saw it.

Marian's face.

It had been easy to ignore when she wasn't looking for it. Now that she knew the truth, all Raquel could see were the features of a woman long dead and buried. *I used to kiss the tip of her cute little nose and say it looked like a teddy bear's. I used to kiss her cheeks and delight in their shape. I used to...* Once upon a time, Raquel had loved a girl with her whole heart. The future was theirs. A world that neither of them deserved waited for them. Those nights of lying naked in bed and talking about their wedding, their kids, their careers and their future house with a white picket fence were going to last forever. Raquel was going to grow old staring into those eyes. She may no longer recognize the woman she saw in the mirror, but she would always recognize the woman she loved.

She stood before her now. Seemingly ageless.

"Yes," Lisa finally said, her tone a striking blow to Raquel's ears. *Marian! How have I never heard it before?* This was the same tone Lisa espoused whenever her melancholic tendencies overcame her. Only now Raquel realized that the reason she always winced whenever Lisa got like this wasn't necessarily because she worried for the girl, but because it reminded her of someone else.

It was the same tone Marian had when she broke up with Raquel.

Lisa pushed her hair out of her face. "Yes," she repeated. "My mom was your ex-girlfriend."

"So you knew?"

Lisa snorted. "How do you think I found you?"

Raquel's jaw dropped at that admission. "Found... me." She thought back to the night they met, how she had been dumped by a young woman who wasn't interested in dating older anymore. How she happened to bump into Lisa at the next bar she went to.

How Lisa *happened* to have an empty hotel room for them to share, compliments of some friend Raquel had never met.

The pieces were coming together, but hadn't quite snapped into place. Raquel was too overwhelmed by more than one detail manifesting at a time. Lisa was Marian's daughter. Marian was dead. Lisa had known who Raquel was from the very beginning.

Did that mean she... went looking for Raquel?

"Oh, my God." Raquel leaped up from the chair, knocking it far back behind her. "You can't be fucking serious. This has gotta be a prank of some kind." She looked around the room, searching for any cameras from some young and hip TV show that made its living pranking old women like her. "This has gotta be a lie. I simply can't believe that you... that this is..."

Lisa remained on her bed, legs tightly pressed together and arms wrapping across her stomach. "I was gonna tell you. I simply didn't know how."

"*That* was what you wanted to tell me?" Raquel faced the windows, her view of the city tarnished by the taller building next to Lisa's. This was not a place where the sun shone brightly. Nor was it a place for romance to blossom. No, this was a place where relationships came to die. "You wanted to tell me that you were Marian's daughter. That you had *found* me... for what reason? To fuck me?"

Lisa covered her face again. "I'm sorry."

Was she crying? Was *she* crying? When Raquel was the one who felt like the biggest idiot in the room? A woman who shuddered in disgust when she realized she was finger-fucking Marian's daughter on a weekly basis? *Incestuous!* She was going to be sick. Lisa may not be blood-related to her, but this was... if she were Marian's daughter, that meant it was like screwing her stepdaughter!

In another life, I would have raised you!

Raquel was faint again. She made sure her purse was attached to her hip before swallowing the bile rising in her throat and turning toward the young woman who was out to destroy her. "Tell me that it's a lie, Lisa. Tell me this is some disgusting prank I don't see the humor in. *Tell me!*"

It had to be true. Because she couldn't lose Lisa. Not now. Not like this!

Marian couldn't come back to haunt her. Raquel may always be scarred by what that woman did to her young and malleable heart, but scars were simply that – even Ms. Tithe had told her that scars were merely the remnants of closed, *healed* wounds. There was still room for love in her heart. Hadn't she been eager to offer it to the first person to make her genuinely smile?

"It's true, though." Lisa peered at her through two spread fingers. "I found out about you after my mother died. She still had her old journals from when she was with you. Even some photographs. Some... I was probably never meant to see."

The Polaroid nudes! Oh my fucking God! Raquel attempted to fall back into the desk chair again, but forgot how far back it had gone. Instead of meeting the faux-leather of a beat-up chair, she discovered the carpeted floor. Lisa did not rush to help her back up.

"I had no idea my mom was like that..." Lisa continued. "She had always been kinda homophobic when I was growing up. I never came out to her, but when I found out that she had been with a woman before my dad..."

Raquel couldn't take it anymore. This "confession" was quickly going somewhere that would ensure Raquel threw up all over the place. She was better of scurrying up to her feet and high-tailing it out of there. Now.

She didn't say goodbye. She didn't invite Lisa to text her later, or to come by the condo.

As far as Raquel was concerned, the moment she stepped onto the sidewalk, the process of forgetting Lisa had begun.

Chapter 17

Raquel called out of work the next few days. Her boss threatened to cut off her head if she didn't address the winning bid of the luxury apartment, but Raquel was in such a perturbed haze that she offhandedly suggested that someone else take on the project – and the commission. Not only did that shut up her boss, it got him off her ass.

It also made her lose out on a commission that was supposed to help pay for the Christmas she wanted to spend with Lisa.

That wasn't happening now. While Lisa hadn't been in a hurry to get into contact with Raquel, when she did, it was when Raquel was already deep into her wine collection and spending her days holed up in her dark apartment. She blocked Lisa's number and told the concierge of her building to not let the girl around anymore. Emails were blocked. Twitter handles blocked

– not that Raquel had realized Lisa was following her business account on there until she received a DM. Everything felt dirty. Dirty enough that Raquel almost nuked her whole Twitter account before realizing she needed it for work.

It still had to be a lie. It couldn't be real. Lisa wasn't Marian's daughter. No, no matter how Raquel read into it or thought about the facts, it couldn't be real. That was too cruel – both of the universe, and of the young woman who had overstepped her bounds.

Whether from the broken heart or from the change in seasons, Raquel came down with the stomach flu. When she wasn't throwing up in her toilet or having fever dreams in her bed, she was dragging herself to the kitchen to get cold water and more wine. Her doctor warned her to lay off the alcohol. She didn't listen. She'd rather throw up wine than puke up more water.

The only person allowed in her vicinity for those few weeks was Paisley, who grabbed Raquel's bottle of wine and downed a whole glass the moment she heard the news. "That is *fucked* up!" Paisley announced, as if Raquel had never put those words to her feelings. "Did she, like... stalk you or something?"

"I have no idea." Raquel was strewn across her couch, sweatshirt hiding the scars now ripped open in her heart. This was long after she recovered from the stomach flu, but outside of work, she couldn't bring herself to dress up for anything. Not even Halloween, which was on the horizon. "I'd rather not think about it. All that matters is that she knew who I was when we met."

"That girl's messed up in the head. Maybe she got obsessed with her after you-know-who died."

"You can say her name." Raquel rolled over on her couch, eyes heavy. "I had no idea Marian had died. Let alone from cancer." What a way to go. She may have broken Raquel's heart into a million fucked-up pieces, but she didn't deserve to die like that.

"When you think about it," Paisley continued, "the math adds up. Your ex was probably pregnant with that girl before she left you."

Raquel hadn't thrown up in about two weeks, but she was liable to start again.

"Sorry I mentioned it," Paisley muttered, after seeing poor Raquel rush to the bathroom. "Sorry I even thought about it."

It was difficult for a lone wolf like Raquel to find support in her own so-called community. She had been in and out of LGBT groups since she was a teenager, but the older she got, the more she eschewed them because of her hectic schedule and lack of interest. Now, however, she found herself wishing she had a few gay friends to talk to about what had happened. *They would understand. Maybe.* Back when she was a kid, older-younger relationships were the norm. If gay girls her age weren't dating someone from school, they were shacking up with the "elders," who ranged between thirty-five and sixty. *Can't believe we called thirty-five-year-olds elders!* Went to show how different things had been in the '90s. Everyone was navigating the gay rights era with the HIV epidemic nipping at their heels. Raquel had sat through a number of safe sex talks, enough to tell her that she lived in seriously dire times. Even Marian had been moved to tears on more than one occasion.

Her being fucked over by a woman much younger than her wouldn't be looked at too terribly in certain LGBT groups. Problem was, she no longer knew where they were, and she didn't know how they would take to the "truth" anyway.

Therapy was absolutely no help. When she finally divulged everything going on to Ms. Tithe, the therapist's eyes widened as she sat in stunned silence for almost ten minutes. *"What was the girl's name again?"* she continued to ask, even though Raquel could only say the name *Lisa* so many times. By the end of the appointment, Ms. Tithe had inexplicably announced that she would no longer be able to work with Raquel. An email full of alternative therapists in the city was soon in Raquel's inbox. The nerve!

Work became her one escape when she finally recovered from her stomach flu. Her boss commended her for getting back to work so quickly, not that he knew anything about her love life – and she intended to keep it that way. These were the people who would see her relationship with Lisa as something "unfavorable" to the image of their company. If Raquel were lucky, she'd be let go from the agency with a decent letter of recommendation. *"She does good work, but watch out for the cradle robbing. Sick, ain't it?"* Yeah, that would be fairly decent.

Between breaking up with Lisa and preparing for the regional conference, Raquel sold one apartment and one small home on the far side of town. It was enough for her to take it easy for the rest of the year, but why would she? So she could mope around her house, feeling sorry for herself? *Fuck that. I'm going to Paris.* Maybe Milan. Amsterdam. Yorkshire. Somewhere in Europe that would take her far away from America and what haunted her there. Although she entertained a Caribbean getaway, the thought of going somewhere tropical only made her think of Lisa and how delightful she was in Hawaii.

Raquel hated to admit how much she thought about Lisa.

It wasn't merely the circumstances of how they broke up. It wasn't that the more Raquel thought about it, the more she should have realized the similarities between Lisa and her mother. It was... well, it was how she felt while she was dating Lisa. The comfort of the relationship. The thought that it might be long-term. Fantasies of getting married and living together.

Being in love.

That was the part that hurt the most. Because no matter how good Raquel's mental gymnastics were, she couldn't stop remembering how good it had felt to be in love again.

She could only imagine how Lisa felt.

It didn't matter. Lisa had hidden who she was, knowing that Raquel would be disgusted to date the daughter of her ex-girlfriend. *It's so... incestual.* The knowledge that Marian was probably pregnant – something that Raquel had sometimes suspected, granted the suddenness of their breakup – with Lisa while they were still together made it even worse. *I'm like... her mom!* Jerry Springer might as well show up and announce to the whole world that, yes, Raquel *was* the mother! Didn't matter if she didn't know about Marian having kids. Didn't matter if she wasn't related to Lisa. Fact was, it was close enough for her to feel sick to her stomach, and that was all that mattered.

"Are you gonna be okay for the conference next week?" Mr. Filmore rapped his knuckles against Raquel's desk on his way out of the office. "No more stomach bug, right?"

Raquel mustered her best, most professional smile as she looked up at her boss. "No problems, Mr. Filmore. I received the info about the panel and was preparing my introductory statement for Women in Real Estate."

"Excellent. You know I'll be in the front row, right?"

Yes, and you'll be making sure I don't make our agency look bad. Raquel wasn't dumb. Did her boss think she was dumb? "Looking forward to it, sir."

Mr. Filmore went to bug some other hapless employee, leaving Raquel to stare at the checklist beneath her folded hands. *Days Without Crying: 5.* She would make sure it said six by the end of the day. Not like she hadn't been through a bad breakup before. At least this time she knew what to do. She knew what women of a certain lineage were capable of doing.

I know I'm getting older when I still think of her as a grown woman. The thought of Marian being old enough to have an adult child really put things into perspective. Marian may be dead now, but...

Ah, shit. There were the tears breaking Raquel's streak. Every time she seriously thought about Marian dying, the tears came back. *Why am I crying? Why do I care?* She hadn't seen Marian in over twenty years. Why would she cry to hear that she had died? Was it imagining what it would have been like to live through the death of a romantic partner? Was it imagining Lisa as she dealt with her mother's death?

Was it everything crashing down upon her at once? For some reason, life was a bitch like that.

Raquel did what she had done almost every night since brushing herself off and getting back to work. She swung by the liquor store around the corner from her apartment and indulged in her choice of the evening. Sometimes she drank the whole thing the moment she got home. Other times, she savored a sip and put the rest back in the cabinet – perfect for getting through the weekend. *I'm becoming an alcoholic.* She thought that every time she took her purchase up to the register and looked the middle-aged man in the eye. Probably judging her, although she didn't doubt that straight-up drunks stumbled in there half the day. At least she looked like a functioning alcoholic.

She didn't care. The worst part about breaking up after falling in love was the aftermath. This was the second time in her life. A pattern had nevertheless been established. Raquel got her heartbroken, and she danced with addiction. No wonder she wasn't cut out for emotionally heavy relationships. They turned her into *this*.

It only got worse after she made that realization. Because why did it matter? Everyone she ever loved turned out to be a traitor of some kind. What gave her the right to think she could be in a real, healthy relationship?

How dare she?

Raquel opened her closet and stared into its depths, a glass of whiskey in her hand. The effects of the alcohol were already settling into her bloodstream. It was a miracle she opened that door without dropping her glass or falling on her face.

"Maid Marian..." Raquel slurred through her chapped lips. "Wherefore art thou, fairest Maid Marian?" That had been one of her nicknames for her ex-girlfriend, back when they thought it romantic to watch every Robin Hood movie ever made. Marian had chastised her for mixing up Shakespeare with other English legends. Raquel didn't care then, and she didn't care now.

She was looking for that shoebox. She was looking for the end of her world.

She knew it was in there somewhere, fucking up her ability to entirely move on from the ghosts of her past. *That's how that brat was able to find me.* Raquel had done well in purging Marian from her life after so many years. She had dumped everything except a few of her most treasured keepsakes from that time. Like the photos. What was she supposed to do with those, anyway? They weren't for looking at anymore. The only people who would want them were the kind having no business with such intimate photos.

I have no business with these things. Yet she found the box, and she didn't think twice about yanking it from its hiding place and tossing it onto her bed. The ice in her drink clinked against the glass.

"Remember when you used to write cutesy shit like *Marian Mendes* in your journals?" Raquel took a generous drink of her alcohol while calling out a box full of dead memories. "Then you asked me what I thought about it. Wasn't the alliteration the *cutest?* Wouldn't it be awesome if we could get married and have the same last name? We talked forever about moving to Hawaii and getting hitched there."

The lid to the box was askew. Raquel finished her drink and placed her glass on the nightstand. For a few moments, she paced before her bed, wondering when the best time to yank off the Band-Aid was.

She wanted to see Marian's face. She wanted to see the face she had been staring at for months.

"Instead, I took your *daughter* to Hawaii!" Raquel knocked the lid off and beheld the contents. Stacks of Polaroids and a few trinkets rattled around the box until it finally settled on its side again. The first of a few photographs spilled onto the comforter. Raquel flopped down onto her bed and picked up the first one. "Were you ever gonna tell me about a kid, huh?" Finally, she had Marian's face in her hands. A shadowy, blurry face of a picture that had been taken when Marian first realized she was the subject of a nude photoshoot. She had launched at Raquel, yelling at her to put the camera down before her nudity was on display for the rest of her life and beyond. "Or was it good enough to dump me for your baby daddy? How long had you been cheating on me, anyway? Months? Weeks? A one-night stand you thought you'd get out of your system?"

That was a question that had burned inside her for years. When had the cheating started? Raquel always

assumed the worst with that one. *Weeks. At least.*
Toward the end, Marian had been distant. When she
wasn't complaining about stomach pains and a foul
mood, she was staying away from Raquel under the
guise of "trying to get her shit together." Marian had
always been a bit sensitive when it came to her moods.
While Raquel assumed it was PMS related... she never
realized, until it was too late, that her girlfriend had
been running around with a guy.

Apparently, that guy was Lisa's father. The man who
paid for her insurance.

*Not only was I screwing Marian's kid... but that
bastard's, too!*

Raquel slammed her hand on the bed. The
photographs flew up in the air, some of them landing
upside down. Raquel didn't care. She was too far gone
in her bad memories.

"I thought you loved me," she muttered. "Instead, I
was... what? A fling? Releasing your homosexual urges
into the wild?" She turned over, picking up a random
photograph. "Did you ever think of me when you were
with him? Did you look in your daughter's eyes and
wonder if she'd turn out like you? Gay, anxious, and
fucking me?"

She couldn't get over it. *How* could she possibly get
over it? How was a woman supposed to move on from
having her mind blown and heart torn in two in one
instance?

"I should've purged you from my life when I had the chance." Raquel took one last, long look at the photographs she had kept for over two decades. Why? Because she was afraid of letting go? "Instead, I invited more of your bad energy into my life." She gathered the photographs back into the shoe box and pushed herself off the bed. "I couldn't get enough of your shit, I guess. Had to leave some bread crumbs for your progeny to follow." It was the only explanation. Refusing to get rid of these photos meant a piece of Marian's cosmic energy was still embedded in Raquel's soul. It was probably easier than pie for Lisa to find her.

With shoebox in hand, Raquel stumbled into her living room. She didn't possess a fireplace to dramatically fling it into. Nor did she risk starting a fire in her kitchen for the sake of shaking the wool from her soul. Instead, she pulled out a large pair of scissors from her junk drawer and didn't hesitate before cutting the first picture in half.

It unceremoniously fell back into the box.

"No more of this." For someone full of liquor, Raquel had no issue slicing Polaroids in half. "No more of you in my life, Marian. Fuck you."

One by one – and sometimes two by two – the nude photos were cut up into a pile of indiscernible paper. It would take a forensic scientist to piece them back together and tell a tale of one naked woman posing for her lesbian lover. *"For them to be torn apart like this,"* that scientist would say one day, *"implies that a breakup occurred. One the cutter refused to cling to any longer."*

How empowering. *Blech.*

When she was done, Raquel gazed into the box and slowly shook her head. Twenty-something her couldn't believe she had done that. *You don't understand, old me. It had to be done. You won't believe what has happened. It had to be done!* She pulled out a few rubber bands from the junk drawer and ensured that the lid wasn't about to fly off and spill its puzzle pieces everywhere. Only then did Raquel tuck the box beneath her arm and head down to the garbage bins behind her building.

She stood in nothing but a tank top and sleep shorts in the chilly November night. Yet before the cold could settle into her bones, she opened the lid to the nearest dumpster and rid herself of Marian's remnants.

Maybe *now* they could both finally be at peace.

***

It was the weekend before the regional conference, and Raquel was celebrating the sudden closing of a house that had been on the market for only two days. Paisley insisted on treating her to a drink at one of the upscale bars downtown. Nowhere near where Raquel had gone with Lisa. They both made sure of that.

The martini was also Raquel's first bit of alcohol since she dumped Marian's old photographs into the dumpster. *The fog cleared the following day.* No longer was Marian's bad energy haunting her ex-girlfriend, which meant she could sober up and attempt to move on with her life.

Attempt.

Raquel had sobered up, but she would hardly call the weeks since she broke up with Lisa *moving on.* Every time she thought about her, Raquel choked up and had to distract herself before she turned into a fool. As long as nobody else could tell...

"Here's to you continuing to kick ass." Paisley held up her glass for a toast. "And helping me stay in business, too."

They toasted to that. First thing out of Raquel's mouth was whether or not Paisley was still seeing that young stud she rebounded with after breaking up with her husband.

"Who? Gavin?" She scoffed. "You really have been checked out for a while."

"Yeah. Sorry."

Paisley shook her head. "Anyway, *no.* After he started asking me to sugar mama for him, I walked. I'm in the middle of an expensive divorce, and this fucker thought he was going to get some of my money too? As if. At this rate, my husband might get alimony from *me.* Can you imagine?"

"It's a brave new world out there," Raquel said. "Husbands getting alimony and lesbians dating their ex's kids."

Paisley pursed her lips. "Have you talked to the girl since then?"

"Hell, no. She stopped trying to contact me after the first couple of weeks. Figured she finally took the hint. I have no idea what happened to her." That was how Raquel preferred her breakups, after all. Cold, clean, and considerably distant. As soon as the cord was cut, they were no longer on speaking terms. Marian had taught her. Hadn't she also taught her daughter? "Let's talk about anything else."

So they did. For an hour of their mini-celebration, they talked of future career prospects, where they had yet to travel, and whether or not they should pitch a new home selling and design show to HGTV. As much as Raquel was down for that, she made Paisley promise that they would wait another year before getting too crazy with the audition tapes.

Paisley had to leave first. She offered to share a ride with Raquel, but that wasn't in the cards. Raquel was more interested in sitting at the bar with her final drink of the night and staring at her phone. With the rabble of friends and dates sharing the evening around her, she was content to believe in a world where she had truly moved on from her relationship foibles. *Look at everyone here. They're so happy.* Save for one man with his date at the far end of the bar – and the bartender, Raquel supposed – the upscale place was nothing but women gabbing and goading each other on. The fruit cocktails and beer bottles were unearthed. The decibels were climbing. When Raquel and Paisley arrived two hours before, they had been two of the only people in the bar. *We should've come around this time.* Not that Raquel would have the prime seat at the bar. The perfect place to see a beautiful woman enter and look around for some action.

Raquel was old and experienced enough to recognize that look on a woman's face. *She's looking for a good time.* Based on the stranger's reaction to the number of women in the room, she was pleased with the parade of pussy before her. Had Raquel stepped into one of the last lesbian nightclubs in America?

The woman sat a few stools down from Raquel and ordered a dry martini. *At least she has good taste.* Raquel nibbled on her olive while keeping her eyes to herself. She had a million questions about the woman sitting next to her, though. How old was she? What was her story? Did she know she looked like she was interested in picking up chicks? Would she be interested in someone older than herself?

"Hey."

Raquel looked to her left. There the stranger was, pushing up her generous cleavage and threading her fingers through her soft hair. "Hi," she said.

"You come here often?"

What a tired line, but it worked to get the conversation going. "Not really. You?"

"First time! Had a friend say this was a good place to make more friends."

Raquel never did ask for the stranger's details. Not even her name. For by the time Ms. Dry Martini asked Raquel to come back to her place, the decision had already been made.

No. Not tonight. Possibly not for a few more nights. Raquel had gotten involved with Lisa after being dumped the same night. It wasn't a good omen. Besides... she should take some time to herself before hooking up or shacking up with anyone, regardless of age.

The only decision Raquel made that night was one she knew would change her life for the better. When she returned to the dating scene, she would go out with women closer to her own age. With any luck, that would keep her out of trouble.

Yet, somehow, she also knew that the universe would have something up its sleeve for her. It always did.

Chapter 18

"This is the drink station." A man with a guard over his facial hair and rubber gloves on his hands showed Lisa to one of the most important places in the hotel kitchen. "Learn it. Love it. Make nice with Barry over here, because he single-handedly fills the flutes of champagne for the lushes to imbibe. We went over how to best carry the trays, yeah?"

Lisa rubbed her hands together before touching the white apron around her waist. "Yup! Kimmy showed me all her tricks, and I've been practicing at home!"

"Good, because guests don't like it when you spill glasses of champagne all over them. We may not be the fanciest hotel near the airport, but we're constantly booked for a reason. Excellent service."

Lisa nodded along through the last of her tour. She had been working in the hotel restaurant for the past two weeks, but this was her first conference. Barry assured her it was more of a rite of passage than a litmus test... but if Lisa could prove herself competent when surrounded by tons of half-drunk, stressed-out people attempting to network in their industries, then the promotions would come sooner rather than later.

Honestly, she needed the tips and fires lit beneath her ass. This was one of her first service industry jobs, and she couldn't afford to fuck it up. Even a crappy hotel job was better than what had happened after Raquel dumped her.

In the weeks since that god-awful moment, Lisa had fallen into a stupor that rivaled anything Raquel ever told her about. *I didn't think it would hurt me so much...* She knew her time with Raquel was limited. As soon as she discovered the truth, that would be it for their relationship. While Raquel had been worried about the age difference getting in the way, Lisa had spent the whole honeymoon period with the knowledge that there was one thing that had the power to fuck them both over.

Because it was never meant to be a real relationship. Nothing more than sated curiosity for a girl who had always been taught to deny who she really was.

Lisa had dropped most of her writing work, knowing full well that she wouldn't be able to pay rent without it. The less she did, the less she was assigned, after all. Until she was eventually demoted to "part-time" which came with its own pratfalls. Hell, what was Lisa working for now? The whole reason she had moved to the city was to be closer to Raquel, the woman she desperately wanted to get to know. Now that it was over... there was nothing keeping her in town. Raquel had made it clear she wanted nothing to do with her ex-girlfriend's daughter, even if she had been calling that grown daughter *girlfriend*. Lisa faced the end of her lease with grace. She packed her meager things, spent the last of her money on a small U-Haul, and high-tailed it to a cheaper city, where she shacked up with the first group of roommates that would have her over Craigslist. They were willing to waive her deposit until she found a job. The first thing to pop up was this gig at one of the airport hotels.

It was thankless, cheap manual labor that sometimes left Lisa crying for reasons that were unrelated to her breakup and moving to a new city in such a short amount of time, but at least it was better than being homeless. Her father had scolded her for not moving in with him – didn't his daughter know that his most recent girlfriend had moved out and he now had some extra room? – but Lisa would rather eat dirt than move in with the guy responsible for originally breaking Raquel's heart. No matter how Lisa looked at it, she was backed up into a shitty corner, and the only way out was through the legs of the beast.

At least this job paid a few bills. At least her new roommates were cool with her being gay. At least she wasn't in the same city as Raquel anymore, where she saw that face on billboards and bus stops. *At least.*

Yet it didn't help that the first convention Lisa was assigned to work was for a bunch of real estate hobnobbing. Lisa knew that her ex-girlfriend was going to some real estate conference before Thanksgiving, but she couldn't remember exactly when and where it was. Even if it were a different convention, Lisa's mood was not improved, because she was surrounded by reminders of that torrid affair she carried with her mother's forgotten memories.

"You're starring in the show in ten minutes, Lisa." Her supervisor poked his head into the staff room, where Lisa stared at her phone while avoiding a single wrinkle in her hotel uniform. The black trousers and blouse did nothing to accentuate her body. Not like her summery outfits had... let alone the sheer maxi dresses and robes that had turned Raquel *so on* that it was a miracle they made it into Lisa's suitcase. Not that she knew what to do with them. Sell them, maybe. God knew she needed the money. "Now's your chance to go to the bathroom, because once they see you, you're gonna be everyone's best friend."

"Thanks!" That was the cheeriest she could sound before her supervisor left the room. She was saving the rest of her energy for the conference's first-day mixer.

It was as boring as she anticipated. Everyone was at least thirty, dressed in their frumpiest business casual and, in some cases, so jet-lagged that they looked twenty years older. That didn't mean they lacked the energy to descend upon Lisa the moment she walked out of the kitchen with her tray full of champagne flutes. *"Ooh, fancy!"* more than one attendee exclaimed when they say her coming. *"They really went all out for this event, huh?"*

Lisa maintained her practiced smile – *and* maintained a perfectly balanced tray upon her hand – as she made the rounds in the mixer. The attendees continued to decimate her platter, sending her back to the kitchen more than once to pick up more flutes. She was lucky that the kitchen was so close to the conference room. Otherwise, her phone in her pocket would register about two thousand more steps over the course of the night, and her feet weren't sure they were up to the arduous task.

She didn't see Raquel, and she wasn't sure if she was relieved or saddened by that fact. After all, she had been in love with the woman... but that didn't mean she wanted to embarrass herself by seeing her in the flesh yet again. *What would I even do?* She had practiced that response more than once. Should she see Raquel, she would immediately go into the break room and declare to her boss that she had massive, explosive diarrhea. It really was that bad, and she *really* needed to go home. Now. Possibly for the rest of the conference.

There were plenty of other guests to keep her occupied, though. When they weren't drinking themselves into giggly stupors with cheap champagne, they were flirting with each other and discerning who had the best hotel rooms at the conference – sometimes both occurred at once, much to Lisa's mild surprise. However, she could live without the reminders of how she first seduced Raquel. *I wanted her to seduce me...* A girl had jumped the gun. Who knew it was possible?

"Finally got a break?" Kimmy, one of the other waitresses on duty, joined her at a card table in the break room. "Me too. Don't know how we both got breaks at once, considering how busy it is out there..."

"Guess it's finally dying a bit." It was nearing nine, and most of the guests had moved on to dinner and their rooms. The only ones milling about in the conference room were those who were there to do some serious networking, and those who came in late and wanted to rest up a bit before settling in for the night. Lisa's shift would soon come to an end, and she'd be back in that house she shared with other people for a fraction of the rent.

"Got any plans for your weekend?" Kimmy rubbed her hands together. "Some of the other girls and me are heading down to Bruno's for a birthday party. You should come! Make some friends around here."

Lisa considered it for a few seconds before saying, "No, thanks. I'm still settling in and getting a routine down. Maybe I'll be up for exploring soon. Right now I'm trying to pick up as many shifts as possible so I can pay the deposit on my place." They wanted her first month's rest, for fuck's sake.

"Be careful with those routines, girl. That's how you get yourself."

"How so?"

Kimmy shrugged. "You get too comfortable and never want to try new things. Like beer pong events at Bruno's."

At least that got a chuckle out of Lisa. Quite possibly the first one she enjoyed in a few weeks. "Thanks for the reminder. I'll keep that in mind."

She had another ninety minutes before the end of her shift. Lisa was assured that it would mostly include standing around, waiting for one of the conference stragglers to need something, and end with her helping the night shift start the cleanup and prep for the first real day of the conference. She was also assured that she would get used to the routine before the end of the month.

She hoped so. Lisa was in desperate need of a job that would offer an escape from her toxic thoughts.

Toward the end of her shift, she handed in her platter and apron before marching back toward the conference room to help clean up trash and tables. The fastest route was through the lobby, which employees were allowed to use as long as they made it snappy and didn't linger long enough to catch the attention of guests.

Lisa was almost to the other end of the lobby when two people crashed through the front doors with their luggage.

"I am *beat!*" An old man with a pocket protector and a silver walking stick hobbled in front of the woman accompanying him into the lobby. "We're finally here! What a day."

The night auditor on duty welcomed them to the hotel and asked if they had a reservation. Only then did Lisa turn around and see who else had come to the conference later than late.

Raquel. Dressed for business-casual travel in her floral long-sleeved blouse and high-waist jeans that accentuated her long legs. Her hair hanged loose around her shoulders. The bags beneath her eyes suggested that she had spent most of the day traveling. *I had heard the weather back in the city was terrible.* It was only an hour away by plane. Theoretically, Raquel and her boss would've been at the conference hours ago. *Should've taken a car, I guess.* Six hours by car. Of course they didn't want to drive like Lisa had in her U-Haul.

Raquel hadn't seen her. She was too tired and too focused on checking into the hotel to notice one of the employees standing a few feet away. As soon as Lisa realized she was in the clear, she jetted into the conference room and prayed to God that Raquel never came in while the cleanup commenced.

Her heart was aflutter as she helped dissemble tables – only to take them into another conference room for set up. For the last half hour of her shift, Lisa blindly followed orders while her body slowly gave out from fatigue and her brain gave out from overstimulation.

Raquel was there. It had happened. Even though Lisa had moved a few hours away, she *still* bumped into her ex-girlfriend a few weeks after being dumped.

Was it fate drawing them together again? Not like Lisa had worked for this one! *What if she sees me? Will she call me out in public?*

Lisa went from fearing for her sanity while at work to thinking over her options as soon as she arrived home an hour later. While she showered, brushed her teeth, and lay in her cramped bed in a bedroom smaller than her old studio apartment, she contemplated everything this meant and what she should do about it.

Because Lisa was a woman of action, wasn't she?

I wanted you, Raquel, so I went after you. She had wanted to explain herself the moment she was found out, but was never given the chance. No matter how many times she attempted contact with Raquel, she was brushed off as if she were contaminated.

This was her chance. To at least explain herself and start over again.

Lisa knew that reconciliation was hopeless. She had always known that there was no happily ever after with Raquel Mendes, the woman who had made it her life's mission to sleep with every co-ed in her city. *The woman who once loved my mother.* Lisa crawled out of her bed and peered into one of the boxes she had yet to unpack. There, in the depths of darkness, she found the envelope full of her mother's old photographs.

Mom... Even in the darkness of her room, she could make out her mother's face. That smile. That glimmer in her eye. That tell-tale sign that she knew something was wrong, but couldn't articulate what.

In another life, Marian would have never broken up with Raquel and raised Lisa as their own. *Raquel would've been my mother, not my lover.* When she thought of it that way, she knew what it must have felt like in Raquel's scarred heart. How disgusted she must have been when she realized she was sleeping with Marian's daughter. *The things we did... it must have felt incestual to her.*

Was it bad if Lisa didn't feel the same way?

Of course she didn't feel that way about Raquel. Raquel had never been her mother, after all. Never even knew about Lisa's existence until the night they met. Countless conversations about Marian had revealed that Raquel knew nothing about what happened after the breakup. Not the marriage to Lisa's father. Not Lisa's birth. Not even Marian's cancer and subsequent death. It must have been a giant shock. One too great for Raquel to overcome so she could talk about it with Lisa.

I have to tell her. Lisa resolved that as she climbed back into bed, the photo of her mother slipped beneath her pillow. *Everything. Including how messed up I am.* All she cared to accomplish was a clean slate for both her and Raquel, so they could move on with their lives.

Even if seeing her at the hotel had invoked something animalistic deep within Lisa's heart. She hadn't simply seen the woman she once obsessed over, until she knew every public detail about Raquel's life long before meeting her face-to-face. She hadn't simply recalled every sexual act they performed together over the course of their short relationship.

She had felt something else. That same something that had challenged her perceptions of reality near the end of her reality.

Now that the breakup was already done, she realized it wasn't a sense of foreboding. It was something that was *supposed* to be good.

Love. Or, more specifically, the act of falling into it.

Lisa had to act quickly. Both for her sake, and Raquel's.

Chapter 19

The mic bumped against Raquel's unsuspecting chest and blasted feedback across the room. People slapped their hands on their ears and braced themselves against the screeching monstrosity that now prowled in their midst.

The sound had gone straight to Raquel's teeth. Yet she couldn't be bothered to react, because she was still processing the presence of her ex-girlfriend standing at the head of the aisle.

Lisa had barely flinched.

What is she doing here? That question repeated in Raquel's head as the MC attempted to get her attention. *What is she after? Oh my God, have I gone insane?*

"Raquel!" the MC snapped. Only then did Raquel realize that it was her turn to say hello.

"I... oh!" She brushed her hair out of her face. Sitting up straight in her chair made her cleavage the most prominent thing in the room. Out of the corner of her eye, she watched to see if Lisa was paying attention. Of course she was. She always said her favorite thing about Raquel's wardrobe was how it showed off her curves. "Hello, everyone. So sorry about that. Bit out to lunch after the crazy travel mishaps I had yesterday! Maybe I need more coffee."

A nervous chuckle reverberated among the peanut gallery. While Raquel hadn't made any friends with her mishap, she was at least preventing the making of enemies.

"My name is Raquel Mendes... thank you for having me." She had forgotten to include her agency or, hell, her city! Few people there recognized her name. Maybe they knew her face from the ads in her city, but "Raquel Mendes" held nowhere near the amount of weight that Laney Dickinson did. This was Raquel's one chance to blow a little smoke up her boss's ass.

Could it be helped, though? Lisa was still there, proving to not be a manifestation of Raquel's addled brain.

The MC began the panel while Raquel continued to stare in Lisa's direction. *Tell me I'm not seeing things... tell me I haven't lost my mind.* This was stalker levels of whatthefuckery.

So why was she about to cry?

Get it together. Keep your shit together. Don't fucking *lose your shit in front of these people!* Raquel had already screwed up once. She wasn't about to do it again!

What was more important? Her career? Or staring at the ghostly apparition on the other side of the room?

She didn't know how she got through most of the panel. It helped that Raquel was only called upon to answer a question a few times, and she had rehearsed her practiced responses so well that she was able to present a respectable delivery. Not that Mr. Filmore was impressed. Every time Raquel looked at him, he was shaking his head and mouthing to ask if she had stage fright. *God. I'm tanking my career.*

Raquel had been fine when she first sat down. Then? *Lisa!*

"It's all right, darling." Laney Dickinson personally came up to Raquel after the panel was finished. "We were all there once. Why, I remember my first day as weathergirl back in 1991. You may not believe this now, but I was so piss-scared that my mother called me afterward to ask me if someone dumped a bunch of ants down my drawers!"

This wasn't happening. It couldn't be happening.

"Tell you what." Laney slipped Raquel her business card. "Give me a call when you get back home and we'll set something up. Just us girls." She had seen Mr. Filmore coming up from behind. "Know what I mean?"

Before that year, Raquel would have hoped that was some flirtation on Laney's part. Now, she held no hope.

Nor did she entertain thoughts of elevating her career by impressing *the* Laney Dickinson.

"Well..." Mr. Filmore said, once Laney trotted off to fulfill other obligations. "That could've gone a lot worse. Also could've been a whole lot better!"

Raquel spun around to see if Lisa were still standing in the room. Not only was her post empty, but most of the room had cleared out, leaving her alone with her boss and a few other stragglers. Everyone was off to get dinner and perhaps hit up the cocktail hour in the hotel bar. Raquel was more than grateful to be hauled off for cocktails.

She didn't know the people Mr. Filmore invited along. They could've been from lunch with the treehouse people, or they could've been people he picked up while Raquel was supposedly preparing for her panel. After the first round of introductions, however, she was content to get smashed on cocktails.

All right, so she didn't get *smashed*. Even though she wanted to, since she still couldn't believe what a riot of a day it had been. *Maybe that wasn't Lisa, after all.* Lots of young women could look like Lisa from a distance. It was a sign that Raquel still wasn't over her.

Anytime would be great, though. She thought that while tapping her fingers against her cocktail, attempting to listen to the conversation going on around her. She needed to pull herself together before Mr. Filmore determined she was unreliable on these trips and decided to never bring her along again. *That would* really *tank my career!*

The bartender came over to ask if they would like anything else. Raquel ignored him, until he presented her with a napkin that had a line of recognizable handwriting on it.

No. No!

Raquel hadn't seen a lot of Lisa's handwriting during the course of their relationship, but she would never mistake those loops and harsh lines that represented "dots" above i's. There had been enough love notes in their relationship for Raquel to instantly mark Lisa's handwriting.

"Excuse me," she announced to the small party around her. "Ladies' room."

Once she was safely inside a stall, she unfolded the napkin and read Lisa's note. Although her instincts told her to dump it in the trash.

"Meet me outside your room at eight."

Eight! That was in twenty minutes!

Raquel ripped up the napkin and flushed it down the toilet. She didn't know why. Maybe it helped her detach from the reality that Lisa was in the same building as her, *and* trying to arrange a meeting. Maybe it got rid of the evidence, in case anyone came looking for proof that Raquel had inadequate tastes.

Or maybe it simply felt good. Anything to still her beating heart, honestly.

She couldn't stop thinking about it. How could she? From the moment she saw Lisa in the conference room, her mind had been running with impossible thoughts. Impossibly *impure* thoughts. It was bad enough that Raquel recognized the fluttering of her heart and the tantalizing possibilities of starting over again. Now, she must face the fact that seeing those pale pink lips and that fussy hair, even from a distance, was enough to warm her body and remind her of the passion that exploded when she and Lisa were in the same room.

Why? she asked herself. *Why the hell am I still attracted to her?*

Finding out who she really was should have been enough to kill Raquel's libido around Lisa. Knowing that she was Marian's daughter – and the child that instigated the breakup twenty-three years ago – was akin to having her whole world smashed into a million pieces. It had been enough to dump Lisa on the spot and never speak to her again. But, Raquel surmised, that was only truly possible if Lisa weren't physically around her. Seeing that soft face and the outline of Lisa's form was enough to send Raquel into her usual tizzy. Not so long ago, both had been enough to turn her into a feral beast, intent on giving and getting pleasure.

Apparently, it wasn't so different now. Almost as if who Lisa was didn't really matter.

What do I do? Raquel smacked her hand against the stall. *What if she's stalking me? This might be unsafe!*

Every fiber of Raquel's being urged her to go to Lisa and hear her out. If nothing else, maybe she would find out the real truth behind their relationship. First, however, she had to convince herself to not take any drastic measures. Like slapping Lisa. Or kissing her.

She made up an excuse that she wasn't feeling well. Mr. Filmore was less than impressed, but also so absorbed in his conversation with his new friends that he brushed Raquel off without anything more than a, *"Eh, feel better by tomorrow."* Raquel thanked him for understanding before heading toward the nearest elevator. Until then, she didn't wonder how Lisa knew which room was hers. The alarm bells started going off somewhere between the third and fourth floors. *Stalker! She's totally a stalker!*

It was too late to change her mind, though. The moment the elevator doors opened, Raquel saw her again.

Lisa.

She was still dressed in the somber black blouse and trousers from the conference room, but her hair was no longer perfectly perched atop her head in an uncomfortable, yet practical, bun. Instead, Lisa's hair was left hanging at the nape of her neck, the sparkling clasp embedded in its tangles. It looked as if it had begun sagging down the back of her head the moment the conference ended, and Lisa could never be assed to fix it.

She also picked at her arm while looking the other way. A small tic Raquel had come to learn meant Lisa was nervous as hell.

The doors closed when Raquel stepped out of the elevator. That movement summoned Lisa's attention, which was soon pressed upon Raquel until the end of time.

"You came," Lisa said, loudly enough for Raquel to hear down the hallway.

Raquel did not approach. "Didn't think I would, honestly." If there was one thing she needed to be right now, it was firm. Firm enough to lay some ground rules with this girl, and firm enough to walk away if it came down to it. Raquel wasn't above going to the hotel across the street and renting her own room if she had to.

Lisa continued to pick at a mole on her arm. Without the usual amount of makeup she wore on her dates with Raquel, she almost looked... older? Or had she aged ten years since Raquel dumped her in that tiny apartment? *No, it's my mind playing tricks on me.* Most women looked older when they didn't wear all the makeup they poured onto their faces.

Still, did it have to be so jarring? Raquel had seen Lisa without makeup plenty of times before. That was the definition of an after-shower romp or waking up the morning next to one's girlfriend. Was it so strange now because Lisa had that solemn look on her face?

If Raquel were a man, she'd be wondering if her ex-girlfriend was here to tell her that she was pregnant.

"What do you want?" Raquel's voice contained the tiniest squeak. Tiny enough that only she could hear, but loud enough to shake her inner resolve.

Lisa stood up straight, still clinging to her arm. "I wanted to talk about what happened."

"Is there anything to explain? I think it's pretty obvious what happened."

"You don't know the whole story."

"Do I even want to?"

Lisa paled. "P... please," she muttered. "You can kick me out if you want... *after* I'm finished. I've had a lot of time to think about how I would explain myself to you. Even before we broke up... I was planning on doing it. It's what I wanted to talk to you about so badly."

I bet. It was going to come out eventually. *Bet she didn't plan on the way it did happen, though.* "Did you stalk me so you could find me here?"

"No! I work here."

"You *work* here." It was the most likely answer, after the way Lisa effortlessly blended in with the staff and had access to a bartender delivering her messages. "Did you get a job here because you knew my conference would be coming through town?"

"No. I swear. It's a total coincidence I'm here while you are, too." She sighed. "I know it sounds too ridiculous to be true. Trust me. I get it."

Do you? Raquel stepped out of the way as someone came out of their room to use the elevator. The old woman spared a quick glance to the couple in the hallway, but said nothing. Nor did she look back at them as soon as she was in the elevator.

They couldn't be out here.

"Shouldn't you be getting back to work?" Raquel sweetly asked.

"My shift ended at 7:30."

"Of course it did."

"I'm not lying." Lisa dropped both of her hands with another sigh. "I know I look like a crazy stalker, but I'm not. I could actually get in trouble if my bosses see me hanging around outside your room. I *need* this job! Please... look, if I'm gonna risk my job by showing up on the security cameras right now, can we at least talk? I'm sure you've got some questions for me."

For a start...

"Fine." Raquel removed her keycard from her purse and approached her door. She kept one careful eye on Lisa, because God only knew if she had gone so far off the deep end that she might try something funny. "You can come in for a few minutes, but don't think it's an invitation to do something I wouldn't."

Lisa stepped back while Raquel opened her door.

This was a bad idea, wasn't it?

Chapter 20

Lisa sat down at the table by the curtained window, a mug of the hotel's complimentary tea in front of her. Raquel had heated up the water in the hotpot as soon as she entered the room and flung her purse onto the bed. It wasn't until she barked at Lisa to sit down that it became apparent Raquel intended to play hostess for someone she didn't even want in her room.

"Let's start with what you're doing here." Raquel sat across from her ex, mug of Earl Grey in her hand. She leaned back, showing off the cleavage Lisa had been trying to not stare at for the past few hours. *God, shoot a tractor beam to my face, would you?* Raquel was as gorgeous as the day Lisa first laid eyes on her in real life. *Us... a hotel... it's happening all over again.* In all the wrong ways. "I had no idea you moved."

Lisa explained that she let her lease run out and moved as far away as she could afford. "I knew it was over," she said. "I had no reason to stay in the city. I was better off getting a job in a cheaper town and saving up some money while I figured out what I wanted to do." Being a digital nomad around Southeast Asia had popped up in her head more than a few times, but that still required some money and forethought. "This was the first place I could get any kind of job quickly. There's a reason why they have such a high turnover here, I guess." Yeah. She *guessed,* because working there for a little over two weeks hadn't taught her a damn thing, apparently. The stress, the unreliable hours, the grumpy managers... none of it was worth the minimum wage she made. "I remembered you saying something about a conference around here somewhere, but honestly hoped it wasn't this one. Lo' and behold."

"Yes. Quite the coincidence."

"I'm not stalking you, okay? I took the chance to talk to you when I saw it!"

"You were definitely stalking me before." Raquel didn't wait for Lisa to explain herself. "I saw some of it in that journal you kept."

Lisa couldn't breathe. She definitely couldn't sip the tea in front of her. "Can I start from the beginning?" She pulled her cross-body bag off the chair and exposed its contents. This was going to be a long night, if Raquel would let it happen.

Raquel glimpsed into her ex-girlfriend's bag and looked away again. Had she recognized the photographs

Lisa brought with her? Including the one she had slept on the night before? *I feel like a little girl.* She hoped that was not how Raquel saw her, although Lisa was barely dolled up and wore the same uniform some of the underaged employees sported. *Instead of sleeping with stuffed animals, though, I'm sleeping with pictures of my mother.* Some days she swore she was over most of the grieving process. Then she would wake up with tears in her eyes.

No wonder she had pursued some of the unhealthiest forms of distraction.

"Start wherever you like." Raquel brought her mug to her lips and blew the steam away.

Lisa inhaled a deep breath and used those precious few seconds to figure out what she wanted to say.

"I knew I wasn't... well, I wasn't straight... long before I found out about you. Ever since I was in middle school, I was attracted to other girls. Not that I ever did anything about it. I was too shy. So I pretended to be into boys. You should've seen how embarrassing I was when One Direction hit it big. I basically threw a dart at the board to decide which one I pretended was my boyfriend."

Raquel propped her head up on her hand and languidly looked in Lisa's direction.

"My mom found out that I was sneaking around with a classmate and flipped the hell out. Long story short, she showed a homophobic side I had never really known about before and scared the shit out of me. I had no idea why it would be such a big deal if I liked girls. Now I know that it was super personal to her." Lisa stared at a photo of her mother, taken while touring the Grand Canyon ten years before. *It was on her bucket list.* If only Lisa had known how important that bucket list would become in the near future. "I didn't find out about that until after she died."

Raquel flinched.

"I was going through her stuff." *Because I had to move.* Lisa's father had barely done a damn thing when he learned his ex-wife was dying of cancer, but he showed up to help his daughter go through things and pick up the legal pieces left behind. Lisa had still been a minor, after all. *My father took me in for my senior year of high school, but I left as soon as possible.* Lisa was willing to take on the extra debt to move to another city for college and pay for a dorm. Living with her father was too painful – a reminder of what had happened to her mother. At least in a dorm, she could pretend that her mother was still at home, waiting for her baby girl to come home. "I had never gone through my mom's stuff before. It was like sneaking stuff out of her purse, you know." Lisa continued to stare at the photo in her hands. "I didn't think I would find anything scandalous. Maybe an old boyfriend or something. She never talked much about the time between high school and marrying my dad."

Raquel narrowed her eyes. "I was during that time."

"Yes. I know that now." Lisa sipped the hot tea and immediately put the mug down again. "I found some of my mom's old journals... and photos."

Lisa pulled out the pictures she had shoved into the bottom of her purse. She wasn't proud to say she had them. Nor had she looked at them much since first discovering them six years before. Yet there they were. Nudes and semi-nudes of Raquel when she was barely twenty years old.

Raquel gasped, slamming her face into her hand. "You've gotta be kidding me."

"I thought these were of my mom. Because why else would she have pictures of a naked woman?"

"I can't believe she kept those after..." Raquel cut herself off.

"I read through the journals and discovered that my mom had been with 'this' woman..." she gestured to the photographs of a younger Raquel, "long before she met my father. It was the most shocking thing I've ever learned about her."

"Your mother..." Raquel tested the word, as if she still could not wrap her tongue around the idea that Marian had a child. "She was very much in the closet when I met her. She never really came out of it, even when we had friends who were more understanding than most. She couldn't imagine a world where what we were didn't matter."

Lisa couldn't help but chuckle. "The exact opposite of you, right?"

"In many ways."

"It took me a long time to reconcile this part of my mother's past. I couldn't understand why she would hide it from me. Nor did I understand why she blew up at me for liking girls when *she* liked them, too!"

While Raquel's face softened, she refused to say anything. It was enough to make Lisa keep going.

"After I discovered your name, I searched for you. On the internet, I mean." It was Lisa's turn to blush. "I wanted to know what kind of woman my mother fell in love with. I also really wanted to know what happened between you, but her journals didn't go that far."

"She probably burned that one," Raquel muttered.

Lisa ignored that. "I wasn't expecting you to be so easy to find. Even with a name as simple as yours, I knew it was you the moment I saw all your real estate stuff show up online. I mean... I recognized you..."

Raquel put a finger on one of her nudes. "From these, right?"

Lisa couldn't bring herself to answer.

"Well," that was accompanied with an amused snort, "says a lot if you could recognize my professional headshots using nothing but these grainy photos from when I was nineteen."

"Thank you for not getting a bunch of plastic surgery."

Raquel opened her arms, as if to say, "*No problem.*"

"Anyway... the rest is history, I guess."

That earned Lisa a hearty guffaw. "Yeah, right! The story is only starting!" Raquel jammed her finger into the table. "Like the part where you stalked me, right? That would be a good thing to cover now."

"I didn't...!" Lisa slumped down in her seat. "Guess I could see how it looked like that."

"So you did stalk me?"

"Not like *that*. I may or may not have gone to college in the city because I wanted to get away from my dad's place. And, um, because I was trying to build up the courage to contact you about my mom."

"Why did you think I'd want to talk to you?"

That was a genuine question, wasn't it? "Because you knew my mom so well, apparently. That and I was really curious about you."

"Was this before or after you developed a crush on me?"

"I don't know. Before? After? It's kind of a blur, honestly." Lisa was hyperfocused from the moment she was accepted to college in the city. Between doing her schoolwork and attempting to have some semblance of a normal social life, she was following Raquel's career and wondering what it was like for her mother to date this woman. Somewhere in those forgotten years, Lisa replaced the thoughts of her mother... with herself. "When I broke up with my first college girlfriend, I started going older. It took me a little while to realize why that might have been."

"Uh huh."

"I'm serious!" Lisa sat back in her chair after almost impaling herself on the table. "Look, I didn't suddenly become gay after finding out my mom liked girls, and I didn't start being attracted to older women the moment I discovered your existence. Those things always existed, but maybe that's why it was so easy for me to be into you."

"Let's fast forward." Raquel tapped her finger on the table again. "To the part where you happened to find me after my date dumped me."

This was the part Lisa had been dreading the most.

"You were dating one of my old classmates. I knew that girl from a few classes I had with her in the English department. The whole reason we had more than a few conversations was because we were both into older women, but other than that, I couldn't stand her. I honestly wondered if that was the kind of girl you really went for."

Raquel snorted again. "You have no idea what she was like."

"There were rumors about you around my campus. Kinda like a hushed thing, you know? Not many girls were willing to admit they slept with older women, or how easy it could be to find one for a few nights. I know that sounds corny as hell, but..."

"It sounds even cornier coming from older women."

"What I'm saying is that more than a couple of my acquaintances went out with you."

"Not surprising. Not like there are a lot of colleges in that town, and it seemed like I mostly date college students."

"I kept trying to come up with these meet-cute ways to get to know you." She didn't have the guts to go through with any of them, though. They either sounded too contrived, or Lisa feared she would be laughed out of Raquel's presence. *What if I wasn't good enough for her? What if she immediately recognized me as her ex's daughter?* Those what-ifs plagued Lisa. Until... "When I heard Jackie was going out with you one night, I asked her how it was dating you. She was so rude about it. Said she was only going to dump you."

"Sooooo you..."

Lisa sighed. "I knew it was the perfect opportunity to meet you. I got a decent hotel room and hoped I would see you in your favorite hotel bar after she did the deed. If she even did."

"*How* did you know I would be there?"

"Your social media posts would often show you checked in there." Lisa didn't add that Raquel often looked like she was alone whenever she checked in late at night. The occasional selfie she posted from the hotel bar always showed her alone, anyway. One post had even said, "*My favorite place for some recharging.*"

"Oh my God. That's a thing?"

"Yeah. It is."

Raquel's jaw dropped. "I'm too old for this shit."

"I almost didn't have the nerve to approach you. I wanted to know you... like I *wanted* you so badly!" The frustrations Lisa had harbored for more than a few days. Ever since the day she unearthed her mother's biggest secret, she peered into a portal that was never meant for her to traverse. *Maybe my mom was trying to protect me form the mind-numbing world that is falling in love with you, Raquel.* What began as mere curiosity turned into a crusade to meet the woman who had known the "real" Marian. Lisa wanted answers. She wanted to hear the stories that her mother would never part with before she died. Even with a few months between her diagnosis and her death, Marian never once implied she had some things to tell her only child. She took her lesbian history to her grave.

She wanted to take Raquel's existence with her, too.

Lisa held back a sob that would have shaken the table. Raquel kept to her chair, yet her countenance betrayed the concern lurking deep in her heart. How dare she be a decent person? How dare she have empathy? Concern? Love in those big brown eyes of hers? *How dare my mom break up with you, Raquel. How dare she cheat on you. How dare I ever be born.*

That was the first time Lisa admitted that her mother had cheated on this woman. It was also the first time she would recognize the feeling in her heart wasn't disbelief... it was anger.

How dare *anyone* cheat on Raquel! Even Lisa's mother wasn't exempt from that anger!

"I was selfish," Lisa confessed. "When I realized I had an opportunity to talk to you, I didn't introduce myself as your ex's love child. I introduced myself as a woman who wanted to fuck you. Like that hadn't been my plan all along!" She had gotten them a hotel room, after all! Everything was a story she concocted before talking to Raquel. Anything to throw her off the scent of somehow knowing this girl she had never met before. "I didn't think we would have a relationship. I honestly didn't think you would ever want to talk to me again after that night. I was supposed to walk away with my curiosity about you sated. But, then..."

"Then you happened to walk right by my open house. With your body hanging out for me to admire." Raquel shook her head. "You trying to tell me you didn't plan that too?"

"No. I planned that." Lisa had no explanation, other than she had fallen for Raquel. Curiosity hadn't simply been sated. It had been ignited into an uncontrollable blaze. "I was hooked on you. I understood things about my mother I never anticipated." A tear fell from both of Lisa's eyes. When she said that out loud, she realized how disgusting she must have sounded. *I wasn't thinking about my mother anymore. I was only thinking of myself. When did I lose the connection between Raquel and my mother, and only saw Raquel?* "I sound like a fool. I know."

Raquel finished her tea. "You do. Like a young fool."

"How many young fools go after their mother's old flames and seduce them, though?"

"Probably more than you'd think. The real question is, how many of those old flames are women?"

Lisa bit her lip. "Can I ask what happened between you two?"

"What is there to say? One day things were fine. Next day, Marian was saying it was over and that she had found someone better suited for her. I watched her run off with some guy. It must have been your father."

"Guess we eventually learn that our moms aren't superheroes, after all."

"Ha! You thought your mom was acting like a homophobe? You should've met my aunt. She made being a bitch look like an Olympic sport. Unless I was fucking dick, she never wanted to talk to me. So we don't talk."

Lisa shuddered to think of that being a reality with her own mother. *What if she never came around to me being gay?* "I have assumed that she reacted like that to my sexuality because she saw too much of herself in me. She was very... defensive, about it."

"Sounds about right. Maybe you made her think about me and how she fucked me over."

A breath was hitched in Lisa's chest. "I'm so sorry, Raquel. I know I'll never be able to get that bad taste out of your mouth, but I want you to know that I never, ever meant to hurt you. Or scare you, for that matter. I... I really wanted to tell you the truth. Even when we were together, I had a million questions I wanted to ask you about my mother, but I kept them to myself. I was falling really hard for you, and I was so afraid of fucking everything up. I don't know how long I thought the charade was going to last. Or how you would feel the longer we went without me telling you... but I wanted to tell you. *So* badly."

"Badly enough that you ended up here, too?"

"It's a coincidence!" Even saying it made her sound like a loon. How was Raquel supposed to buy that? "Never mind. It's over." Lisa hid her face behind her hair, which was in the way of her life. *Why do I care what it looks like now?* She had spent her relationship with Raquel being so meticulous about her hair. Making sure it went with all her outfits. Keeping it clean and out of the way – or down and easy to stroke and grab. Everything she had done during that relationship was to keep them both in the fantasy of this older-younger relationship that spawned from one crazy night. Except Raquel had been played the whole time. She must have felt like an even bigger fool than Lisa.

"We definitely can't ever look at each other the same way again," Raquel said.

Lisa winced. The tears were really flowing now, but she kept them sealed tight behind her throat, so she wouldn't choke or embarrass herself any more than she had.

Raquel didn't show any contempt for the tears being spilled in her hotel room. She simply grabbed some tissues off the TV stand and handed them to Lisa, who snatched them in her fingers.

"I should have known better." Raquel stared out the window. While the curtains were closed, there was enough of a sliver for them to see blinking airplane lights. "Like you were chasing after your mother's old relationship, I was still trying to cling to the same one by dating women half my age."

"What do you mean?" Lisa asked between sniffs.

Raquel finally looked back at her puffy face. "I was never the same after Marian dumped me. I've told you that."

"Yeah, but..."

"When I finally jumped back into dating, I never dated older than you. Didn't think about it at first. Then I woke up one day, and I was thirty-two and still dating college girls. A part of me wanted to believe that I would recreate that relationship again. Although I know now that it was never possible. Nor would I ever have a real relationship with that mindset."

"Did you think you were having a real relationship with me?"

Lisa had never meant to sound so desperate, but a part of her cried to be recognized. If not by Raquel, then by someone who could reassure her that she wasn't broken and would one day move on from this mess she created.

"Yes."

She hadn't expected to hear that. The shock on her visage must have been visceral, for Raquel could barely look away.

"You were the first person I've dated since..." Raquel couldn't bring herself to say Marian's name. Not in present company. "Who made me feel like there was something more than sex in the equation. Don't get me wrong. I was completely using you for sex in the beginning."

For some reason, that didn't offend Lisa. *Like I wasn't doing the same thing to her.*

"Except you kept hanging around. You kept teasing me like it was the first time. You kept giggling and acting like it was your birthday every time I slightly spoiled you. You wanted to spoil me. It was nice."

"Just nice?"

"It was wonderful." Raquel folded her hands. "Except had I known who you really were, I wouldn't have ever slept with you. It would've been wrong."

"Why do you think I never told you?"

"Which is why I reacted the way I did. The whole situation was terrifying. Can you imagine being in my shoes? Facing the fact that I was sleeping with my ex-girlfriend's daughter? When I didn't feel like an incestuous nitwit, I just felt... *old*. The perspective was too much. What was I doing with someone young enough to be my own daughter?"

"For what's it worth..." Lisa forced her reddened eyes to look in Raquel's direction. "I never thought of you as a mother figure. You were my girlfriend." A small smile twitched on her face. "I couldn't believe that you were my girlfriend after following you online for so long, but a part of me wanted to believe that we could be together. Forever, you know?" Her hands fumbled together in her lap. "Guess that's not happening now. Not if you see me as, like, your daughter. Not if you don't trust me because I kept it from you."

Raquel was silent. Then, "You're not my daughter. That's the important thing to keep in mind here. We're not related. I had no idea you existed. I didn't even know Marian was pregnant when she left me."

"Are you worried about what people might think if they find out?"

"Oh, honey, I've got so many other things to worry about. You think me having a twenty-something *girlfriend* isn't bad enough? By the time anyone who wants to ruin me finds out about how we're tangentially related, I'm already finished. I can't think about that. I have backup plans in case my career bottoms out. Hopefully it won't, but... God, after that panel today..."

"I'm sorry if my being there threw you off."

"You think? I thought I was seeing things!"

Lisa leaned across the table. "Did you ever see my mother in me? When we were together? Did I ever remind you of her? In a creepy way?"

Raquel's eyes widened. "No. You were... you. Anytime I thought of her, it was because I was already living in the past."

Then maybe there's hope. Dare Lisa entertain those thoughts? "So you might have never found out if I never told you." *I scrubbed all traces of my mother away.* No more photos. No more journals. No more of the same damning evidence Marian had left out for her daughter to find years after the fact.

Funny how things always came back full circle.

"When we were together," Raquel continued, "I only saw the girlfriend I was falling in love with."

Something throttled Lisa's heart and made her lose every bit of breath in her lungs and drop of blood in her veins. "You were falling in love with me?"

"Yes," Raquel coolly admitted. "You trying to say you weren't head over heels in love with me? Because the alternative is that I was totally delusional during the course of my relationship, and I've got bigger problems than I originally thought I did."

Lisa didn't know why she giggled. There was nothing funny about what Raquel said. Giggling didn't make Lisa feel any better about their breakup. Closure might come from this conversation, but she didn't hold out any hope that they would have their own happily ever after. *The one she couldn't have before. The one I've always dreamed of.*

"If my mother was the one that got away for you..." Lisa began, "then I guess that makes you the one that gets away from me. I'm gonna be in therapy forever."

"One day you'll meet a lovely young twenty-something who makes your heart flutter and your pussy hot, and you'll discover that she's my daughter." Raquel shrugged. "So the cycle continues. Maybe we're in a cursed situation."

"Who started the curse?"

"Someone really mad about the concept of love."

Lisa tilted her head. "Do you believe that age is only a number?"

"No," Raquel didn't hesitate to say. "I don't."

Lisa was silent.

"I've been in a lot of relationships with women from a different generation. If there's anything I've learned, it's that there are differences that provide unique challenges you don't see in relationships between people of similar age. You and I had different childhoods. We grew up in different climates. You keep talking about One Direction."

More nervous giggling erupted from Lisa's tear-covered lips. "Who were the hot boy band when you were a kid? New Kids on The Block?"

"Oh, *honey...* when I was a kid? Like twelve?" Raquel had to think about it. "Huh. Guess it was the Kids. Kinda all a blur now."

"You might say they were a bit before my time. Like literally before I was born."

"*Don't* do that to me. I'm trying not to see you as a little girl with pigtails and a diaper. Anyone born after 1990 is permanently a toddler in my imagination."

"Yet you were dating so many girls born after 1990!"

"You have to understand... it was a different concept in my stupid brain. When I see a twenty-two-year old, I assume she was born in the '80s. As soon as Clinton became president, all babies were permanently infants."

"I guess I get what you mean. There are kids going to college today who literally cannot remember 9/11."

"Seriously. Stop it." Raquel quickly devolved into laughter.

"Sorry."

The awkwardness they summoned gradually dissipated. For a moment, however, Lisa could pretend that this was simply another night in their relationship. One of those times when she looked into Raquel's eyes and saw her girlfriend, not a woman of her past. *Will I wake up at forty-five tomorrow and wonder what the hell I was doing right now?* Raquel wasn't forty-five yet, but she probably thought that frequently.

"I hope you know that I don't regret anything," Lisa said. "Except for not telling you sooner. Maybe this hurts so much because I actually had hope that we might have something more one day."

Raquel was silent for a moment. "Do you remember that morning in Hawaii? When we ate the mango?"

That wasn't the only fruit you ate that day. "Yeah?"

"You asked me what happens when you get older. When everything stops being so new and you start comparing everything to things that have happened to you before."

Oh, Lisa remembered. Specifically, she remembered the way that mango bled its juice down Raquel's hand when she crushed it. "Yeah." She had to swallow the sexual memories before they engulfed her.

"I was projecting my own issues into that conversation. You see, I've been comparing everything in my life to those two years I had with Marian. My job, my house, my relationships... they all came back to her. I was obsessed with her in ways that don't compare to you being obsessed with me. I dated younger women so I could pretend to be twenty again. Back before I hated everything and had my heart broken."

That wasn't news to Lisa.

"I should have been embracing the present. I should have stopped seeing aging as some forbidden process I'm not allowed to experience. Just because fruit gets a little ripe, does that mean it's still not delicious? Fuck it. I love ripe apples. And ripe bananas! Those are the best."

"I love me a bruised banana," Lisa said with a smile. "Maybe that's the real reason I'm dating older."

"Watch it, young lady."

When the laughter died down, Lisa said. "I also remember our first night together. When you made me feel like having sex with you was one of the greatest honors I'd ever have. Because you were a *queen*. I didn't think of my mother once that night. It was only you and me. I loved every moment of it. I was so sure I had done the right thing by seducing you."

Raquel got up from her chair and took her empty tea mug back to the hot water pot. After contemplating the remaining teabags, she turned around, her aura transforming before Lisa's swollen eyes.

"The worst part," she said, her voice cool and her demeanor far more collected than it had been earlier. "Is that this whole time I've still wanted you, like I used to have you."

Shudders rippled through Lisa's unsuspecting body. She clutched the edge of the table and became more self-conscious about the tears she had shed and what they had done to her face. "Not a day has gone by when I didn't think about what I had lost when you broke up with me. I was in love with you." She eased her grip on the table. Raquel slowly approached. "I still am."

Raquel stopped one step away. When she lowered her head, Lisa thought it was to whisper something into her ear.

Instead, she was bequeathed a kiss that rivaled the very first one they shared a few months before.

Everything melted away as if it had never existed. There was only them... and the memories, yes, but memories that existed on the fringe of their forbidden love, not at the forefront of their minds.

Their minds were too occupied with the sinful thoughts that tended to lead two perfectly well-meaning women astray. One moment they were living their lives, and the next? Indulging in the kind of carnal pleasures that they would either come to regret as they reached an older age...

Or treasure for the rest of their natural lives.

Lisa already knew which outcome she was destined for. She only hoped that Raquel felt the same way.

Chapter 21

"Can I ask you a question?" Half that sentence came out in a huff of air because Lisa plopped down to the hotel bed with the full-brunt of her weight.

"Really?" Raquel had both hands on either side of Lisa's bent torso, nose turning upward and head slowly shaking. "Now? You wanna ask me a question *now?*"

"It's important."

Raquel held herself back from devouring Lisa with a maniacal sigh. "Your whole body is important," she muttered. "Hope you know that. Hope you know that you should have my mouth on every..."

"How did you know you were gay?"

Lisa never anticipated an exasperated look like the one she got when she asked Raquel such a left-field question. Let alone when they were on the verge of reconciling some form of their relationship. "You gotta be fucking with me right now."

"I'm serious." Lisa's fingers trailed up the length of Raquel's arms. "I wanna know."

Raquel bit her lip as she drank in the sight of Lisa sprawled out on the bed beneath her. *I must be torturing her to death right now.* Lisa didn't relish the thought. She was too preoccupied with fretting over what Raquel must be thinking right now.

"If you could see what I do right now," Raquel muttered. "You'd be gay as hell too."

"That's not an answer."

Raquel's knee hit the bed. Lisa's legs spread without forethought. Because when Raquel kneed the bed with *so* much purpose, a girl had no choice but to acquiesce. Sure enough, Raquel's knees made a grand ascent up her girlfriend's thighs.

"I knew I was gay because I was a horny teenager who couldn't stop thinking about kissing girls. Boys were gross. You know the drill."

Lisa relaxed her shoulders against the bed. While it was wonderful to have Raquel between her legs again, she had forgotten what the little jolt of anxiety was like. The one that reminded her of who they were to one another. What Raquel might think if she realized Lisa's true identity. Well, they had mounted that bridge and now possessed a lit match in one hand. They could burn the bridge connecting them or continue to the other side. Neither would probably be enough, though. They were insatiable when it came down to it.

"I sure do know." She also knew what Raquel meant when she said that a single view could awaken a girl to her true sexuality. Because, right now, Lisa had a fantastic view of Raquel's generous cleavage. Everything else she worried about slipped away. All she could remember was what it felt like to be in this woman's loving arms. "It really was that straightforward to you, huh?"

Raquel's lips grazed her young lover's forehead before descending to her cheeks. The closer her lips came to Lisa's, the closer her knee came to touching the seam of those hotel uniform pants. "When most of your dreams include making love to beautiful women, how could it be more complicated?"

Eyes closed, Lisa welcomed the kiss that pushed her all the way down to the bed. Raquel was on top of her, the weight of an older woman representing more than her body. It was the weight of experiences and memories, both old and recent. Every time Raquel's heart beat, it brought with it more of the kinds of memories that renewed the love between two kindred souls. Even Lisa no idea how much they had in common.

"Don't you wanna ask how it was for me?" Lisa brushed some hair out of Raquel's face. Anything to see better in those deep, brown eyes.

"How was what?" Difficult to gaze into a woman's eyes when they were clouding over in lust. Not that Lisa didn't appreciate what she did to Raquel. Nor was she about to push aside how joyous this union was bound to be, as soon as they properly got to it. (Whenever Lisa would let that happen.)

"Me realizing I was gay."

"Are you trying to tell me..." Instead of unbuttoning Lisa's blouse, Raquel slowly pushed it up to her lover's chest, biting her lip until it bled. "You'd rather talk about your cute little baby lesbian history instead of showing me?"

Lisa laughed, but she didn't know if it was from Raquel's demands or the way she gave them. "I realized I was gay when I started crushing on this girl at school. Really bad." She could still remember that day now, when Tessie Kay first walked into Lisa's high school and proceeded to stomp all over her pubescent heart and loins. *I wanted to comb her hair... then finger her until she exploded.* She was allowed to comb that untamable black hair only once, at a slumber party hosted by a mutual friend. A moment Lisa treasured until she found the first girl willing to make out with her and teach her how to tongue. "She had curly black hair and tanned skin. Lots of nice curves." Some curves remained in her face now. Lisa had to hold herself back from suffocating herself in Raquel's cleavage. "She looked like you, before I knew you existed."

That got Raquel to lift her head and cock one of her manicured eyebrows. "You really like teasing me, huh?"

Lisa threaded her fingers through some of Raquel's hair. While it wasn't as untamable as Tessie Kay's, it was a testament to a woman's ability to look as different from her peers while also harkening back to times of old. *You can't possibly be related to her. Yet you're so similar in appearance. I love it.* At least Lisa could certify that she had a type... and it wasn't simply *older*.

"I like being with you."

"You make it sound like you're in love with me." Raquel's warm hand spread against Lisa's exposed stomach. Every breath Lisa took was pushed right into the palm of Raquel's hand. Breaths. Bodily warmth. They both naturally had those life-giving things, yet Lisa was amazed in that moment. "A finicky young thing like you... in love? Older women like me have long learned about the dangers of a young and fickle heart."

In love... Yes, it was true. Lisa entertained fantasies of being with Raquel for a reason. She wasn't merely beautiful, experienced, and successful. She had a big heart that had loved so hard it was broken for so long. Too long. Lisa may or may not have been on a mission to heal the broken heart of Raquel Mendes, whether she thought it was accomplishable or not.

Lisa liked to think she knew her own mind. If it said she was in love... why would she not believe it? "I've loved you longer than you've known me."

Raquel hesitated before pulling open the blouse encasing the top of Lisa's torso. Black buttons disappeared beneath their bodies and into the folds of the hotel comforter. A gasp tore up Lisa's esophagus and gently echoed in the small room. Loud enough for even the neighbors to hear. *I know how thin these walls are...* Lisa had only been working there a few weeks and already heard enough complaints from guests to last her the rest of her life.

"You think you're so adorable," Raquel muttered through clenched teeth. "Yet you have no idea how irresistible you really are."

Lisa looped her arms around that head quickly coming for hers. "You're so irresistible that I moved to a city for the chance of seeing you."

"Oh, my..." That purr coming into Lisa's ear sent shivers down her spine. So happened that when her spine shuddered, her whole back arched and pressed her against Raquel's chest. There was no denying her now, not that Lisa dared to do so. *It was my hope to be back in your arms like this. I simply didn't think it would happen.* They had both said the F word. Forbidden. A love already forbidden due to their age difference, now tested by the revelation that they were already connected in the grand scheme of the cosmos. "Well, when you put it that way..."

There was no other way to put it. Lisa didn't have the chance, because her lips were back on Raquel's, and there was no denying what this did to their undying need to be together.

Lisa could hardly believe it. She had barely believed it the first time they hooked up, and that was after a semi-elaborate plan, engaged over more than a few years, was put into action. Was it possible for them to truly be in love? To have fallen in love over such a short amount of time? Did Raquel really, *truly* love her? Was her heart slowly fusing back together after watching it shatter twenty years ago? *Her heart has been broken for as long as I've been alive...* Longer, when she thought about it.

She didn't want to think about it.

She wanted to make love. To throw herself against Raquel's body and indulge in the inferno engulfing her body. Kissing Raquel wasn't enough. Feeling her press down upon skin would never be enough. Lisa needed more. She needed the sweat, moans, and inner devotions of having sex with a woman she loved more than anyone else – and the love must be mutual.

This time, it was Raquel who interrupted the physical expression of their emotions for one another. "I lied, you know?"

Her voice was directly in Lisa's ear. Her knee agonizingly pressed against the pelvis of a woman about to already burst. Her chest was covered in a fine layer of sweat, a testament to how hot this moment was.

"What did you lie about?" Lisa squeaked.

"The first time we did this." Raquel pulled away, leaving Lisa half naked and alone on the bed. Yet

Raquel was not about to leave. She pulled back the covers of the bed and yanked her blouse over her head. Her bra did not hesitate to follow the rest of Raquel's clothes over the side of the bed. *She looks like a goddess.* Lisa was in as much awe now as she had been the first time Raquel undressed before her. There wasn't a curve or an inch of skin that wasn't as divine as the first day Heaven touched Earth. It wasn't merely romantic devotion bringing Lisa back to Raquel. It was the promise that women stayed beautiful forever, regardless of what the rest of the world said. Being with someone like Raquel was a peek into the future. A future where women grew into thcir bodies and commanded their countenances with the experience and knowledge that led them through life. Lisa barely understood what was in store for her, but this was a blessed lesson one did not learn dating their own age.

This didn't feel so forbidden anymore. It was more natural than wanting to lie naked beneath the shining sun.

"I called you my serf. A slave, I guess." Was that a tinge of blush to Raquel's cheeks? She was embarrassed about it! *No, not you! How could you ever be embarrassed?* "I didn't mean it literally."

"No shit." Did she think Lisa was that young and naïve? "It was roleplaying. It was hot."

"I took things in that direction to deflect from the pain in my heart." Raquel silently forbade Lisa from undressing herself. Instead, she gently opened the front of that black blouse and stroked the mounds of Lisa's breasts. One of her nipples had already fallen out. A tease to the woman sitting before her. "I was trying to reimagine the relationship I had lost. In the process, I made sure those girls I slept with knew that I was the one in charge. That I held all the power, so my heart could never be broken. I barely had my ego bruised."

Lisa inhaled a sharp breath. It was the only way to fend off the sparks of lust claiming her as Raquel grazed that hardening nipple in Lisa's bra.

"I shouldn't have called you those demeaning names. I should have called you what you really are."

Lisa leaned forward, her lips begging to kiss Raquel's again. "What's that? A princess?" It followed Raquel's logic that princesses became queens one day. Much harder for a lowly serf to rise in power.

"No." Raquel propped herself up on her knees, her nudity radiating beauty in the low light of the hotel room. "You're a goddess."

The surprise on Lisa's visage was palpable.

"Goddesses are ageless, you know. They can appear as youthful maidens or wizened crones. They bring joy and beauty wherever they go, but they will also cut you wide open if you offend them. Goddesses are powerful. They're worthy of worship and praise. That's what I should be focusing on when I'm with you." Raquel wrapped her arm around Lisa's shoulders and brought

Hildred Billings

her closer. With the tiniest gasp filling her chest, Lisa braced her hand against her girlfriend's arm. Her thighs spread as she balanced herself on her knees. The perfect opportunity for Raquel to unzip Lisa's trousers and slip her fingers inside. "I shouldn't be taking from you. I should only be giving."

Lisa forced her eyes to remain open as the first stroke to her clit occurred. An incredible feat, considering how deft Raquel was with her finger. "So what does that make you?"

"This is Heaven, hon. We're both divine."

Lisa could go along with that. It was Raquel's way of saying they were equal in their own way. They weren't mother and daughter. They weren't older sister, younger sister. They weren't cool aunt and wayward niece trying to make her way through a crazy world. They were simply two women celebrating the fact that they were in love.

Finally, Lisa closed her eyes. It was the only way to survive the finger sliding down her slit and searching for her opening.

"Think I found your most sacred place," Raquel quipped.

"Not quite." Lisa bit down on her lip, hard, holding back a cry of pleasure as it threatened to tear her in two. "You've gotta dive a bit deeper to find that."

They both landed on the bed, Lisa's trousers coming down as soon as Raquel could manage it. It didn't take long for the length of her finger to dive deep into Lisa's body.

"Done," Raquel said with a Cheshire grin. She really was the happy cat perching on the docks, enjoying the fruit of the world. She soon plunged that smile into the modest depths of Lisa's cleavage.

Yet Lisa was far from *done*. Even when Raquel stroked her to her first mild orgasm and kissed her so tenderly that it felt like their love physically manifested as a single peck. It wasn't enough for Lisa, however. She wanted to revel in their strong bond and the reassurance that they would have many more nights like this in the future.

She wanted to know that Raquel loved her as much as she was loved.

"Is this what you want?" Raquel sweetly asked. "For you, anything."

Lisa kept her eyes closed and breathed in the sweet air blowing between them. "Whatever you want. I'm all yours."

"A goddess belongs to nobody, dear."

"Sometimes she can." Lisa pressed her lips against the white of her lover's throat. "Belong to someone, that is. Maybe I want to be yours."

"Maybe I want to give you whatever you want."

"Then do it. Give me what I really want."

Raquel sat up, her finger abandoning the sacred space deep in Lisa's body. They both took the opportunity to finish undressing the last of Lisa's clothing. Soon, both of their outfits piled onto the carpet.

Lisa rested her bare foot on top of Raquel's thigh. "I can't stop thinking about that morning in Hawaii. Ever since you brought it up."

"You mean when we ate breakfast together?" Raquel kissed the tops of Lisa's knees. "Or when I ate you like that mango."

"Both."

With a proud growl that only women like Raquel could utter, she spread open Lisa's thighs and launched her face between them.

It was the forbidden taste of a fruit untouched by true devotion. Until the moment Raquel's lips touched Lisa's, anyway. Until the moment her tongue fearlessly searched for one goddess's treasured relics.

Lisa's belonged to her whole body. From head to toe, she felt like the kind of holy vessel that broke boundaries and protected the lovers that knew not who they loved – or why fate worked in such strange and mystical ways. Songs would be written about the way she guided hearts and loins to their one-true homes. The very first ballad was currently sung against her body right now. Its echo reached for her innermost spot and touched her tender core.

She didn't know who she was anymore. Who Raquel was. What were identities but ways for the common man to categorize and record people into the annals of history? Right now, in that bed they never should have lay upon together, they had no names, no histories, and no cause for relating to the real world.

When Lisa came, she wasn't even sure she was still mortal.

***

If Raquel had any more room to doubt that she was in love with this young woman, every single one was dashed by the emotions overwhelming her.

She did a damned good job hiding the tears she wanted to cry and shielding her heart from the misery it still claimed to harbor. *You stupid thing. Too stupid to realize that it's time to move the fuck on already.* It should know that this was real when it no longer associated the woman before them with the woman who hurt it so much so long ago.

So, so *long* ago.

There wasn't a spot on Lisa's body that Raquel didn't want to be a part of. What wasn't a quest to pleasure her was a pilgrimage to change their insular world. The nape of Lisa's neck and the cleft of her inner thigh as it turned toward her stomach were worldly wonders to behold. The soft little moans coming through that tightening throat were enough to lure Raquel off the comfortable ship she sailed and plunge into the warm, loving waters of the unknown. Lisa wasn't a mere siren, however. She didn't do this to harm Raquel. She did this because, like her lover, she was in desperate need of love and to love in return.

It was only right that she scream in pleasure.

"Oh my *God!*" Did she know she was a sonic treasure when she shouted like that? Did Lisa know that it only enticed Raquel more? To kiss her? To touch the spots that made girls tremble and women empowered? To massage the wounds in her heart while getting a little rough with the softer parts of her body? It was a miracle Raquel was able to do so much with only her own body. Fingers, mouth, and the brunt of her strength overtaking them both... it was enough to sate her, even without being touched in return.

She lived for how tight Lisa became every time she climaxed, how she moaned into the pillows and gave up her inner fire with a mere flick of the tongue or come-hither of the finger. There was no such thing as drowning in the wet waters of Lisa's arousal. Not when Raquel was willing to sacrifice herself at the altar of renewing everything she once thought lost.

She was on a mission to give. In a grand contrast from the first time she made love to this body, nothing Raquel did was about exposing herself to a bigger ego and the consolation prize that was going home with another conquest beneath her belt. This was about bringing Lisa into a circle of indestructible forces.

So Raquel was completely blindsided when Lisa eventually toppled her and insisted on giving something back.

Her hair was loose and wild, a fluttering shield to the outside room – unlike Raquel's hair, which was a tousled bramble and only good for recounting how much they tossed and turned in bed together. Yet Lisa was strong enough to get on top of Raquel and grind against her, as if that was the one thing she had wanted all night.

God knew Raquel was into the idea now.

"You okay with giving up some of the power?" Lisa snatched Raquel's hands and held them above her head. Fingers grazed against the cheap headboard of an airport hotel room. "Do you think you could give some of it up to someone like me?"

The surprise gradually dispersed from Raquel's face. "I thought I already had."

She was woefully incorrect.

Who knew how many women had tried to make love to Raquel like this before? She had no idea. She always made sure the relationship never advanced far enough – either in or out of the bedroom – to discover how many women out there had the ability to make her forget where they were or why they were in love. Hell, it had been years since Raquel even entertained the concept of romantic love. A love for sex, conversation, dating... she was well acquainted, but she didn't understand kissing ruby-red lips and acquiescing to her fluttering heart.

When she opened her eyes and saw that shrouded face above her, both youthful in its façade and aged in its demeanor, she knew it was time to give in to the temptation that had haunted her for twenty years. She simply had not been ready until the right woman came along.

Raquel didn't think about who Lisa was. *She's just Lisa. She's that girl I fell in love with. What else is she to me?* Sometimes, when Lisa's eyes became heavy lidded or she tilted her head in such a way, Raquel could see the shadow of Marian in the room. But it didn't frighten her like it had a month ago. It didn't seize her soul and force her to remember a time when she loved only one other, and now fate had sent her round two. Nor did it choke her throat and make her bow down to the hell she once experienced at the hands of another woman. Breaking hearts and turning one's back on a lover were not necessarily genetic traits. Raquel had nothing to do with Lisa's upbringing. *She's right. She knew of me longer than I knew of her.* Lisa's obsession had turned into infatuation. Then, as she got to know Raquel... had it turned into true love?

Young women were prone to making drastic, terrible decisions. That was part of the appeal of being young and foolish, even if it meant a lifetime's worth of regret. *I was drastic at that age. Closing off my heart to everyone who came near me.* Now, nothing about Raquel was closed off. Not her body, and most certainly not her heart.

Lisa gave as good as she got. She didn't hold back a single drop of her desires as her tongue descended Raquel's body and made a grand show of dipping between two thighs ready for the taking.

In that moment, Raquel was as young as she wanted to be. She was twenty again. Nineteen. A foolish fifteen and exploring another girl's kisses for the first time. Thirty, and wondering what life had in store as she only continued to get older. When Raquel turned forty, she had looked at herself in the mirror and tore herself apart. Sagging, lines, wrinkles... cellulite that had followed her from her first post-pubescent growth spurt.

None of that existed now. Or, if it did, it was something Lisa aspired to behold and to have for herself one day. Raquel was an inspiration. She merely needed to accept it.

That acceptance came when Lisa remained on top of her and rode them both into the kind of climax that felled lesser women. It did a bang-up job on them, too.

Lisa jerked the last of her energy against Raquel's thighs before collapsing beside her, hair strewn across her sweaty face and chest heaving with breaths. "Holy shit," she said through that veil of hair covering her face. "I don't think I've ever been so spent in my life."

Her eyes turned toward Raquel. "And you fucked my ass once."

"Did I not a few moments ago, too? Or does it not count if I'm using my finger?"

"We need a shower."

Raquel used the last of her energy to laugh. Lisa rolled onto her side.

"Would it scare you if I say I really do love you?" Lisa's grip tensed against Raquel's torso. "Like, I imagine us being together a really long time. Living together... maybe... getting married one day?"

Her voice ended on a tentative squeak. Lisa may be brazened enough to strut up to Raquel in a hotel bar and make her night, but when it came to lifelong prospects, she could barely contain her hesitations.

Raquel couldn't blame her. That was heavy stuff to talk about so soon after reconciling.

"It doesn't scare me." Raquel locked Lisa into a lover's embrace. The scent of one woman's body filled Raquel's head with the sort of contentment she usually only fantasized about. *A scent wholly her own. I've never encountered anything like it.* Now she knew that Lisa had been wearing perfumes similar to her mother's, and it hadn't even been on purpose. Yet didn't she know that scent was the biggest memory trigger?

She wasn't wearing that perfume now. She simply smelled like sweat and sex. So happened that was exactly what Raquel wanted to smell.

"I was falling in love with you only recently." A butterfly kiss touched her cheek. "I don't know why I couldn't do it again."

"Because I make you think of someone else." That sheepish tone was accompanied with a tender pick at a bump on Raquel's chest. "Because it feels wrong."

Raquel had to carefully consider her response to that. A feat, since she was so tired. "I was shocked when I found out the truth, but a part of me was also looking for reasons to end our relationship." She couldn't believe that she had possibly found *the one* after such a long time of closing herself off to the world. "We should take things slowly. Figure things out as we go. I'm sure that we'll find the level we're the most comfortable with in no time."

A titter touched her shoulder. "As long as we can have plenty of nights like this one."

Raquel couldn't help but smile. "I think we've established that I can't keep my hands off you."

"I can't keep my hands off you, either." Lisa entwined her hand with Raquel's and lifted both into the air. "You have such a way with words. Calling me a goddess and stuff."

"You must know your worth. That goes for me, too."

Lisa snuggled against her with a sigh. They had a whole night of being together ahead of them. The first of many nights to come.

Epilogue

The early afternoon drizzle almost put a damper on Lisa's visit to the cemetery. As romantic as it was to stroll through the green fields while a dense fog settled over such a sacred place, Lisa was not dressed for the weather. Or the occasion.

She carried a small bouquet of red carnations with a sprinkle of baby's breath. The carnations had been her mother's favorites. The baby's breath was an addition the florist insisted upon as soon as she heard what they were for. Lisa had to admit that the little bouquet was beautiful. *Mother would have adored it. Pictures all over Instagram.* Marian had missed the Instagram craze, but she was an early adopter of most forms of social media. She insisted it was the best way to keep tabs on troublemakers. *She always said that with a wink, as if she meant me.*

The cemetery was one of the largest in the state, with recent land acquisitions and expansions bringing the total area to a number Lisa could barely understand. Even so, it was never difficult to find her mother's grave. There was a statue of a dreamy angel only a few yards away, and Marian had the best view of the old oak tree at the top of a nearby hill. It was the best spot Marian had been able to afford after she realized her cancer was terminal.

"Hey, Mom!" Lisa always tried to greet her mother's final resting place with a big smile, even if her heart sank deep into the pit of her grieving stomach. She bent down, emptied the vase of rainwater and debris, and fanned the flowers in a flattering arrangement. Lisa's heels prevented her from kneeling or staying bent down for too long. "Sorry I haven't been by lately. It's been a super busy... year."

She shivered in her cashmere sweater and the leggings that were better suited for the beginning of autumn, not the cusp of Christmas. *This is the fanciest I've ever looked in front of your grave, Mom. Not even the black dress I wore to your funeral looked this good.* Granted, Lisa lived a slightly more expensive lifestyle now... and she went to events that required her to look her Nordstrom best.

"You know that though, don't you? Bet you've been keeping tabs on me all year, passing judgment and coming up with all sorts of opinions about how I'm

---

living my life." Lisa sighed. "Although I like to think that wherever you are now, you've chilled out. About the gay thing. Both of our gay things."

She was silent for a while. The crisp chill of the fog cut through her sweater.

Luckily, there was someone to keep her warm.

"I can't believe she lied about her age until the very end." Raquel wrapped her arm around Lisa's shoulders and snapped her other hand to her waist. The bell sleeves of her dress draped through the air, as if she and Lisa were attending a royal cocktail party at the cemetery instead of making a stop-off. "She always liked shaving off two years. I guess she liked the number seven so much she pretended to be born in double sevens."

"Maybe you don't remember how old she was."

"Honey, I like my ladies young, but that would've made her sixteen when we met. Bit young for me, even when I was a kid."

Lisa shook her head at her mother's insistence that she was born in '77, not '75. "We could always have it changed, you know. I'm trying to believe that wherever she is now, she's not concerned about how old people thought she was."

"She didn't want to look older than thirty-five," Raquel muttered. "What, did she think it was more tragic if she died before the midlife mark? What an attention..."

Lisa laughed. "Down, girl. She ain't even around to defend herself anymore."

"Oh, really? You hear that, Marian?" Raquel loomed over the grave marker. "I get to say whatever I want and you have to take it, but I'll refrain, because we're in polite company." At least her tone was good-natured. Lisa turned her whole body toward Raquel so she could fix the hair coming out of the clasp at the back of that mess of curly black hair. "You're really too much, hon."

"Huh? What do you mean?"

Raquel chuckled. "Standing in front of your mother's grave, silently flaunting your lesbian relationship... I love it." She nuzzled a half-kiss into the crook of Lisa's neck. Surprise laughter rang across the solemn cemetery. "Like I love you."

Somewhere, Marian was watching this spectacle. Lisa only hoped that her mother was relieved that her only child was well taken care of and loved. *You would know firsthand how capable Raquel is of that, Mom.* They had long moved past the awkwardness that came up every time they acknowledged the fact that Lisa was Marian's daughter. Lisa squeaking closer to twenty-five helped chisel away the veneer of untouchable youth and perpetual daughterhood. She was her own woman. A grown woman with quirks, a hefty personality, and responsibilities she took seriously.

In the year since she and Raquel reconciled at some regional real estate conference, Lisa had come into her

own as a charming woman who did what she did best –
seduce the older set into giving her whatever she
wanted. From the moment Raquel introduced her as a
long-term girlfriend, Lisa was shaking hands and coyly
flirting her way through the real estate world. Mr.
Filmore found her the most delightful person in the
room, a feat Raquel took full advantage of when it came
time for her to ascend to the #1 position at her agency.
Raquel was making hay while the sun shined in her
favor. That year alone, she had made $14,000,000 in
sales. That wasn't her cut, unfortunately, but she had
enough savings socked away to retire whenever she felt
like it. Lisa's student debt was a thing of the past. When
she wasn't in the condo they shared, taking care of the
day-to-day affairs while Raquel's face was plastered on
yet another freeway billboard, Lisa was at high-society
clubs and open meetings, schmoozing with the wives
and newly independent children of the wealthy. Some
of them yearned to move or strike out on their own.
Lisa was a flattering devil who knew how to point them
in Raquel's direction.

She also threw a mean cocktail party, like the one
they were due to attend as soon as this rendezvous at
the cemetery was complete.

Lisa had wanted to stop by and say hello to her
mother before she no longer had the chance that year.
Their holiday season was booked with parties and
travel, since Christmas was to be in Italy and New

Year's in New York. The winter season was prime for networking, both for Raquel's business and Lisa's personal life. While she had moved away from her online friends in the sugar baby chatroom, she had adopted a small circle of women both her age and older who knew what it was like being partnered with people who worked hard and forged professional identities for themselves. On the side, Lisa was slowly chipping away at a Great American Novel that would probably never see the light of day. Yet it gave her something to do that was purely for herself.

Raquel had stressed that they take things slowly, and Lisa hadn't disagreed. Nevertheless, they had moved in together that past summer, and Lisa joked that they would be married within another year. Rarely did she feel the distance between them. They were partners before they were mere lovers. Lisa was not a trophy wife to keep quiet in the home when the breadwinner was away. She was a source of advice and opinions. A woman who acquired her own experiences while learning from Raquel's. Occasionally, people looked askance at them. Few said anything.

For every person who assumed Raquel was Lisa's mother, there was someone looking at them with seething jealousy. They may or may not have gotten off on it.

"Do me a favor," Lisa said before they left the cemetery. "Tell this lady you're gonna love me forever."

"Hm? Do you think she doesn't know it yet?"

"Doesn't hurt to say it, right?"

Raquel tilted her head with a small smirk on her lips. "What can I say? I have a lot of love for a certain kind of lady." She looked down at Marian's grave. "That's why we're in therapy together." Too bad Ms. Sally Tithe refused to see them after discovering they had been talking about each other the whole time, but the new therapist they got wasn't a disappointment. The fact they could openly go to couple's therapy together only made them a stronger pair with no inhibitions about who they were and what they wanted from their life together. It helped that the therapist was a genius at helping them come up with dialogue when faced with opposition.

"Give me a moment, hon." That's what Raquel said when Lisa expressed she was ready to go. "I'll be right there."

Lisa made her way to the car. She lowered the visor and primped in the tiny mirror, hoping she didn't look a dewy mess for the 4pm cocktail hour at the Women's Club downtown. Raquel was to drop some hints that a certain neighborhood was all the rage, and Lisa's job was to charm the pants off everyone in the room. Figuratively, of course.

"Crap." She realized that some of her makeup was running. Luckily, Raquel kept a stash of tissues in her glove compartment. "What a time for..."

A little black box fell out of the glove compartment. Lisa bent down and picked it off the floor before realizing what it was.

Sure enough, when she opened the lid, she was greeted with a solitaire diamond ring.

The wheezing gasp erupting from Lisa's mouth was enough to summon her girlfriend from across a freakin' cemetery. She hurried to put the engagement ring back into the glove compartment before Raquel noticed what she was doing. By the time she was in the driver's seat, talking about the fine mess her hair was now in, Lisa was plastered beneath her seatbelt and pretending she hadn't seen anything.

"Did we have plans after the party?"

Raquel considered that before turning on the ignition. "Well, we should grab dinner. Beyond that, we'll see where the night takes us, huh?"

Lisa could barely contain her excitement. To the point she opened the glove compartment and pulled out the ring box the moment they hit the first red light.

Turned out a solitaire diamond was the perfect accent to her cashmere sweater and legging ensemble. It was not, however, conducive to eating the mangos someone brought back from their trip to Hawaii and insisted on sharing with everyone at the party.

Hildred Billings is a Japanese and Religious Studies graduate who has spent her entire life knowing she would write for a living someday. She has lived in Japan a total of three times in three different locations, from the heights of the Japanese alps to the hectic Tokyo suburbs, with a life in Shikoku somewhere in there too. When she's not writing, however, she spends most of her time talking about Asian pop music, cats, and bad 80's fantasy movies with anyone who will listen…or not.

Her writing centers around themes of redemption, sexuality, and death, sometimes all at once. Although she enjoys writing in the genre of fantasy the most, she strives to show as much reality as possible through her characters and situations, since she's a furious realist herself.

Currently, Hildred lives in Oregon with her girlfriend, with dreams of maybe having a cat around someday.

Connect with Hildred on any of the following:

Website: http://www.hildred-billings.com
Twitter: http://twitter.com/hildred
Facebook: http://facebook.com/authorhildredbillings
Tumblr: http://tumblr.com/hildred

Printed in Great Britain
by Amazon